Beyond the Wildwood

A Collection of the Creative

Benjamin X Wretlind

Beyond the Wildwood: A Collection of the Creative

Copyright © 2023
by Benjamin X. Wretlind

Cover image by Nejron Photo

Printed in the United States of America

This is a work of fiction. All the characters, locations and events portrayed in this novel are either fictitious or are used fictitiously.

No part of this book may be reproduced or transmitted in any form or by any means, electronic or mechanical, including photocopying, recording or by any information storage and retrieval system without permission in writing from the author.

ISBN-13: 979-8385969098

First Edition

www.bxwretlind.com

For Troy Hutchings

Contents

Introduction 3
    Crinkum-Crankum, Etc. 5
Short Stories 7
    Over There 9
    The End and the Beginning 25
    Driving the Spike 49
    A Table for Two 60
    The Pink Teddy 63
    In the Bedroom 70
    Out Shopping 74
    The Royal 82
    Pig Boy and Gator, Chicken and Pa 91
    Sprouts 102
    The True Face of Ferris Fernando 111
    The Fiftieth Floor 123
    Them Rabbits 135
    The Great Machine 138
    Wren 150
Novellas 153
    The Retribution of Nathan James 155
    Sunset on Maior Pales 195
Articles 285
    Anthropology in Science Fiction & Fantasy: Looking
    Forward Through the Lens of the Past 287
    Religiosity in Fiction: Cults, Religion, and the Sci-Fi
    Thriller 311

    The Virtue of Heredity 318
Art 323
    Moon, Lighthouse, Clouds, Water 327
    Abandoned House by a Cotton Field 328
    Monument Valley 329
    Farm 330
    Blue Door (#1) 331
    Abandoned Church in Fall 332
    Dark Gate 333
    Summertime Roots 334
    Red Door (#3) 335
    King Salmon Creek 336
Biography 337

Introduction

When I originally published my first volume of collected stories, *Regarding Dead Things on the Side of the Road*, I added a whole slew of tales that probably should have never seen the light of day without a good spanking and complete rewrite. That original collection was then cut to fourteen of the best of those short stories and released once more (after a good talking to) back in 2021.

"Wait!" I hear you scream. "Does that mean this collection is full of crap?"

Not at all. In fact, I find that this collection, which contains fifteen short stories, is better for the work I put into them *after* they were pulled from earlier versions of *Regarding Dead Things*. And as with that other collection, I have added more material: two novellas and three articles. I've also thrown in some art, because, well, all those paintings I've done won't see the light of day past my living room/gallery if I don't do *something*.

I opted not to throw in any poems, however.

Except one.

Because that one poem is where the title of this volume comes from. But first, I must tell you the tale of how I came to be *Beyond the Wildwood*.

Like many good stories, it all started "back when." For me, that meant high school. Specifically, it started in a creative writing class led by an eclectic teacher who has never returned any of my emails.

But I digress.

Like many creative writing classes, one of the main goals was to put together a literary magazine, and yours truly was selected as the Editor-in-Chief. What that meant, I don't know, but it did get me an A when all was said and done.

When it came time to select a name for the journal, the teacher led the class in a brainstorming exercise. Titles were thrown onto the chalkboard (yes, the kind with *actual* chalk) and we slowly whittled them all down. About the time we were near the end, my co-editor, who had been the Editor-in-Chief the previous year, looked at the board and said aloud: "That could be a poem."

"You mean like one of those magnet poems?" I asked. "The kind refrigerators are made for?"

Indeed, that's exactly what it was. For the next two hours—after school had let out, mind you—my co-editor and I sat down to write what would turn out to be a poem titled "Crinkum-Crankum, Etc." We both immersed ourselves in the creative process, taking what were essentially disparate words and phrases spit out by about thirty different high school brains all with different levels of "creative juice" and coming up with a poem that—to our surprise—actually *made sense*.

You can be the judge of that, of course. Poetry is analyzed differently by different people or even differently by the *same* person years apart. Still, I love the poem, and it is the memory of creating it that I keep with me to this day.

So, here you go: the only poem in this book (if you don't count the haikus written by a robot in one of the novellas later on).

Crinkum-Crankum, Etc....

Phantom images
pierced by shards of imagination....
In the crystallized blackness — beyond the wildwood —
there lies a world without borders.
...From a farther room you can see more than black and white
and the shadows in the rain escape eloquence —
dreaming, scheming, and screaming as they smash through
    the boundaries to a whiter shade of pale.
Paper volcanoes
of diamonds and rust
lie near sand castles in the snow. As we operate the rattling
    machine,
it becomes obvious that we are all bottled,

but not contained.

        — Co-authored with Tracy Pearson

Short Stories

Over There

This story had a two-pronged focus: one, write something for a writer's anthology; and two, explore therapy through the written word. Think of it as gestalt without the chair. I believe it was the fact that there are semi-autobiographical elements in this story which led it to be selected for inclusion in Dream: Tales from the Pikes Peak Writers *in 2022. Those who have read several of my short stories before might recognize the character of Harrow. He goes by different names, but his purpose is the same.*

The man without the hat was not the first Harrow had picked up this week, but he was the first with shoes. Most of them walked barefoot.

The wagon, pulled by two stocky horses with contrasting colors—one ashen, one red—slowed as Harrow pulled back on the reins and gave quiet instruction. He regarded the man standing in the middle of the desert, the man with nothing but ragged clothes covered in dust, the man with shoes too clean to have been on his feet for long. He was slender, as most people in this day were, but only the stubble of a few days' respite from a razor covered his face. Even so, there were telltale signs of exposure to the elements: skin red, crusted saliva around the mouth, pinched eyes.

"Afternoon," Harrow said as the wagon matched the

speed of the man.

The man did not look up, nor did he speak. Rather, he continued a slow plod through the desert toward the horizon, a determined gaze fixed upon the unreachable.

"Give you a lift?"

Again, the man said nothing, but an inkling of awareness crossed weathered features. Harrow noted the man's affect and appearance. It was no different from most of the people he picked up along the way. Gaunt, expressionless, soulless. Some of them started their journey toward the horizon early, some late. Some started in the middle, as it was clear this man had.

The man stopped and Harrow pulled on the reins just enough to rest the wagon. He looked at Harrow, then slowly took in the horses resting in the scorching sun, the jockey bench where Harrow sat, the wagon bed and the iron tires wrapped around maple spokes. Harrow sensed the man was processing, absorbing as much information as possible and calculating a response in a brain no doubt slowed from shock, exposure to the elements, or a lack of water. Maybe all three.

"Where are you headed?" Harrow asked.

"Over there." The man's voice cracked as he pointed in an ambiguous direction with a weak jerk of an arm. Harrow noted cracked lips, red with sores. He'd been wandering for a few days.

"Well, hop in. I can give you a ride. There's some water in a bucket and an extra hat for your head."

"Much obliged." The man ambled to the back, stepped into the wagon, then fell in apparent exhaustion on a pile of brown wool blankets. His eyes remained open, fixed on the cerulean blue sky at the end of the world.

Harrow turned. With a quick jerk of the reins, the horses obeyed, and the wagon moved on.

"What's your name?" Harrow looked back. The man was now upright on the blankets, a tin cup of water in a shaky hand cemented to his lips. He finished the last of the water and let the cup drop on the wagon bed.

"Wendel."

"Apt name."

"Yours?"

"Harrow."

"Odd name."

The wagon continued forward, wheels creaking against the hard desert ground. Every so often, a rock jostled the two.

"You say you're headed over there," Harrow said after a moment. "What's over there for you?"

"I don't know. Don't know where I'm going." The man turned around. "Not sure where I've been."

"Not much out here at the end of the world save a horizon you can never catch."

"No. Suppose not." Wendel crawled forward and took up an empty seat next to Harrow. "Mind if I sit?"

"Not at all. I enjoy the company. You been traveling long?"

"All my life with no destination in mind. If you mean lately, I don't know."

Harrow could not respond to that. The two men looked ahead of the wagon at the vast expanse of scrub brush and wide open sky. The rugged terrain was daunting to look at, and yet peaceful in its way. In the distance, to the left and right, huge rock formations erupted out of the desert floor, defiant fists stabbing heavenward.

"Where you headed?" Wendel asked.

"Avernus."

"Funny name."

"Ever been to Whynot, North Carolina? Dinosaur,

Colorado? Last Chance, Iowa?"

"Can't say as I have."

"Funny people make up funny names."

"What's at this Aver— Av—"

"Avernus. It's a place to rest. Just over yonder. You can relax among friends, put your feet up and do nothing all day."

"Sounds mighty nice. Fancy, even."

"I don't know about fancy, son, but a rest is a rest after a man's long journey."

They sat in silence for another moment. Harrow glanced over at Wendel and noted with bemusement that the man's leg rhythmically bounced up and down. Wendel looked right, then left, then right again. He was nervous, or perhaps skittish. Impatient.

"You expecting something?" Harrow asked.

"No, no. Just...just not sure where I am or how I got here. Eager to get out of this desert, though. With all that's been going on in the world, I want to block it out, put it behind me. Feel like I've been walking for days."

"Can't all be bad."

"Can't say any of it was good. Been running my entire life for a place to put my feet up and relax. Feel like I'm chasing the horizon, round and round."

"The horizon?" Harrow chuckled. "You just keep running? Sounds tiring, if you ask me."

"Sad life."

"Sad. Tiring. A man runs all day, but what if, instead, that man didn't worry so much about that horizon, about what's over there? Some say the destination can be a let down."

"I don't know about that. Has to be better than this."

Harrow looked at Wendel. There was a definite maudlin quality about the man, a defeatist attitude, but one tinted with perhaps a little realization. "Might feel different if you let yourself enjoy the journey."

Wendel scoffed. "Enjoy what? The nagging boss, the never ending list of things to do? The grass that grows the moment you cut it or this expanse of dirt? Should I enjoy the angry people on the street, the news in the papers? No, mister. I been trying to find enjoyment my whole life, and I can tell you, it ain't where I'm coming from. It's over there."

Again, Wendel indicated an ambiguous direction with the jerk of an arm.

"I see. You know, some people pay for enjoyment."

Wendel sighed. "I'd pay a mint just to get there, anywhere, over there."

"Hmm." Harrow turned his attention from Wendel and looked ahead of the wagon, ahead at the distant horizon this man so impatiently wanted to get over. The wagon wheels creaked and groaned in rhythm to the clomp, clomp, clomp of the horses' hooves. A tiny white cloud disrupted the endless sky, and Harrow smiled.

"How much longer?" Wendel asked, interrupting Harrow's revelry.

"Maybe two, three days. We'll rest when the sun sets."

"Got a book to read?"

"Nope." Harrow smiled wider. "But I have something that might help you pass the time when we settle the horses in for the night."

—

"What is this?" Wendel looked at the pill Harrow had placed in his hand. The sun had set, and the glow from a fire between the two gave the pill a reddish tint.

"You wanted something to do, right?" Harrow smiled. "This will help."

Wendel pinched the pill with two fingers and held it up to

his face, squinting. "What's it do?"

"Let's you sleep, dream. Passes the time."

"Dream?" Wendel looked at Harrow across the fire. "Why dreams? Do little for a man to rest his soul."

"Oh, I've found dreams to be an excellent way to heal whatever the past has thrown at you, escape the present, and find a different path. And the best part is that you're doing so while you're still on the path you're destined to take."

"Huh. Sounds like a pitch. You a peddler?"

Harrow nodded. "I've been known to peddle some things here and some things there."

Wendel looked at the pill again. "Why is it so large?"

"Well, it's not a horse pill, but you'll want to take a drink to wash it down. Works pretty fast. Have to warn you, though. It has a kick. Might be out a while."

"I see." Wendel regarded Harrow again with a distrustful look, a sneer maybe. "And what is this going to cost me?"

"Cost?"

"Yeah. You said some people pay for enjoyment. I reckon that's what you meant. You peddle in these dream pills, but all peddlers have a price."

"Yes, well." Harrow slapped his palms down on his thighs. "I suppose I could trade something with you. What do you have?"

Wendel scoffed and handed the pill back to Harrow. "Got a lot of nothing, mister. Picked up a few coins somewhere. Maybe a little dirt, too."

"I see. Well, I got no use for coins. They're just small percentages of a whole. Incomplete and valueless. You ain't got nothing else?"

Wendel stood up, patted his clothes, then reached into a pocket. He withdrew the coins Harrow said he didn't want along with a small toy. He dropped the coins on the ground and looked closer at the thing in his palm. It was a carved soldier, the kind you buy at carnivals. This one was kneeling, aiming a rifle snapped off as one might be if shoved in the pocket of a man's pants.

The quizzical expression on Wendel's face interested Harrow. "What's that?"

"I don't— I don't remember." Wendel turned the little toy around in his fingers. "Don't know why I have it."

"Seems like an odd thing to take with you."

Wendel nodded slowly. "Must have meant something to me."

"How so?"

"That's just it. I don't know. I—" Wendel shook his head. "I can't recall."

Harrow shrugged and held the pill out for Wendel to take. "Well, if you can't remember, must not be that important. Maybe it was already in your pocket and you just never noticed."

"Maybe." Wendel kept his eyes on the toy. "I just feel— It feels— I don't know."

The fire crackled and one horse made a quick snorting sound. Aside from that, the silence between the two stretched on for a minute as Wendel turned the toy soldier around in his fingers.

"Trade?" Harrow asked, breaking the silence.

Wendel looked up. "Pardon?"

"Trade. I don't take coins, but I'm not above bartering at a gentlemen's level. The way I see it, you can either spend the next two days chatting with me or you can disappear into a dream to pass the time. Either way, we'll be at Avernus in a day. It's how you get there that matters."

Wendel looked back at the toy, then slowly held it out. His hand shook a little.

—

The pill worked fast and as advertised. In less than ten minutes, Wendel was asleep in the wagon bed, under the stars. Off to the side, a waning fire painted Harrow's face in devilish desire.

—

The boy is four, maybe five. He sits in the living room of a house filled with old people with their wrinkled apple faces, those his mother claims are her brothers and sisters and aunts and uncles. They are laughing at something someone is saying, paying no mind to the boy. The boy is paying no mind to them, only that they are doing what makes them happy, things that old people do when the sun sets, when the rains come as they do late in the day. When the work moves indoors, play moves indoors, too.

Surrounding the boy are play things, toy soldiers and blocks and a little wooden bowl that may have once held butter made from cows but now serves as a mountain or an obstacle for the invading toy army to attack and overcome. Perhaps today it is a fort, and the little soldier on top holding a rifle and aiming at something is the only survivor, the last stand against the invading hordes, against the other little men frozen in a rictus of war with their cannons or hand guns or bayonets or waving flags poised for a return to action.

The toy soldier on top is the boy, and the boy is making his last stand.

Behind him, out of sight but not out of awareness, the boy's brother stands by a wood stove set up in the living room to provide heat for the old people doing what old people do when the sun sets. The boy knows his brother is doing something with a metal pot the boy had wanted to use as a second fort until his brother took it away, made it his own for what he called an experiment.

The boy doesn't know what an experiment is, but he is curious. He stands, abandons the battle for the wooden overturned bowl. Although he does not know what an experiment is, he understands that if his brother is successful, he will have something new he can play with, something of many colors, of reds and greens and yellows and blues and purples and pinks all blended together, a magical rainbow crayon he says he can use to paint the world. The boy watches as his brother puts the metal pot on the wood stove, as he carefully peels away the paper around each crayon, as he drops them in one by colorful one, as he creates a New Thing.

As he watches the crayons go into the pot and melt, the boy has a feeling he cannot put a name to but recognizes what it is doing to his stomach, to his brain. He wants what his brother has, he wants his own magical crayon of many colors to paint the world. He wants to create the New Thing himself, but he does not have the pot or the colorful wax coloring sticks his brother has.

"Why are they melting?" the boys asks.

"Because wax melts, dummy." *His brother is not kind and drops another crayon into the pot.*

"Can I have it?"

"No."

The boy is angry. He wants to cry but remembers the last time he cried over something he could not have, his brother hit him with a belt and said that's what Daddy would do if he caught him crying. So the boy watches his brother, aware of whatever feeling he has in his stomach that he cannot name. He watches with eyes that want to fill up with tears but will not because he does not want to be hit again, because he wants to be a big boy like his brother.

His brother drops the last crayon into the pot. It is pink and it melts quickly enough. It joins the other colors, and soon enough, the pot is filled with a rainbow. Rainbows are pretty, they are magical, they have pots of gold at the end and the boy knows if he can have a rainbow New Thing like this, he can paint a pot of gold himself and buy whatever toys he wants.

His brother carefully picks the pot up. "Watch out. This is hot. I'm going to cool it off in the kitchen."

"Can I watch?"

"No. This is mine. Make your own. You got things to melt. It ain't like my things should ever be your things."

The boy wipes away a tear that has fallen on his cheek before his brother sees it and hits him with a belt. He turns away, looks at the floor, at the battle for the wooden overturned bowl frozen in time. The toys he has are red and yellow and blue and green. They are, themselves, a rainbow. If he cannot have the magical rainbow New Thing his brother has just finished making, he can make his own. Some of his toys are made of wax and they would melt. Maybe the other ones would, too. They would blend. All he needs to make his own New Thing is a pot to melt them in.

The old people are still talking and laughing at each other as the boy's brother leaves. The boy turns from the stove and picks up the wooden bowl, puts all his toys inside, all except the one aiming his rifle, the one that once protected the fort, the one that was him. That toy soldier is his favorite and he does not want to lose it. That toy soldier he tucks away in his pocket.

With the rainbow of toys now in the wooden bowl and his brother in the kitchen and the old people turned away, the boy returns to the stove. He carefully places the bowl in the same spot his brother had placed the pot. He waits for it to heat up, for the toys of many colors inside to melt. He is excited. The feeling in his stomach is gone and the tears have dried up. If he cannot have what his brother has, he can make his own New Thing and it will be better than what his brother made. When the toys melt and the colors mix, he can paint the world and a pot of gold and make his brother feel the thing in his stomach.

Maybe he will cry and Daddy can be mad at him for a change.

—

The wagon wheels creaked as they traveled the desert floor. The sun was high and the heat had returned. Harrow saw another white puff of cloud in the distance, a collection of whatever moisture could be pulled out of the arid world around them. In other places, that cloud would likely grow into a storm. Here, it would eventually go away, replaced by yet more blue sky and more heat.

Wendel stirred. He was in the back of the wagon on the brown wool blankets, stretched out. Harrow heard him and turned to look.

"Where are we?" Wendel asked.

"Told you it had a kick."

"You weren't wrong about that, mister. How long have I been asleep?"

"A night and a morning. Any good dreams?"

Wendel took a drink of water out of a tin cup and poured the rest over his head. He mussed up his hair and wiped his face dry with his hands before taking the seat next to Harrow on the jockey bench.

"Think I went back in time," Wendel said. He looked around before continuing. "Damn desert looks the same as it did yesterday."

"That's an illusion. The horizon is always just over there, but the mountains to the left and right have grown larger."

"Plants ain't much to look at."

"No, they ain't. So tell me. What was this dream you had? I'm always interested in what my customers experience. Makes for good advertising."

"Just so...odd. There was a little boy, about four or five. Think he was me, but I don't know. He was playing with some little toy soldiers."

Harrow reached into a shirt pocket and held out the toy he had taken as payment for the pill. "Like this?"

"Yeah, that's it. In fact, that's the same toy the boy in the dream...." Wendel trailed off. Harrow glanced his direction and saw the man's eyes drift backward into memory, fixed on a moment rather than any object in the present.

"Go on."

"That's just it. I don't think I can. The boy was playing with the toys and there was a stove. I can't recall what happened. It felt like a memory, though, but some piece of it is missing. What's in that pill, anyway?"

"A few odds and ends. Magic. Whatever you want to call it."

The wagon rolled forward for a quiet minute.

Finally Wendel spoke up. "You said dreams help heal whatever the past has thrown at you. What did you mean by that?"

"Dreams are many things. They can be memories, the brain working out problems, or just random thoughts laid out in random ways. Things in the past can seem lost sometimes, but they're nothing but memories we haven't processed, load-bearing walls in the construct of our house. I think sometimes dreams help us repair that wall if it's causing us to behave certain ways later in life."

"If this was a memory, you'd think I'd remember more."

"Maybe. Maybe not."

"Always thought dreams meant nothing."

"No." Harrow chuckled. "They're something so much more."

"What do you mean?"

"Think about it this way. If I gave you a book with a thousand words, you could make up a thousand stories, right?"

"I suppose."

"But you can't make up stories that included words that were not in that book. In that way, you're limited to what you have."

"I'm not following."

"Your memories are those words. Your brain won't make

up what it doesn't know, so there are holes. Those random images are not random, are they? They are the words in that book being shuffled around until they make up a new story. What if we could put those words back in the order they first appeared? What if we could patch the holes by using the words of another man's book? Another boy's book?"

"Guess I don't get it." Wendel sighed as his leg rhythmically bounced. "Wish I could go back and figure it out."

Harrow pocketed the little toy and smiled slyly. "You can. For a price, of course."

—

"I'll take a shoelace." Harrow pointed to Wendel's shoes as the two sat apart from each other around another nightly campfire. "You ain't got nothing else I need."

Wendel obliged, removing first a shoe, then pulling its lace through the holes. He passed the lace to Harrow in exchange for another pill.

"We'll be at Avernus tomorrow, so make this one count."

Wendel nodded and swallowed the pill without washing it down.

—

There is the boy again and the wooden container with the toys inside on the stove in the living room. The old people are still talking and laughing at whatever it is old people talk and laugh about. They have their backs to the boy and do not see the first signs of pending trouble, do not see the first flame ignite a piece of wood on the side of the bowl, a piece that drops from the bowl onto the floor.

The boy's eyes are wide as he tries to cover up what he's done by throwing a nearby cloth over the flaming piece of wood. In his haste, the wooden bowl tips over, spills the contents of the melted toys onto the floor.

The fire spreads. The old people have turned to see what the boy has done. Some of them are yelling. All of them are on their feet. One of them pulls the boy back from the stove while another tries to put the fire out by batting it down with a blanket. Rather than go out, the fire grows. A spark catches a curtain. Another catches a throw rug. In seconds, the living room has exploded into a firestorm and the boy is pulled farther away by the old person, farther away from the fire, farther away from the experiment that was supposed to end in a rainbow crayon with which he could paint the world. It is gone, like the bowl, the stove, the curtains, replaced by flames, by screams, by shouts of direction and the words of unintelligible panic, by the heat and movement and a dozen different smells vying for attention in the boy's nose.

The boy is in the grass now. It is wet. He is scared and does not yet know what he has done, what he has wrought upon his mother, his brother, his father, the old people still in the house. He hears glass break and sees flames erupt from a window. The night sky, so often full of stars, is now fading, turning a reddish gray, covered by smoke rising from the house and lit from the fire. The boy fears he is not far enough away. He can feel the heat. He is not far enough from the fire in the house, from the angry old people, the glances in his direction, the people running from the trough in the barn with buckets. He wonders why they don't use the water from the well, the well Daddy said to never go near, the well his brother said was home to a troll, the well he once saw Mommy toss a coin.

His brother. The boy looks around. He cannot see his brother, cannot hear his brother. He does not know if one of the old people grabbed him and pulled him out. He had left the living room to go into the kitchen. Is he still inside? Is he safe or did the fire reach him, wrap its devilish fingers of flame around his body, drag him to the place Mommy said bad people go?

Wendel now recognizes himself. He is standing in the grass off to the side, his uncle's house engulfed in fire to his right, the boy in front of him. He watches the boy, the boy who is backing up, the boy who does not see how close to the well he is.

The boy who was his brother.

As rapid as the fire had taken over the house, a surge of regret and guilt—pent-up emotion trapped behind bricks built of self-doubt and denial, of projection and displaced anger—bursts through and floods the tangles of Wendel's mind. He feels his throat constrict even as his eyes grow wider with the realization that it was he who egged his brother on, he who pushed him to place a wooden bowl on a hot stove, he who was responsible for the fire...he who forgot his brother had died in that well on that night so long ago.

Wendel takes a step toward the boy still backing toward the well. He wants to warn him, to say something to the boy who was his brother, who would still be his brother if things had turned out differently.

He wants to, but he does not.

There is something in the grass the boy left behind, something that blends in with the green but stands out because it wants to stand out, because it needs to be a beacon of light in the flood of emotion that threatens to drown Wendel, a buoy on which to cling.

He reaches down and picks up a toy soldier, the kind that is kneeling, the kind that is aiming a rifle. He tells himself he will hold on to it, that he will cherish it, that he will always remember what he did until the day he dies.

Maybe then he can forget.

Harrow backed the wagon up to a pit. Far below, the rotting bodies of men and women and children clambered over each other, stretched out to find purchase on the vertical sides, to find a way to climb out of the pit. They moaned and cried and wailed and screamed. There was room for a million more in the pit and then some. No doubt, as Harrow completed his delivery of this man, he would return to the desert and find another and another. Perhaps they will recall why they were chasing the horizon in the first place, why they wandered in the desert with no destination in mind. Perhaps they won't need a pill to remember.

It's a nice thought, but they all need a pill. True sins can leave voids in the brain, empty spaces where memory should be. The pill helps fill in past transgressions with facts from someone else's point of view.

As the horses pulled the wagon forward and the still sleeping body of Wendel tumbled out of the bed and into the pit, Harrow reached into his pocket and took out the little toy soldier. He regarded it for a moment, turned it in his fingers, then tossed it to land among the detritus of a million other payments made for a chance to learn the truth, a million other reminders of the wages of sin, the price of guilt.

The End and the Beginning

This story started out on one path, but it soon became obvious there was a second. In essence, it was two different stories that were parallel and needed to be told at the same time. Written in 2003 or 2004 (my memory is foggy), it appears here for the first time in print. There have been some modifications over the years, but nothing that would take away from my original vision (which was, also, foggy).

She is standing. It's something she didn't think was possible, but the voices told her to try. Can she walk?

She doesn't think so, and sits back down on something she can't feel but must be there. There's light in the room, but she can't see anything.

There's a voice, but she doesn't understand anything else it says. She thinks it might be her voice.

—

"So, you haven't seen this guy for thirteen years."

"No, I've seen him here and there." Rebecca looked across the table at her friend. Josey had a sense for the bizarre, but maybe this was a bit too much.

"And you've spoken?"

"Twenty words, maybe. That's total, mind you. Nothing else. He didn't live in Tucson; he just passed through every once in a while."

Josey sucked her margarita through a tiny straw. Her eyes shifted back to the left, then right, but never once settled on Rebecca. "And now he's dead?"

"Died last year in a desert north of Nasariya, Iraq."

Rebecca had no idea what Josey was thinking, but she guessed it had something to do with the apparent change in her demeanor over the last few weeks. Rebecca, on the other hand, couldn't help but think of him.

"He has a name, right?" Josey's words broke the silence. She finally looked up at Rebecca and managed a weak smile. "I mean, most...ghosts...were people once, and people have names."

"Edward."

Josey stopped in mid-suck, her eyes opened wide. "As in Martin? Edward *Martin*?"

Rebecca nodded and turned her eyes away.

"Dammit, girl! What the hell is wrong with you? Eddie wasn't exactly the catch of the day, you know. You left him high and dry for a reason. He didn't leave you."

"I know." Rebecca fought back the memory of the supposed end, or at least that drive so many years ago. No, he didn't leave her, but maybe her inaction gave him no other choice.

Josey looked at her watch. Quickly, she stood up from the table and grabbed her purse. "I'm late. You do what you think is necessary, but you need to think of Scott and the kids as well. You can't just up and leave them, especially for a...well...ghost."

"I know."

"They're memories, Rebecca. Nothing more."

"So why am I thinking of him so much?"

Josey shrugged and took her last drink. "I don't know. Just don't go nuts on me."

Rebecca sat back in her chair and watched Josey leave. She felt a wave of sadness as tears welled up, ready to fall. She didn't want to lose her composure in public, but maybe this once it wouldn't matter where she lost it. Composure was a front, a cover to hide behind. But what had she been living behind for the last thirteen years? She thought of her visions while driving through the city, her dreams while sleeping next to her husband, her wild imagination as she lay in a hospital bed years ago wishing Eddie would stop by, even if it was to just say "Hello."

Her life was a lie.

―

She hears him. This time she knows she's not the one talking. She hears everything he says to her, but none of the words make any sense. It might be a different language, but there's Familiarity in the voice.

The light is gone and she is no longer standing but lying down on something she can feel but doesn't recognize. It might be a bed or maybe the floor. It might even be a cloud.

She doesn't think she's flying.

She laughs.

The sound of her voice travels far, resonating in the corners of what might be a room or maybe a cave. It doesn't matter where she is. She just wants to know why she laughed.

―

The Veteran's Cemetery was situated such that its gate would be inaccessible to anyone when the summer's rains came. The road dipped into a dry wash, then climbed up over another hill. A yellow sign—riddled with rust and bullet holes—warned drivers not to cross the wash when water was present.

There was an irony to it, considering the lack of rain over the past three months.

Rebecca eyed the entrance to the cemetery and pulled in, her heart pounding. She felt like a schoolgirl meeting a blind date for the first time. What would he look like? Was he blond, tall, fat, stupid? Muddled somewhere between comparative thoughts, however—knocking on her heart with quiet, methodic raps—a nagging sensation pulled at Rebecca's soul; she knew she was close to him, but couldn't decide if what she sensed was the physical or the spiritual.

He was dead, after all.

The narrow road wound through the gravesites, most stone crosses or embedded headstones. The newer stones were obvious, their white granite texture unmarred by years of the scorching Arizona sun or the relentless assault of sand. In contrast to the white, small American flags at each site waved in the gentle breeze.

A caretaker looked up at Rebecca's car as it sped by. She met his gaze, his eyes sunken deep, wrinkled skin folding over on itself. For a moment, Rebecca thought her life was an open book, and anyone could read the pages of her history without so much as asking a question.

She slowed the car down around a corner and parked under a palo verde tree. The gravesite she wanted—no—*needed* to see, was among the newest, along a row of fallen soldiers, airmen, sailors and marines who gave their life in far-away deserts. Eddie's mother had pointed her in the right direction, smiled, then closed the door.

"Well, Josey," Rebecca whispered, as she stepped out of her car. "You once told me I'm a dreamer."

The wind picked up, and the hot desert air tossed Rebecca's auburn hair about. "Maybe I'm just tired of living this nightmare."

—

The voice is back again; this time she recognizes a word.

"Rebecca."

Is that my name?

She still doesn't know who's talking, but she's sure it's not her. From the feeling in her throat, she doesn't think she's talked for a very long time. She's thirsty, but she knows she's not allowed to have anything to drink.

She doesn't know why, though, and this troubles her.

—

Rebecca's mind raced with images of Eddie—images from the distant past, some from not too long ago, all interspersed with visions from her dreams. She knelt down in front of the white cross. The flag stopped waving, the wind now relegated to those events which existed outside of the conscious moment, like a tree falling in the woods miles from anyone who cared.

Rebecca closed her eyes and prayed. She honestly couldn't say if the prayer was directed to God, directed inwardly, or cast in vain upon the ghost of her lover. Whatever the case, she prayed for a reason to emerge behind all this madness.

"I saw you at the gas station, yesterday." Rebecca's words floated in the air above the cross. She half-imagined them taking form and absorbing into the ground, coming to rest in the ears of the deceased recipient.

The ghost of Eddie remained silent.

"You didn't say anything to me, but I could tell in your eyes that you still thought of me."

The flag fluttered slightly, then fell motionless once again.

"You know, I think about you constantly—on the road between here and Bisbee, on the drive to work, passing any number of restaurants we might have eaten at."

Still, the ghost said nothing.

"Why do you suppose I think about you so much? You know, it seems not an hour goes by that you don't cross my mind. I don't know if you could have said that about Kathy—that was your wife's name, right? I know I can't say that about Scott."

Rebecca sighed and ran her fingers over each letter on the gravestone. "So what is it, Eddie? Is this newness or just the excitement of the unknown—wondering what it would be like to be together after so long? We've both been married for a long time, so there really isn't anything remarkably exciting or mysterious about our current relationships."

The flag fluttered again. Rebecca took note of it and suddenly realized there was no more wind. Her heart skipped a beat as her mind wandered off to a place not too far from insanity, but still on the safe side of reality.

"Do you think that's why I spend so much time thinking of you? It kind of feels like a first date, you know? You remember—it's all you can do *not* to think of that other person."

Rebecca felt sadness well up inside of her, starting with her chest and crawling past her throat. She swallowed, hoping to stem the flow of inevitable tears.

"We've known each other a long time, though. Is there another explanation to all of this?"

Rebecca wiped an errant tear from her eyes. She smiled weakly and silently wished the flag would flutter one more time.

"Josey thinks I'm crazy." Rebecca let loose a short laugh. "She thinks I'm seeing things. I wonder what she'd think if she knew I was talking to you right now. I guess she really never understood what you meant to me. I should tell her sometime, don't you think?

"I'm glad you sat down the other day after she left. I was beginning to think I was alone in this world. It's funny the way things work out. One day, you're surrounded by people you love, high on life. The next day, you sit at a bar and everyone around you fades away. It's just you and the bartender."

Rebecca sighed. Another tear formed and fell silently onto her cheek. It rested for a moment in her makeup before rolling ever so slowly down her face.

"I should have given you another chance, you know. You were gone, off to see the world in your uniform and I...didn't think I could wait."

The ghost said nothing, but in her heart—in that one last chamber of sanity that survived through the years—Rebecca didn't really expect anything.

"I never stopped loving you, Eddie. I think you know that."

Rebecca stood up. She wanted to leave and hoped she'd said enough to calm the curiosity that drove her to this position. With a parting kiss directed at the ghost she knew *had* to be there, Rebecca turned to go.

"I'm sorry, Eddie. I'm sorry for everything."

The flag fluttered once more.

—

"Rebecca, wake up."

She hears the voice and wants to respond, but her eyes refuse to move. She tries to move her hands to her face, but they feel tied down.

No, they're not tied down, but she still can't move them.

For some reason, she's not worried about this. A weird feeling of pleasantness has come over her, like someone constantly saying, "It's okay."

There's a wet spot beneath her. She's still thirsty and knows someone needs to change her sheets.

She thinks about this. She wonders what sheets are and why someone needs to change them. The thought of sheets leads her to another word: bed.

She must be in a room, not a cave.
She smiles. A room is nicer than a cave.

—

Rebecca sat on the edge of her couch and watched her smallest child climb the side of the bookshelf. A glass of rum and Coke sat on the coffee table. Not her favorite drink, but certainly *his*. Her visit to the cemetery a few days ago lingered in the back of her mind, and painted the present with colors from the past. Since that day, she'd slept maybe three hours total, skipped work, and generally ignored the task of keeping a household. Dinner came in a bag from McDonalds, the kids met the bus in the morning with their hair uncombed, and Scott slept downstairs more than once.

In Rebecca's hand, a letter dangled.

She wiped at a tear and took a drink. She'd read the letter a thousand times, and not just recently. It was written on heavy paper, the ink still sharp, the letters crisp. In her world, this letter was the invocation to a lifetime of wondering, waiting, wanting. She remembered when it arrived, shortly after she became engaged to Scott. He didn't like the idea of her ghosts coming back for more, but really there was nothing he could do to stop it. Ghosts don't go away.

Ghosts wait.

Rebecca sat back into the folds of the couch and looked at the letter again. She didn't need to read the words to know what it said; after years of longing, she could recite it.

Know when the sun sets on our lives, we will have lived together like God intended — as One. Despite your present situation, I still look upon you as the savior of my life — the woman who awakened my senses, brought me to life, and let me grow as a man should. You are half of me, Rebecca, and I can't let that go.

When there's a knock on the door of your life again, answer it.

"Don't climb too high, Megan." Rebecca didn't need to

look and see where her child was. The most recent model addition to the household routinely tried in vain to get a blue vase from the top shelf. Perhaps it was the color, the gold leaf around the edges, or the stupid-looking cat on the side — whatever the reason, the child wanted it, and every day she climbed a little higher.

Eddie had given her the vase, years ago.

Megan climbed down from the bookshelf and walked over to the couch. She held out her hand like a drink should be in it. "Juice."

Rebecca put the letter on the coffee table, wiped her eyes one more time with a tissue, and obliged her child.

The doorbell rang, filling the cavernous house with chimes that sounded more like the trumpets at the gates of Heaven than small electronic tones emanating from a cheap speaker somewhere down the hall. Rebecca caught her heart somewhere between her throat and her nasal cavity. Her breath stopped. A dreaded silence engulfed the house, stopping every nuance of living. The clock was silent. The air conditioner said nothing. The air refused to move.

"Juice." Megan pulled on Rebecca's shorts. "Want juice."

A million thoughts swam like brine waiting to be devoured by the whale of reason. Each idea — *he'd come back, he's not dead, he's behind the door* — screamed its possibility with the voice of demons, the pitch rising with each iteration.

What the hell?

Rebecca slowly turned from the kitchen and walked to the door. Her hands shook; fingers wiggled back and forth as if moving them around would calm her fears like some ethereal massage. Other possibilities rose out of her sea of thought — *the mailman has a package, the kid next door wants to play, someone wants to sell the Suck-o-matic 4000 vacuum cleaner* — and each one of them quickly sank back to the stagnant ocean floor of her mind.

What the hell?

She thought of the flag fluttering without wind, the recent dreams she'd been having, the chance encounter at the gas station the other day when she swore he'd been standing across the way, watching her with a smile. Josey didn't buy it—and in so many ways, neither did Rebecca.

Ghosts aren't real.

When there's a knock on the door of your life again, answer it.

Rebecca stood behind the door, afraid to look through the eyehole. *It wasn't a knock*, she thought.

The doorbell rang again. Rebecca jumped back, held her breath, and opened the door.

Josey waved tentatively from the porch. "You said noon, right? Lunch?"

Megan tapped her mommy on the leg. "Juice *now*."

Damn.

—

"Can I put things in perspective for you?" Josey put the letter down, folded her arms and leaned back into the couch. "He's dead."

"Physically."

"No, Rebecca. Not just physically. He's dead, period. Spiritually, sure he's probably up in Heaven or down in Hell doing whatever it is spirits do. But emotionally and physically, he's rotting away in a pine box six feet underground in a cemetery just north of town."

Rebecca sighed. "You have such tact."

"How did he die?"

"I told you."

"No, you said *where* he died, not *how*."

"I don't know." Rebecca crossed her arms. She stared into the blank space in front of her and imagined Eddie standing there, watching. "Is there something else we could talk about?"

Josey leaned forward and grabbed her purse. She pulled out a folded piece of newspaper and handed it to Rebecca.

"I found this the other day."

Rebecca looked up for a moment then back down at the clipping. "You found this, or you went to the library and looked it up for me?"

Josey smiled but said nothing.

"Megan, get down." Rebecca opened the clipping. There was a picture of Eddie in uniform, standing among a few other Marines. He smiled for the camera while the others struck macho poses like boys standing in front of a mirror at home checking out their developing bodies, thinking they might impress someone at the next dance. The tent behind them was propped open, their worldly belongings shoved into bags or strewn across cots. Everything was covered with sand, and even though the picture was black and white, the effect—or perhaps just Rebecca's imagination—painted the whole bright beige.

Rebecca read through the article while Josey stood up to get Megan off the bookshelf. She found herself smiling every time Eddie's name was mentioned, even if was followed by "...died in a mortar attack..." and "...killed by enemy fire." The article felt like a connection—a conduit—to the final moments of Eddie's life. It was almost like jumping onto an expressway in reverse and seeing things for the first time as they unfolded. Her body crossed the Great Divide between now and then, floating through some parallel universe to be with her lover.

As her eyes skimmed over the words unimportant to her, her mind passed through places she'd been a thousand times before, asking the "what if's" but still failing to find the answers.

What if he *did* knock at the door?

What if I could take it all back?

"You're thinking something, aren't you?" Josey sat back down on the couch, a little closer to Rebecca. She put an arm around her. "He really turned out to be quite good looking, if you ask me. He was a stick, remember?"

Rebecca smiled. "Thin as a rail." She passed the article back to Josey. "Do you think I'm crazy?"

"You're a nutcase. Freak. You're one fry short of a Happy Meal and two quarts short of a gallon. Basket baby."

"But I loved him. Doesn't that say something?"

Josey tapped Rebecca on the leg. "Sure it says something. It says that life begins and life ends. It says that we live, we love, we die." Josey shook her head. "I really don't think there's anything else it could say. Keep thinking about what could have been, and what should have been will never be."

"Who fed you that line of crap?"

"You did. About a year ago."

Rebecca sat in silence, staring into the void that was her life. There was Scott, the kids, the friends, the house, the stupid dog and even dumber cat. There was a Durango in the garage, an Altima with her husband, three televisions sets, two computers, a movie room and leather furniture. She was surrounded with everything thirty-five years of life dictated she should have.

A tear pulled itself out from the corner of her eye. She never felt so empty in her life.

—

There is another voice in the room, and she doesn't recognize this one. At least the first voice had Familiarity if not a name to go with it. This voice is different, female, and it's telling someone to go home.

She wants to ask what a home is, but again her mouth refuses to move. Her arms won't move either. It seems she was just standing not too long ago, but now she has no legs.

She wiggles her feet. Yes, she has legs.

The light is back, but she still can't see anything. Maybe if she opened her eyes.

She thinks for a moment and tries to put together everything she knows: voices, bed, light, room, thirsty.

A pain explodes in her arm, but she can't scream. She wants to punch whoever made her arm hurt, but she knows any movement will cause more pain.

Quickly, the pain subsides.

She thinks she's smiling now.

She knows she's waiting.

—

The desert had a quality all its own, and on some occasions Rebecca could feel the aura of ancient seas and mystical civilizations well up inside, making her either weary of the next step or alive with the energy contained in every breath. Standing beside Eddie's gravestone, the heat overwhelmed her.

She looked up across the rest of the cemetery to the desert beyond and the mountains in the distance. Years of living in a valley of manufactured green had conditioned her to the signs of impending danger.

The longer she stared, the more the atmosphere around her moved in slow motion. She could almost see the moisture dance on thermals and make love to the sky. Drop by drop, they propagated and coalesced, creating impossible images of vapor in the azure field of blue. Out of crystal clouds would be born, grow and become alive.

The danger was real enough.

Inevitably, though, the clouds would die, and in their fit of death they would expel cold air onto the world below. The air would sink and rush in to replace the weakened atmosphere seared by the sun.

It was the wind Rebecca worried about, and she could see it in the distance, swirling in eddies and picking up sand and dust, maybe even the ghosts of those that lived and died on the desert floor. She'd been in that wind before, and knew its dance would lead to disaster. A wall taller than any skyscraper would soon enough scream across the land and suck dry whatever it touched.

That wall was closing in on her, and her time with Eddie would have to be short.

Rebecca knelt down in front of the gravestone.

"Look what you're doing to me. I can't even go to work, anymore. I keep seeing you everywhere, and not only when I'm awake. These dreams you're giving me are driving me nuts."

A blade of grass held her attention for a moment. It was new, like all the others growing over the casket of her lover — so much life, born anew and struggling to survive in a hostile world.

"I talked with Josey, again. She showed me an article in the paper about the day you died. You looked incredible in the picture."

The wind tossed the flag about from right to left. Rebecca looked up to see the wall of dust much closer now.

"I think you've filled out quite nicely, actually.

"You know, there was a time I didn't even think about you, not like this anyway. I was happy with my life. Hell, I had a husband that seemed to care, kids that played like kids should play and a bun in the oven. I'd play cards with the girls on Monday nights, go to Scott's functions at work, and even take walks to the same park where we once made love in the grass."

Rebecca noticed the lack of tears on her face for the first time. It seemed she'd been crying for days, and finally nothing.

"I went there yesterday, thinking I could picture us again, your hands all over my body, my head thrown back. You know what I saw?"

Rebecca waited for an answer.

"Well, I'll tell you anyway. You were there, waiting on a blanket. Actually, I think it was the same blanket I used to keep in the back of my car."

Rebecca smiled at the thought of the blanket. So many nights were spent tangled together beneath it. She couldn't remember where it was now.

"Times change, don't they? I think you told me once that what we had was a blink in the eye of God, but what we could have would last forever. So tell me—why can't I get in the shower without you being there? Why can't I go to sleep without thinking you're lying down next to me? Is this the forever you meant?"

A rush of feeling overtook Rebecca. She looked up at the wall of dust.

"I didn't tell you this, but I had an orgasm the other day and called out your name." Rebecca chuckled at the thought. "I really don't think Scott cared to hear that, especially since he wasn't even in the room with me."

Her cheeks felt hot. She was suddenly angry, and could feel it rise through her body like the heat all around her—quick, painful, and searing in its intensity.

"Do you know what you're doing to me, Eddie?"

The wind tossed Rebecca's hair in a fit of rage, a sure signal the wall was about to hit. She stood up. In the back of her mind, she knew she needed to get in the car, but not before saying her peace.

"You're half of me, just like you said in that damn letter. I'm *dying*, Eddie, and you won't knock on the door."

Dust stung her face. Pinpricks of pain enflamed her cheeks as the sky turned red.

"Knock on the fucking door, Eddie! You know I'll answer."

The wall hit her hard, and the little flag fell over.

—

She hears noise, but doesn't know what it is.

"Listen to this, Rebecca."

The Familiar voice is back. She likes the Familiar voice, but she wishes she understood more.

"You should remember this," the voice says.

She doesn't recognize the noise, but she thinks of the word "music".

—

Scott sat across the table, his fork poised someplace between his mouth and the plate. "You're what?"

Rebecca swallowed the last bit of rum and Coke. She looked over at the empty bottle on the counter. "I'm going away for a few days."

"Where?"

"Does it matter?"

Scott put his fork down, and stood up. "No, I guess it doesn't."

"What the hell is that supposed to mean?"

"It means exactly what I said. You walk around this house in some horrible depression. I don't like the way you're ignoring me, and frankly I couldn't care less if you walked out right now."

"It's just for a few days. I need to get my head straight."

"Why not? You're not even *here*, as far as I can tell."

Scott wiped his face and threw his napkin down. He walked out of the kitchen, leaving Rebecca alone with her thoughts and an empty glass in front of her.

Maybe this wasn't such a good idea. Maybe she really didn't need to walk out, but stay at home and try to figure out just what direction her life really *was* supposed to take.

Was she wrong?

Megan walked up to the table and put the blue vase from the bookshelf down. She crawled up on a seat and stared at the cat.

"Ed-dee," she said and pointed to the vase.

Rebecca blinked.

"What did you say, hon?"

"Eh-dee." Megan smiled wide and turned her attention to the cat. "Eh-dee vase."

Rebecca felt her stomach sink about the same time her heart beat its way into her throat. A bead of sweat formed on her forehead. Megan never could reach the top shelf, and even if she did, the vase was too heavy for her to hold in one hand and climb back down without dropping it or falling herself.

"Megan?" Rebecca leaned down to her daughter's eye level. "Who gave you that vase?"

Megan giggled in her seat and pointed to the living room. "Eh-dee. Eh-dee vase."

Rebecca followed the finger with her eyes into the living room. The lights were off, but there was a faint glow creeping in through the window from the street lamp outside. Slowly, she stood up from the table and walked toward the living room. With each step, her heart pounded harder.

Eddie sat on the couch with his hands clasped between his legs, much like he did the first time he met Rebecca's parents. Dirt covered his body from head to toe, and the uniform he wore was tattered in the shoulders and legs. He looked up at Rebecca and smiled, his teeth gleaming white in sharp contrast to his dingy face.

"Knock, knock."

Rebecca's eyes rolled back and she fell to the floor.

—

She feels like she is flying. She is happy. She doesn't know why, but it doesn't matter.

—

"Are you awake?"

Rebecca opened her eyes to see Scott standing at the side of her bed. She squinted at the bright light coming from the nightstand. "What happened?"

"I don't know." Scott sat down next to her. "You collapsed on the floor downstairs, so I brought you up here. I think you drank too much."

"I don't drink too much, Scott."

"No? Well, you stink like rum and I don't remember that bottle in the house yesterday. It's empty now."

"Where's Megan?"

"Sleeping on the couch downstairs."

"And the other kids?"

"Watching TV or something. Are you alright?"

Rebecca sat up and rubbed her temples. Maybe she did drink too much and simply hallucinated Eddie's presence on the couch. It *was* possible. She knew she'd been a different person in the last few weeks—at times someone she hated altogether—but she'd never been so irresponsible around the kids before.

But the vase....

Rebecca stood up, suddenly feeling the swirl of an inebriated mind spin out of control. The room turned in circles, the light danced on the ceiling then the floor. She reached out and grabbed Scott for support.

"Where do you think you're going?"

Rebecca swallowed an intrusion of bile in her throat. "Downstairs. I have to see something."

"Come here and lay back down."

"*No!*" Rebecca took a first cautious step toward the door. "I have to know."

"Know what?"

The door was harder to reach than she thought and got farther away the more she tried. She took another step and found herself within an inch of the wall.

"You missed. You're not very good at this, are you?"

"Not like you. You're a fucking pro."

Rebecca grabbed the handle and swung the door open, half expecting to see either the closet or the bathroom, but definitely not the hall.

Eddie stood in the doorway. "Mind if I come in?"

Rebecca looked up at his face. She smiled weakly and ran her finger across his lips, failing to notice just how much she trembled. Her mind quickly raced back through the events of the day, those of yesterday, those of years ago when they were together — all of the love, all of the passion, all of the purity wrapped itself together in one big package deposited at her feet. There was a reason for everything, despite whatever Josey had to say.

"Are you for real?" Rebecca whispered, but her words resounded through the room and drowned out all other sounds.

"Who are you talking to, Rebecca?" Scott stood right behind her, his breath irritating her neck. It seemed more an intrusion into her private world that he was even there, and a part of her wished he would disappear forever.

Rebecca ignored Scott's question and continued to stare at the face of her lover. Her lips parted, a smile crept across her face, and her eyes opened wide. "This can't be happening."

"Life doesn't end when we die, Rebecca. It just takes a little break."

Scott opened the door wider and looked down the hall. He furrowed his eyebrows and gnashed his teeth a bit. "There's no one here, Rebecca. Who are you talking to?"

Eddie pointed inside the room. "Can I come in?"

"Yeah. Sure." Rebecca sighed and put her hands against her chest, feeling the beat of her heart escalate with every breath she took. "Come on in."

Scott stepped into the hall. He turned around, his face painted red with anger. "You know what? You can just sleep this off. You're a lunatic, talking to ghosts and acting like an idiot. I don't know what's come over you these past few days—Hell, *weeks*—but I'll be *damned* sure I don't have to live with it myself. I'm taking the kids to my mom's, and I'll be at Patrick's house if you want me."

Rebecca completely shut out the voice or even the existence of her husband and followed Eddie with her eyes. She didn't care one way or another that he left. In fact, it would be a good thing.

A very good thing.

Scott slammed the bedroom door shut. She missed the last words he had to say, but none of that mattered right now. Her world dissolved in a flash of light, and what replaced it was a Heaven she'd only dreamt of for years. What mattered now sat on the edge of her bed, caked with dirt and smelling like a dog fresh from a walk in the rain. His hair wasn't quite as trim as she remembered it, but his appearance didn't matter.

Half of her had returned.

Rebecca couldn't find any words to really say what she felt. A few phrases coupled with a few more words that were in no way connected was all she could think of, and none of that needed to come out.

"Hi." Eddie looked as nervous as she felt.

"Hi."

Words passed between the two of them silently, sliding between souls on a silver thread that had never been disconnected despite so long a separation.

"Um..." Rebecca struggled. "Scott can't see you, can he?"

Eddie smiled. "No, I guess not. Ugly as ever, though." He patted the bed. "Sit down."

"Megan. How did she...?"

Eddie shrugged. "I don't know that, either. Maybe innocence opens eyes to things guilt can't see."

Rebecca sat down and tentatively touched his leg. It was real enough, and a barrage of feelings coursed through her body and electrified every nerve ending. It was almost as if a limb she'd been living without for years had returned to its rightful place, sending all the warmth, all the sensitivity, all the pain that might have occurred when it was gone in a rush of impulse that overwhelmed her brain and pushed her body to its limits in a valiant effort to maintain life.

"You're not dead," Rebecca whispered, her fingers making bolder movements across his body. "I know this can't be happening. I can't be talking to a ghost."

"I told you I would knock on the door of your life again. It doesn't matter if I'm dead or alive. Remember when I told you I'd either marry you or die your lover?"

Rebecca smiled. "Yeah. You also said 'There is no other option.' You wrote that down on a Valentine's Day card."

"See? I know what I'm talking about, don't I?"

Eddie stroked the side of Rebecca's face, brushing off a tear. She sighed and expelled any last bit of resistance she might have had to dealing with her insanity. It was a feeling she'd never experienced before, and every ounce of herself told her it was real.

She was insane.

—

She hears the words and finally they register.
"Wake up, Rebecca."
She tries to move her fingers, but her toes move instead. She has been crying, but she knows that no one has heard her.
"Knock, knock, Rebecca."
She is tired, but trying to wake up, trying to open her eyes.
She screams, but her voice is still gone.

—

The first kiss was nothing like the last kiss. Between both of them, though, Rebecca knew there passed a sense of self-awareness and awakening. That she could even feel his lips was something of a miracle, but even more incredible was the warmth she felt course through her body.

She wanted to push him onto the bed and make love to him, like so many times years ago. The strangeness of it all, though, filled her with inhibition. What would it be like making love to a ghost?

Their eyes caught each other in an unguarded moment, and Rebecca soon found herself caressing Eddie's neck softly. Her chest was heavy like a weight of guilt had been slapped upon it. Nevertheless, she felt right.

Eddie kissed Rebecca softly, stirring her with goose bumps that erupted like tiny bubbles gliding across her arms, chest and legs. She reared back and smiled, feeling the awakening like never before. Together, they fell back onto the bed, their bodies, minds and souls tangled together as one.

Rebecca closed her eyes, and gave herself completely to Eddie.

—

"Good. You're awake."
She smells stringent and freshly washed cotton sheets. Slowly,

an eye opens and lets in a little too much light.

"Don't try to move, now. Just relax."

She opens the other eye just a bit. Maybe the light isn't so bad on that side of the room.

Then again, maybe it is.

"When you're ready. Do you want me to close the drapes for you?"

She finds herself nodding her head, unsure of why she is doing it and even more unsure of why she can't just say "Yes." The footsteps of whoever is in the room sound like steel on steel, each step a hammer to the side of her head.

"You have a visitor. Do you want me to let him in?"

She nods her head again. Her eyes try to focus in the light, but all she can see are blurs and other blurs that move. She is not sure she wants to see anyone, but she doesn't think she has a choice.

A blur enters the room and slowly walks toward her. She squints to see it better, but all it does is cover her vision with tears.

"Hi."

She can't speak, but she recognizes the voice. It is Familiar.

"How do you feel?"

The other voice chimes in. "She can't speak right now, but give her time. She'll get better."

"I've been waiting for you."

The blur slowly comes into better focus. She thinks she can see shiny buttons on a coat, but she doesn't want to commit that to fact. She nods her head a little and raises her arm.

She is amazed she can raise her arm at all, but the blur with the Familiar voice takes her hand.

"They always let the newcomers wake up on their own," the voice says. "It's a decompression chamber of sorts. Not very nice, if you ask me."

She doesn't understand this. She wonders what it means to be a "newcomer" and why she needs to wake up at all. She hasn't been asleep, she thinks, but maybe she just doesn't know any better.

The blur becomes even more focused, and the shiny buttons become real. They are attached to a green jacket with red lines on the sleeve. She tries to focus in on the face, but it could be anyone.

She thinks she can make out a smile.

Her lips part, dried skin separating from dried skin. She's still thirsty and tries to point to her mouth with the other hand.

"I'll get you some water."

The familiar blur with the green jacket lets go of her hand. She shakes her head suddenly, thinking she may not see him again and never know who he is.

She forces air through her larynx. "Who..."

The blur smiles, and he bends down closer. He kisses her on the forehead. "Disorientation comes with the trip."

She doesn't understand why the word "trip" is being used. She forces out more air. "...where..."

The smile fades enough for her to recognize the response to her question. Quickly, though it returns, and she feels better.

"This is the holding area for all new arrivals, Rebecca. We're both waiting for passports. I've been here a little longer than you."

"Pass..."

The face becomes clearer. She is not completely sure, but she thinks it's Eddie.

"I know you haven't been told anything, yet, but you might as well know. You stepped in front of a car a few weeks ago."

"Pass...port...to where?"

"Don't know, but they wouldn't let me go without you. Seems that you really are half of me."

Driving the Spike

What started out as the preface to novel never blossomed the way I thought it would. That's the way of a writer sometimes: you think you have it just how you envision things, and then the characters come crashing down around you. They go off and do something else, and all you're left with is the shell of a story. I do have plans to revisit that novel, but for now, here is the preface.

The train sped by, a blur of red, white and blue that cut through the wheat and corn fields, through towns that once hoped to build on its arrival, though farms, through bayous and forests and plains and all things American. The train sped by people who gawked at the miracle of technology without understanding the miracle of finance, by lovers who dreamed of dining in the opulent cars they had heard about before retiring to the gold-trimmed and silk splattered birthing racks reserved for the rich and famous, by romantic idealists who imagined what the land would look like from the Plexiglas windows at 300 miles per hour. The train sped by on rails of iron scratched into the landscape like remnant scars of a vicious battle, oblivious to those who dug the tunnels, shifted the earth, laid the lines, drove the spikes in the heat of summer and death of winter.

The train did not care.

The train did not know it owed its existence to the men and women who died, to the families that suffered the pain of distance and the dissonance of government officials as they debated direction, toll, contract, unionization. The train did not know its name, did not know its schedule, did not care about the millionaires and billionaires and diplomatic officials that road in its belly on that first trip. It did not feel itself on the verge of history as it tore through the land with its magnetic push and spidery webs of communication and guidance lines of copper and titanium, with its satellite positioning systems, wireless sensors, in-cab signals, proprietary software.

The train did not care.

—

Vera sat forward in her leather seat and stared at the setting sun through the massive window of the train. The interplay of cerulean blue, indigo, orange and red above the rolling hills was something she never knew existed beyond glossy photos. Her five-year-old mind was awash with a wonder never explored. Downtown Washington D.C., with its bustling streets and ancient monuments to a nation she couldn't understand, had nothing on the wide open space of eastern Colorado or of the majestic peaks which jabbed their defiant fists into the heavens announcing the Great West.

"Look, Mommy!" Vera cried. Her voice shattered the solemnity of the Presidential Suite. She turned to her mother with wide eyes. "Do you see the sun and the mountains?"

Vera's mother did her best to raise her head and say something motherly. "Yes, dear. How nice." She rubbed her temples and pushed back a few loose strands of gray hair from her sweating forehead.

Vera had known the duties of a First Lady could be stressful, or at least she'd been *told* the duties could be stressful. That's what Nanny said, anyway. Whatever the duties were, Vera thought, why couldn't they include looking out the window every once in a while?

She looked across the aisle at her father who was busy talking with some old, wrinkled people with dried apricot faces. They looked angry. They probably weren't angry, Vera knew, but they always looked that way in their gray or blue or black suits. If she had to wear a suit all day, she'd probably look angry, too.

"I don't see the purpose in sending a whole battalion to Xining," one of the men said. "For what purpose?"

Vera's father, the President of the United States—a designation lost on Vera altogether—sat back in his leather chair and looked sternly at the man in the grey suit. "If we can control their chemical and natural gas processing, medicine, foods and bio-chemicals in the north, we can cripple the supply to the east."

"To Beijing," the man said.

"No, to Pyongyang."

Vera turned back to the window. She couldn't follow the conversation, didn't know some of the words, and that man in the gray suit raised his voice a lot. It seemed strange to her that given the view out the window, no one wanted to look at the sunset.

"What do you see?" An older woman sitting next to her mother with sharply tied black hair traced with white peered out the window. "You know what that is?" she asked.

Vera nodded in response to the woman's question. "The Rock Mountains."

"The Rocky Mountains," the woman corrected. "We're going through them."

Vera wrinkled her nose. "How do we go through them? They seem so big."

"Tunnels were built through them to minimize the delay."

"What does that mean?"

Vera's mother sighed. "It means we'll get off this damn train sooner than later."

Both the woman and Vera looked at the First Lady with matching scowls. If she couldn't look out the window, the least she could do was keep her mouth shut.

—

The train sped through the plains on its way to the first tunnel dug into the first mountain. It did not care there was a tunnel, nor did it care why it was there. The train was programmed to remain on its track, slightly elevated by the magnets beneath, and deliver its passengers to the destination, someplace on the other side of that tunnel. It did not know why its destination had been chosen, only that its directions were clear.

The artificial intelligence onboard the train would handle all the details of why it was going in this direction. It would work out when the train needed to speed up or slow down, when it needed to release pressure on its undercarriage, when it needed to turn on its lights or adjust the comfort baffles. The AI was the train's master. The people inside were just the cargo.

—

Vera returned to her examination of the sunset and the mountains in the distance that seemed to grow larger every second. She had been told the train was the fastest in the world, but without a reference point, she didn't know what fast meant. She had been told this train would to take people to an extraordinary new world of possibilities. This trip was the first of many to come, and Nanny said only special people were allowed onboard. Nanny wasn't included.

"Who dug the tunnels?" Vera asked.

The woman opened her mouth to respond, but the First Lady cut her off. "People who aren't important," she said quickly.

Vera didn't respond. She considered her mother's words, thought them strangely cruel, and finally settled on listening to her own thoughts about who dug the tunnels. Maybe they were giant moles like the kind she'd seen in the zoo last summer, the ones people called naked and looked funny. Then again, no. These were the Rocky Mountains, she recalled. Moles couldn't dig through all those rocks.

A weak shudder ran through the cabin, like a body shivering in the cold winter night. Vera looked up at her mother, at the woman, and then at her father. No one seemed to have noticed. Perhaps it wasn't a big deal—just a part of train travel. Although, she thought, there hadn't been any other shudders the whole trip.

—

Outside the cabin, the train cut through God's country oblivious. It sped by with nothing more than a destination in mind, with the soothing hum of the magnetic track to guide it. The conversations in its belly, the communications beamed from satellite to receiver to server and then to terminal screen in the engineer's pilot house were nothing to the train at all. Even the warning that flashed in the eyes of the engineer as he sipped on a steaming latte was a warning that meant nothing.

The train did not care. It was the AI's job to care for such things and adjust as necessary.

—

Vera looked out the window again at the passing glory that was America. This was the first trip, or so the kind old man who sat her down and buckled her into her seat had said. This was the big one, the end of things that had started long ago, long before she had been born. In her lap she held a pamphlet the man had handed her. It was a guidebook of the train and how it came to be. She could not read much of it, but there were pretty pictures of the train in all its glorious red, white and blue. There was a map on the back that showed a red line — the one they were on — and several dotted blue lines. According to the man who had given her the pamphlet, the dotted blue lines were tracks still under construction. The red line crossed the country from New York to someplace called Seattle.

Vera flipped through the pamphlet looking at the pictures. There were black and white pictures in the front, pictures of old trains and smokestacks and funny people in weird clothing all standing next to a building that said "Union Station." There were other pictures of trains that looked newer but were still said to be "relics of the early days of Amtrak in the last century." She didn't know what "relics" meant, but she liked the pictures. There were many words on a few pages, but on one of them there were words next to an old picture of her great grandfather, another former president. She had never met her great grandfather, but apparently he was an important man once. As she read the words next to his picture, she silently sounded out those she didn't know.

—

What we need, then, is a smart transportation system equal to the needs of the 21st century. A system that reduces travel times and increases mobility. A system that reduces congestion and boosts productivity. A system that reduces destructive emissions and creates jobs. What we're talking about is a vision for high-speed rail in America. Imagine boarding a train in the center of a city. No racing to an airport and across a terminal, no delays, no sitting on the tarmac, no lost luggage, no taking off your shoes. Imagine whisking through towns at speeds over 100 miles an hour, walking only a few steps to public transportation, and ending up just blocks from your destination. Imagine what a great project that would be to rebuild America. —President Barack Obama, 2011

—

Vera read it over again. If Nanny were allowed to be here, she would have helped with some of the more difficult words. Vera looked at her mother and her sad face, then at the woman next to her, her chief of staff. Vera had never been told the woman's name only that she existed to help her mother in whatever way she wanted.

The woman smiled at Vera then pointed to the pamphlet. "What are you reading, dear?"

"Great Grandpa's words." Vera looked down, suddenly feeling ashamed. "I can't understand them."

"Well, then..." The woman shifted in her seat to get closer to Vera. She looked at the pamphlet. "Tell me what you don't understand."

Vera shrugged. "Why are these words here next to his picture?"

"Long ago," the woman said, "people wanted high-speed rail like this because many other countries had them. Your great grandfather knew this, but no one wanted to pay to build one."

"Why?"

"Some people wanted to keep the money for themselves. Some people thought that money should go other places, like hospitals or community centers. Some wanted the money spent on electric cars. Other people thought money should go to the poor neighborhoods so they can have better lives."

Vera's mother choked or coughed. Whatever noise she made caused Vera to look at her. Her mother rolled her eyes then turned away.

—

The AI guiding the train did not notice the warning signs beamed to it from a satellite above. If it had sentience, it might have wondered what had made it recently tired, and then it might have wondered if anyone had adjusted its sensors. If the AI guiding the train had eyes, it would have closed them. Certainly it should have noticed the dark figure in the train's engineering cabin typing away at one of its terminals, feeding the AI code that would alter its awareness. Had the AI paid more attention and identified the threat, it might have ordered the train to slow or even stop.

The AI guiding the train did not notice.

—

The woman next to Vera continued. "When no one could agree on what to spend money on, nothing ever changed. For years it was like this, everyone out for themselves instead of what the country needed."

Vera scrunched her eyes. "But why would people *not* want to spend money on things that would help them?"

"Because there are bad people out there," Vera's mother cut in. "They don't care about anything but themselves."

"Wouldn't this help them? A way to get across the country quickly?"

"Sure." Vera's mother smiled weakly. "But if you're not the right person who says it should be done, half the country will hate you for it. If you *are* the right person, the *other* half will hate you."

"Huh?"

"It's politics, dear," Vera's mother said with an exasperated sigh. "Nothing more."

"Are there still people like that out there?"

"Absolutely. They're the ones who didn't vote for your father."

"What do you mean?"

The train shuddered again, preventing Vera's mother from answering. In the jarring moment, Vera dropped the pamphlet on the ground. The woman reached down to pick it up, then hesitated.

The shudder stopped and the woman returned the pamphlet to Vera.

"What was that?" Vera asked.

"Just turbulence on the rail," the woman answered. "Nothing to worry about."

Vera was worried, even if she was told not to be. She fiddled with the pamphlet in her hand, then opened it hoping to get rid of all the bad thoughts she was having. On the earliest page, there was an old painting of people standing on railroad tracks surrounding a man holding what looked like a hammer. The caption read "The Driving of the Last Spike painted by Thomas Hill. Promontory Summit, UT, on May 10, 1869."

"What is this?" Vera asked the woman next to her since her mother was obviously not going to answer. At least no nicely.

The woman looked at the painting. "That, dear, is a great moment in history. When two railroads finally met in the Utah, the last spike—I think it was golden—was driven to connect the two."

"What's a spike?"

"The thing that holds railroads together, like a large nail."

"Or the thing that's being driving into my head right

now," Vera's mother said. "Honestly, Claire. I have a headache the size of Kansas and this banter you're having with my daughter is making it worse."

The woman—Claire, apparently—sat up straight and nodded to Vera's mother. "As you wish," she said quietly.

Vera was about to protest her mother's intrusion when a grumbling noise, like a soft roar, filtered from the front of the train. It grew in intensity, and as it did so, everyone turned to face the front of the cabin.

—

The train did not care about politics or wars or paintings or what the people inside its belly were saying. The train existed to do as it was told, go where it was told and not to dissent. As such, the train did not see the explosives placed under its rails a hundred feet in front of it, nor did it know the meaning of rebellion. It had been the AI's job to look for such things, and yet there had been no warning, no orders from its master to do anything different.

The train did not hear the screams of the dying as they were thrust through the air, through the cabins, through the windows, born on balls of fire, impaled on steel and carbon fibers, crushed beneath the train's own massive weight. It did not feel the inferno that raced through its innards.

As the sun finally disappeared behind the purple mountains majesty of America, the smoldering remains of the train did not see the mysterious man, wrapped in a black duster, whistling a gentle tune as he watched from a forest high on a hill, his eyes twinkling with what might have been delight or wonder or revenge. The train did not see the other black figures walking through its shredded and burning wreckage. It did not hear the muted gunshots that cut off the whimpers of those who had not yet died. It did not feel the blood pour from the body of a five-year-old girl, as her life flowed over the train's skin and onto the track bed that had become her grave.

The train simply did not care.

A Table for Two

At the outset of my new "career," I wanted to get involved as much as I could with like-minded people. I joined an online writer's group that had been around since the early days of the World Wide Web and quickly felt comfortable with the regular visitors to the site. At first, I was scared to post anything; I read other work, posted comments and tried to stay in the foreground of the background (if that makes sense) as much as possible. By the end of 2001, however, I'd been pulled into posting my own work on a consistent basis.

In the middle of 2002, the group posted a quick "flash" challenge — in 1000 words or less, write something horrific about food. In the realm of literary expression, the craft of flash fiction has never been one I have excelled in, despite the nudge from some who might suggest that it would be worthwhile for me to delve further into the art form, if only to cultivate a proficiency in the art of linguistic brevity (or to be succinct). I had written the first paragraph years prior, but like so many things, it sat like a misfit in a folder on my computer, waiting for the moment to surface and become something. From that paragraph, this story emerged.

"A Table for Two" was published in Goremet Cuisine, *an anthology, in 2005*

Shadows danced undecidedly on the walls to the flicker of a half-wasted candle in the middle of a small card table. Two lovers sat facing each other, staring into the void of their lives and finding companionship in the loneliness. Neither spoke, reserving words for a more appropriate time.

The man sighed and pulled his gaze from his lover's. He looked down at his plate. Dinner had been an exercise in love. The meat wasn't ready, but a side of beans from a can found in the trash a few alleys over and a garnish handpicked from the garden of weeds outside were prepared to round out the meal. It wasn't the sustenance either of them craved, though; it was the moment. If they were to share a moment together—any moment, no matter how trivial—they wanted to savor every precious second. Everything was almost perfect.

The woman stood from the table and smiled at her companion. She slowly walked to another room and fumbled for something on a shelf. Within moments, soft melodies of a solo piano crackled through the air, filling the trailer with atmosphere. She walked back to the kitchen, the curves of her body through her dress taking on a more sensuous quality in the candlelight. She ran her hand across the back of her lover, kissed him softly on the cheek and turned to sit down.

She looked at him and smiled. "I thought the music would get us in the mood a little more."

"I was already in the mood."

Her smile became more whimsical, almost embarrassed by his candor. "I hope the kids are sleeping well."

"At least we'll have a little peace tonight."

Their eyes caught each other again, trapping their souls in a dance that would continue forever. In each, the pit of their stomach turned softly, reminding them of how love really felt. It wasn't enough to be with each other, to raise a family together, to struggle day in to make ends meet. It wasn't enough to want the best for the other and forgo the selfish desires that lead so many into a world of an unhappy marriage. To be bound in love was to give of each other—mind, soul, and body.

"Do you think we'll ever change?" The woman took a sip from a plastic glass of red wine, licking her lips seductively.

"I suppose when the need is no longer there."

"What need?"

"The need to exist."

"I didn't mean money-wise. Are we ever going to stop sharing of ourselves, sharing of our children, sharing everything that's important to us? Are we ever going to *change*?"

The man smiled and stood up. He walked behind his lover and wrapped his arms around her chest. "I think the life we have is a gift in itself, don't you?"

The woman closed her eyes and leaned back to kiss her man firmly, passionately. Slowly, she guided his hands down the curve of her body, resting his calloused palms on her thighs. "I love you."

"I love you, too," he whispered. He pulled up her dress slowly, uncovering a large bandage across her right thigh. "Are you ready to eat?"

She grabbed the knife beside her plate and handed it to her lover. "Be gentle. I don't have much meat left on that side."

The Pink Teddy

Shortly after buying my first laptop with money earned from my first real job, I decided to write a few short stories in order to get my creative juices flowing. I'm almost certain this was written in 1991 or 1992, as the image I had in my head was fresh — a shopping mall and a boy who was probably too young to buy lingerie.

The cashier eyed Greg from behind her little barricade at the register, incessantly tapping a small gold pen. On top of her sharp, pointed nose sat a rudely placed set of thin-rimmed spectacles that immediately reminded any passerby of his old, first grade teacher with the chalk in one hand and the paddle in the other. That, coupled with her thin, silver hair tightly bundled up behind her head, screamed "Prude" to anyone who cared to listen. Not what he was expecting when he came to shop.

"Can I help you?" the silver virgin shrieked.

"Y-yes...I'm..." Greg could never get this shopping thing down right. "I'm looking for some negligee." His face turned red. "Ah. Well...." She looked over her thin-rimmed glasses and down at the man of (she guessed) no more than seventeen. "Yes. We have plenty of that. What kind are you looking for?"

Oh, no, Greg's mind screamed. *Don't start asking me questions like that.* "Uh...hmmm..." He loosened his collar a bit and cleared his throat. He hated shopping for women's clothes, for several of the more obvious reasons. And the fact that Ms. Demeaning was staring at him with the look of some mother on a hell-bent quest to psychologically punish her child, did not help his already nervous state of being. "It's not for me, so—"

"Well!" she interrupted in a sort of half-sarcastic tone, tapping her pen a little harder on the counter. "I should hope not. So, you really don't have anything in particular in mind, do you?"

"Uh...No, not really. I was just looking for some..." he waved his hands in an apprehensive search for words, "something of some type."

The rather tall persona of the Wicked Witch from the East on steroids smacked her lips. "Specific today, aren't we." She glared at him with a look that said "Forget Toto—I think I'll have you for dinner, instead."

"I...I'm sorry." Greg could feel the yellow steak paint its way down his back, telling him to turn around and buy flowers instead. Where did he ever get the idea that his girlfriend might like lingerie? How did he ever muster the courage to step into this store in the first place? Flowers are much easier to buy. Cheaper, too.

"Perhaps if I knew who you were getting this for, it might help." She smiled sadistically as if she had found a way to pin this little heretic to a wall. "Is it for your...girlfriend?"

Greg stood glued to his spot as her eyes became thinner and thinner. He envisioned himself standing in front of a throne in Hell with the Evil One prodding at him with a pitchfork; that pointed tail swinging up in the air, ready to strike him down if he said the wrong thing.

"Come on, you heathen," squealed a thousand voices. "It's for your sexually active, live-in, immoral little girlfriend, isn't it? *Isn't it?*"

Satan, he thought. *She must be Satan.*

"Uh...No, no. It's...um...for my wife." The lie struck him in the face like a steaming pot, the burning sensation spreading throughout his weakening body.

The smile faded as quickly as her hair had, and the pen stopped in mid-tap. There was a pause of a few seconds as she thought this over in slight disbelief, then reared her head. "Oh, your wife. How...sweet." She sighed, put her pen down, and headed around the counter. "Let's see if we can't find something for your...'wife', shall we?"

Greg hesitated for a moment, his mind ablaze with a thought of being led up to the guillotine while a thousand jeering priests threw tomatoes and other assorted vegetables. "Really, it's just my wife. I'm innocent." He heard the crowd erupt in hysterical laughter, as the executioner shoved his head onto the chopping block.

"Ha! That's what they all say," bellowed the beast through his black, blood-stained hood. Below him, Greg could see the heads of those thousands of young, unsuspecting shoppers who had made the mistake of stumbling into this store while the Silver Virgin from Hell had been working. They all stared up at him with a gaze that said "So, you think this is a far, far better thing you do, than you have ever done, now? Should have bought her flowers." He winced as the blade came down in a fury of gleaming metal and dried blood.

"How about this one?" The shriek of the cashier brought Greg out of his day-dream and back into his nightmare. His "executioner" held a small string in her hand that looked as if, at most, all it would cover was the upper portion of someone's clavicle. He stared at it for a moment, trying to think what his "wife" might look like if she wore a thread like that. His knees started to get weak.

"No, huh?" The cashier put the string back on the rack and

began flipping through the rest. "Are you looking for something on the order of purely sexual, moderately sexual, or sort of 'quietly' sexual?"

Greg hated that word; it always made him feel like a dirty ten-year old blushing in a dusty corner of a convenience store with a *Playboy* he had managed to sneak from the magazine rack and hide in the pages of a *Better Homes and Gardens*. "Uh..." He felt his face grow hot again.

"Let me guess." The Wicked Witch took a step back and looked over him in a contemptuous sort of manner. "For you," she sneered, "I'd say 'quietly' sexual."

Greg didn't know whether to take that as a compliment or a downright slam. Judging by the way this lady had been looking him over the last few minutes, he guessed it was a slam.

"What about this?" The woman held out a black strip of translucent lace that might cover a breast (at most).

She calls this quietly sexual, he thought as he stared at it for a moment. "You wouldn't happen to have anything else, would you? Maybe in pink?"

She dropped the lace bandage on the floor, and turned to flip through more of the rack with a look of pure evil on her face. "Pink," she mumbled. "Pink...Ah, here we go. Pink." Pulling out an ambiguous teddy, she turned to Greg, and, with a voice that would make the most fearless man run back to his mother, she growled. "What about this?"

Greg wanted to run back to his mother. He stared at the teddy, trying to see his girlfriend sprawled seductively out on his bed wearing it. It wasn't working.

"Well?" The silver virgin was growing impatient. She began to tap her foot on the ground in the hopes of speeding things up. Maybe a little more sarcasm might do the trick. "Look, perhaps you would like me to try it on for you."

Greg's eyes opened up to their extremes, and he felt his

stomach turn in a fit of utter disgust. To have her try this on would be like watching the autopsy of a month-old cadaver.

"Now, here," began the crumpled shape of the doctor, "we have the chest...I think. Just a moment while I pry this up and check." The sound of cracking ribs fills the room like the sound of a jackhammer through the head of a migraine sufferer. "Yup, that's the chest alright. And as you can see, the breasts have been severely deformed by decomposition."

A tap on the shoulder brought Greg back to reality and the woman in front of him. "Do you want me to try it on?" she prodded once more.

"Uh...no...no...That's alright. I'll go ahead and take it." He wanted to get out of that store as soon as possible and away from this person—whoever she was. He made his way back to the counter and pulled out his wallet.

"It might help things," called the cashier still standing by the rack, "if you told me what size she wears."

For a second, Greg thought it was another slam, but soon he realized that this was, indeed a valid question. What size is she? "I'm sorry. I...don't really know."

The silver virgin contorted her lips and stared at the floor. With a sigh, she looked back at Greg with another evil stare that made him shrink to the size of that teddy. "You don't know what size your...wife is?"

"No...I...I don't."

"Well, how is she built?"

Another question like that, his mind whispered, and it's off to the flower shop. He muddled the image of his girlfriend over in his mind for a second. "She's about...this tall." He held his hand up to his eyes. "And she's kind of, I guess, slender."

"Medium height and slender, huh? Well, that sure narrows the choices down, doesn't it?"

Greg looked confused. "Does it?" he cautiously asked.

The woman leaned against the rack and folded over the teddy. "No. How about her chest? Is it average size? Large? Small? *Nonexistent*"

That flush of red began to come back to his face as he stood at the counter speechless. *Pink flowers or red?* "I...I guess they're...you know...average."

"A medium, slender, 'average'-chested woman. Lessee here." She fumbled through the rack for something that might fit. "Here we go. This ought to fit." With a grunt she put the other choices back on the rack and made her way over to the counter.

"Okay." She sighed as she rang up the cost on the cash register, pounding each key as if they were somehow connected to Greg's head. "That'll be...Fifty-eight ninety-six with tax." She peered over the rim of her glasses and looked at him with a gaze that said "You had better have the money, you little, sniveling rodent."

Greg fumbled through his wallet for the cash. His heart sank to new-found lows as he counted up his bills. Ten...Fifteen...Twenty...Uh-oh. Twenty-six dollars. That's it. *What is she going to do to me? Does she have a pot in the back where she cooks little boys for lunch?*

He looked up at the witch who had grabbed her pen and was tapping again. Her eyes had become thin slits through which a slight red tint could be distinguished. The tapping became louder and louder.

He reached deep into his pockets in a fit of desperation, as his heart beat faster and faster to the rhythm of the pen. He looked up at his tormenter and flashed a quick and uneasy smile. This can't be happening, his mind screamed. Payday was yesterday.

The sweat rolling off of his forehead must have looked strange to the old woman, or maybe it didn't. As far as Greg knew, she could have worked here for thirty years selling lingerie to young punks like himself who saw the word "abstinence" like they viewed the word "parents" — something to rebel against. She might have even expected this kind of money-grubbing the minute he walked through the two glass doors. She might have —

Just as his vital organs were about to cease functioning, Greg pulled two twenties out of his jeans. With a sigh of relief and a fake smile, he handed over the money. The cashier put the negligee into a bag along with the receipt and held it out to the young man.

"Tell me something," she whispered in almost a depressed fashion. "Is this *really* for your wife?"

The look in her eyes held Greg at bay. His world seemed to sink into a pit of deception and dishonesty that he had dug for himself over the years. He stared down at the counter, feeling the weight of his guilt — the weight of a thousand lies that all seemed to center around his present girlfriend — pressing down upon his shoulders. *She knows, Greg. She knows.*

"Yes. Yes it is," he sighed. And, without further contemplation, he grabbed the bag and turned to go. He could feel the silver virgin staring at him as he walked down the aisle to the glass door, past the mannequin sporting the latest in sensual wear, past the racks of lingerie and see-through bras, past the sign on the wall that read "Thirty Percent Off Everything". As he grabbed the handle of the door, a wave of curiosity swept over him like some psychic rush of understanding.

With a cautious glance, he looked back, and on the other side of the store, he could faintly see the old woman, leaning against

the counter...

...crying.

In the Bedroom

This was another flash fiction piece written for a magazine that wanted it. That they didn't select the story for publication is okay. Rejection is part of a writer's life. We write, we edit, we show someone the story, and then we dust off our bruised egos and try again. I do like how this story turned out, however, and I may look to this later for the purposes of expansion.

She bled.

It wasn't so much the amount of blood she watched drip from the small cut in her finger. It was the idea that blood was flowing. It trailed down the side of her hand, rested for a moment on a bend in her wrist, then fell to the floor. The dark red spot at her feet was now a calling card for every bloodthirsty demon in her bedroom. She shouldn't have picked at that scab.

She pulled her hand back and tucked it under her arm. Maybe they wouldn't notice. Maybe they were all sleeping on the far side of the bedroom and the scent wouldn't reach them. Maybe she would live after all.

In the corner of the room, a long stuffed caterpillar looked back at her with lifeless eyes. Its painted smile seemed to widen in the shadows, growing longer with each passing second. Next to it, a ragged bear-its left eye missing-shifted its weight and fell to the floor.

The corner of the room. That's where they had to be. She pulled tighter at the covers and pushed her little body back against the wall. It wasn't fair. No matter what her parents said, the notion that she would sleep better without a nightlight and the door shut was just plain wrong. She was seven. Seven-year-old children needed comfort, solace, and peace. They needed to know that they were protected, even in the cold, darkened recesses of their rooms. They needed to know that someone was there for them, watching over them, listening for any sign of distress. Seven-year-old children needed love.

They certainly didn't need to lie awake in their beds waiting to die.

A branch tapped at the window. She let out a quiet shriek and tightened her grip on the covers. What was out there? Did they wait outside the window, licking their lips, and tasting the sweetness of children on their breath? Were they that hungry?

Did they hear her shriek?

Think about something else. She closed her eyes tightly, trying to force a thought that might calm her nerves. *Think about something else. Think.*

It wasn't working. Another tap at the window opened her eyes. She looked around the room, trying to make out the demons in the dark. If she could just see them, she might be able to escape their grip. She squinted in the dark, knowing there was a dresser in one corner and a toy box against a wall. She couldn't see the details, though. She needed more light.

Her eyes scanned the room again, then rested on the corner of the room where the caterpillar sat watching and waiting. Next to it—

The bear was gone.

Her breath stopped and she felt her heart skip a beat before rapidly pounding against her chest. Where was it? Where was the bear?

The branch tapped louder at the window, blown by some unseen force. It hit the glass almost in time to her heart. Quickly, she pulled the covers over her head and tried to find comfort by burying her head between her knees. Why? Why did they have to come for her? What could she have possibly done to deserve to die so young? Her mind screamed with a thousand reasons, spilling out of her memories like blood flowing from an open vein. Her father would yell at her, then her mother. A teacher made fun of her. The kids next door screamed and fought with her, pushing her around.

She never meant any of it! She didn't mean to be stupid. She didn't try to be careless. She was always careful not to make her parents mad, to step quietly and play quietly with her toys in her room. She tried to remember to brush her teeth, to wash her hands, to whisper. She tried to keep her room clean. She honestly wanted to be a good girl! Why did they have to do this? Why did they have to take away her light? Why did she have to die?

The branch hit the window with a crash, shattering the glass. Rain and wind poured into the room as she screamed.

"Mommy! Daddy!"

She threw the covers aside and jumped off the bed. A piece of glass dug its way into her flesh as she ran for the door. She screamed again, focused on the door. She could make it. It was only another step away.

The door flew open.

"Angel?" The little girl's mother turned on the light. "Are you okay?"

"Mommy..." The girl closed her eyes against the tears that streamed down her face. She grabbed onto her mother's leg and held tight. "I'm scared."

"Don't be, honey. These things happen."

Her mother looked around the room at the shattered glass and the rain pouring in through the window. The branch had broken off and lay against the side of the bed, dripping wet.

"Were you playing with your bear?"

The little girl turned around to look. The bear lay on the foot of her bed, its one eye staring back. In the corner of the room, the caterpillar no longer grinned.

Out Shopping

Following my attempt at flash fiction, the writer's group was presented with a challenge to write a story based on the seven deadly sins. It was a little restrictive, however: you couldn't deviate from the Holiday season and there had to be a little girl...somewhere.

The second and third paragraphs of this story were yanked from the novel I had been writing for the last gazillion years. I rarely delete things I cut out of other works; I paste them into a new document and leave them in a "scraps" folder on my computer. This has proved very helpful on more than one occasion when inspiration has run away from me like the girl in Calculus did when I mentioned the word "prom."

This story also has a point of view problem. I think. When I first posted it, I was given a cat-o-nine-tails style whipping about how I jumped from character to character. It wasn't until someone nicely pointed out to the group that what I had done was write something "unique." Usually, words like "unique" mean "crappy," but in this case the poster felt I'd wrote within the point of view of one person who had a sort of "limited" omniscience.

I suppose. Still, I never sold this story, and I doubt I will. I did, however, have fun writing it.

He watched. More to the point though, he hunted.

The faces of people coming and going from the entrance held the old man's attention. So many lives walking to and fro, so many stories told only on the wrinkles of their faces or the bruises on their skin. Seated on a bench beside a hideous water fountain full of wishes cast in vain, he looked at each person and saw more than the flesh. To him, the souls were clear and told more of the person than any amount of conversation ever could. The sound of mechanical water filled the portion of his ears that wasn't filled with the words of a thousand conversations, an organist trying to attract anyone with a credit card, or kids screaming for attention.

He looked at his wristwatch: nine o'clock. One more hour and the stores would send down the gates, the masses trickle out the door, and the mall would fall silent, resting before the sun rose yet again over the world of commerce. He scanned the souls in front of him, young and old, watching and waiting. A young couple—perhaps lovers—hunched over a glass display cabinet in the jewelry store across the way. The man pointed, the woman said something and then pointed somewhere else. The scene played out as it probably had a thousand times before in the same spot: the man grimaced, then pointed to another location, which the woman ignored and pointed to someplace entirely different. The old man sighed. Life was sure to hand the couple a plate full of failure, frustration and pain. There wouldn't be any satisfaction in preventing it, nor would there be any satisfaction in accelerating their own descent into Hell.

In front of the pretzel shop next door, a small girl stood next to her mother, staring at the old man. He hated that, wishing she would just go away. He didn't need to feel watched himself and he sure didn't need the constant gaze of innocence burning through his skin. The girl stood motionless, trained on the man on the bench. Her mother finally stepped away from the counter and headed off toward the next shoe store or curio shop. She motioned to her daughter to follow suit, finally resorting to a firm pull in the right direction. The girl turned to walk away, stopped, then looked at the old man again. As annoying at she was, there just wouldn't be any sense of accomplishment. As for the mother, she was in her own hell. She had that look about her.

A fat slob of a young man stumbled out of a sporting goods store to the right of the woman and child. He let out a resounding staccato laugh, and then turned to wait for either of the two friends he was with. A stain—ketchup maybe—spotted his white shirt in several places, matching the pattern of acne on his face. The old man weakly smiled at the picture of gluttony, trying to be liked. More likely than not, the fat slob would go home tonight, turn on his television and cry himself to sleep over a pint of ice cream. He'd seen it before: the hapless victim of society, largely held accountable for his genetic makeup and destined to wander through life alone. *Let him have his moment of jocularity*, the man thought. *I might as well take the little girl for all her innocence.*

He continued to watch and wait. In this corner of the mall there didn't seem to be any viable candidates. A family of six, a wave of teenage rebellion, a man with a cigar—all of them baring their souls to the man, but asking nothing in return. He had assumed that during the holiday season there would be a large cache of people to choose from. Unfortunately, it was the thrust of the season—to buy, to spend, to go into debt—that was so pervasive on the minds of the people, that only a few really stopped long enough for their souls to reveal something.

The old man stood up, eased himself upright with a crooked cane, and meandered toward the center of the mall.

There would be other people, probably crowded around a food court shoving fried rice or cheese-on-a-stick down their throats as if they hadn't eaten in days. Holiday music drifted across the man's ears, and he tried to digest it the best he could amid the noise of a thousand people chattering mindlessly. And chatter they did. They chattered about buying this or whether or not she would like that or if they were breaking their budget by getting someone else this. There was anger in the voices, frustration, and mixed in the middle, there was trepidation. There were fathers, mothers, children, sisters, brothers, aunts and uncles—all of them wrapped up in the idea of buying for others, but few of them understanding the idea of giving.

A small, reckless boy bumped into the old man, knocking his cane out from under him. His mother grabbed the boy tightly by the arm, picked up the cane and handed it back.

"I'm sorry," she said, her face failing to hide her anger at the child. "He's a little wound up today."

The old man smiled and looked down at the boy. "It's quite alright, ma'am. Little boys should play." He knelt down slowly, supporting the weight of his frail body on the cane. "Santa Claus knows a boy's heart. Have you been good this year?"

The boy looked up at his mother, unsure of how to answer the old man with the wrinkles so deep. He tried to pull his arm away, but her mother wasn't about to let go.

Undaunted by the silence, the man widened his smiled and stood. He turned to the mother and nodded his head. "Little boys should play."

The mother smiled weakly, nodded in agreement and walked away. The man watched her as she pulled her son alongside, leaning down every few seconds to levy a new set of punishments. He dropped his smile—as fake as it was— and turned back toward the center of the mall.

—

He watched. More to the point though, he stalked.

The old man looked at his wristwatch: ten minutes to closing. The line for Santa Claus was down to three: a skinny kid with glasses that covered half his face, the girl from the pretzel shop, and a mother holding an infant, pacing back and forth while the wonders of Christmas were lost to the child. The stores were finally letting down their gates, some of them for good, others only partially to allow the few remaining customers to leave. The noise of earlier had worn off, replaced more by the repetitive music chiming in from some ancient speaker high in the ceiling. The notes were serenading the old man, covering him with that good feeling that comes with the season. Sure the song was a little slow—a nice relaxing pace for the end of the day—but the words were, as always, magical.

Have yourself a merry little Christmas
Let your heart be light
From now on our troubles will be out of sight

The little girl was staring again, and the old man found himself staring back. She held her mother's hand, but otherwise showed no movement whatsoever. Here was innocence, lost in a world that made her believe Santa Claus was real. *Sure he is*, the man thought. *He's as real as the 42-year old, twice divorced, unemployed former truck driver behind the beard.*

The old man tore his eyes away from the girl and looked up at Santa Claus who was waiting for the next child to come shuffling up the stairs and sit on his lap. Santa leaned over the elf next to him—a young woman who needed a little extra money for the season and wasn't embarrassed by wearing green tights and a rather revealing rag. He whispered something. The elf let out a giggle, rolled her eyes, and shifted a little to the right. Deftly, Santa reached around and pinched the elf on the butt.

The skinny boy with the glasses walked up and stood next to Santa.

"Ho, ho, ho!" Santa bellowed through smoke-laden lungs. "Come here little boy and sit on Santa's lap."

The boy agreed, nervously twitching as he looked over at his mother. She stood stoically, prodding him on with her eyes. It was bedtime, and she was just as tired as he should be. One last trip to the mall had turned into a budget-breaking free-for-all and it wasn't getting any easier. Every year it was the same old thing: spend, struggle for a few months, and pray everyone has a good Christmas. Where was the joy in all of that?

The old man leaned forward on his cane and watched as Santa talked to the skinny boy. The boy nodded a few times, quietly wished for something, then nodded again as Santa asked about his behavior. It was basically the same scene replayed over and over again. Each child asked for a different toy, but each response from Santa was the same rehearsed lie. The man had been watching for a good half-hour, and from what he could see, that was long enough.

The old man turned and looked toward the line. The mother with the infant had finally left, perhaps realizing that her child really didn't care one way or the other. Only the little girl was left, and she was still staring at him.

—

He watched. More to the point though, he readied himself.

The shops were closed finally, and outside the entrance to the mall, snow lightly fell. The song from inside was still playing in his mind, soothing the wrinkles of a life that was growing more and more difficult to lead. He mouthed the words silently while waiting in the shadows.

Through the years we all will be together

If the fates allow
Hang a shining star upon the highest bough

It was growing late, and the old man knew the time was coming. Behind him, laughter rang out from a young woman—the elf now clothed a little more for the weather—and mixed together with some mumbling from Santa. The old man turned in the shadows and stood upright. Santa wasn't alone, but it wouldn't really matter in the grand scheme of things. Life could end surrounded by good company or life could end alone. There was no fine line drawn in the sand that decided when.

He tapped his cane on the snow-covered sidewalk one time and watched a little longer. Santa had changed into something a little less conspicuous and removed the beard. The old man watched as Santa pinched the woman's butt again, then lit up a cigarette.

"One more day of this shit," Santa said. "I'm sick of these kids and their parents."

"You don't think you'll do it again next year?" The woman bounded ahead. "I kind of like the job."

"Of course, you would. There's money in it and you don't have to say 'Ho, ho, ho' all the time. I'm telling you, though, you'd be better as a stripper. Why don't you come and sit on my lap, little girl."

The old man tapped his cane once again and started walking forward. He lightened his step and stayed in the shadows as much as possible, constantly keeping his eyes on the prey. His wrinkled skin began to pull further back, tightening around his cheeks. With another tap of his cane, his eyes turned black.

"What's wrong with you?" the woman asked, her voice changing from bubbly to annoyed. "I told you I'm not interested."

"You don't dress like that and tell me you're not interested." Santa reached forward and grabbed the woman's arm.

"Stop it!"

The old man struck from behind, blood spattering across the woman's face. She screamed and fell back into the snow. Another strike and Santa's body fell forward on top of her, blood pouring from a gaping hole in his head. She screamed again and tried to pull herself out from underneath the now lifeless body of her coworker.

The old man tapped his cane again on the ground next to the woman's head. She looked up, eyes wide in horror. In those eyes her soul was asking a question, seeking an answer, dying to understand. Why? *Why?*

A smile drew across the old man's face, nearly cracking his taut skin. "Have yourself a merry little Christmas," he said, and tapped his cane one last time.

The Royal

I used to own a 1936 Royal typewriter, the "original laptop." It was a heavy beast, too. This story was written in 2003, back when the typewriter was on the desk beside me. I lost it in a flood about fifteen years ago, but I still have that itch to find another. I just hope the one I find doesn't come with something attached to it.

Nocturnal Ooze Magazine liked this story; they published it in May 2004.

Free us.

I read the line over again, my mind racing with a thousand questions that careened around my skull. What did it mean? Free who? Was this typewriter haunted, or was my wife playing a joke on me? Did I bring a ghost home in the tattered carrying case that lay on the floor next to my desk? Who was I expected to free?

With haste, I pulled the paper from the carriage and threw it on the desk. I must have woke last night, climbed the steps to the attic, pulled out a piece of paper, fed it through the Royal and typed out whatever bled from my mind. Yes. That *had* to be the answer.

The Somnambulist Writer.

I pushed the typewriter back and pulled my laptop from

the drawer. Of all the inciting incidents or other nuggets of prose that I encountered daily, this was one event that deserved documentation. I could even drag it out into a short story or a novel if I ever had the real energy to write again. God knows I'd been lacking ideas and motivation for the longest time. Whatever bug nipped at me decades ago to make me write that first novel must have shriveled up and died. I hadn't been bit in a while.

As the screen glowed, I glanced at the typewriter. I purchased it from an antique shop, drawn to its lacquered finish and glass keys. The first time I laid eyes on it, it mesmerized me. Here was the epitome of the writer, the struggling artist, sitting at a wooden desk with his 1936 Royal. The ceiling fan raced to cool the room while the fedora hung on a hook by the door. I smelled the ink, the platen and the musty stink of years of hammering out...what?

I was proud to own it. For years, I had searched through antique stores for the perfect antithesis to my technological world. I wanted that *original* laptop. I wanted to feel the words as I typed them out on twenty-pound paper, each letter applied to the page with a little more effort. I entertained dreams of taking a journey across the country, stopping at every greasy spoon I found, seeking inspiration in the strangest of places.

Steinbeck with Charlie.

No trip like that could take place unless I was at the helm of a '67 VW Samba Bus with its twenty-one windows and unique aesthetic, and no story could be written from the heart unless I pounded it out on a Royal portable typewriter.

Touch-control.

1936.

Hemingway's tool.

I finished refurbishing the bus last year. I don't want a dog named Charlie, and all I needed to find was that typewriter.

Free us.

The words on the paper I'd thrown on the desk drew my attention from the typewriter. The ink bled on the paper as if the ribbon had been soaked, little tentacles of black reaching out from the serif font. I couldn't take this. More questions lit synapses on fire.

What would make me get up in the middle of the night and type such a thing? Why did I come up here in the first place? Was I subconsciously trying to prompt—no, *force*—inspiration from the page? What did I hope to accomplish in those two brief words?

Did I even write them in the first place?

I turned the paper over and pushed it to the corner of the desk. I didn't need to read it again. It was time to put this event to rest and get on with the day. There was planning to do, routes to map, expenses to budget. I was to leave on my journey in a little less than a week, and I still had only the foggiest idea of where I was going.

Out there.

—

My wife was awake when I left the house. I didn't want to say goodbye. It just didn't seem right to leave her alone in that house for a month or two, even if she was initially for the idea. And what was this idea? I needed to leave, if only for a few weeks, to see the country from a fresh perspective. Everything has a story and for every turn in the road, I can type a new chapter out on that Royal.

As I backed the bus onto the street, I caught one last glimpse of my wife standing in the doorway. I didn't need that. She wasn't crying, but in the faint light of morning, I saw the hurt on her face. I don't think she ever understood my mania. She never came to grips with my late nights in the garage pulling out the interior of the Samba. Neither the desk I built inside nor the flushable toilet I installed in the rear impressed her. When I tried to get her to show some emotion toward the tie-dyed curtains I painstakingly crafted and hung over each of the twenty-one windows, all she said was "That's nice." In retrospect, she was really asking me why.

I don't always have answers.

The sun was rising through a thick haze, like a lighthouse piercing the fog at sea—a cliché, but beautiful. It was comforting to know that in just a few hours, I would be at my first stop and my dream could come to fruition. The Royal was secure on the desk, six reams of paper sat in a box next to it, and there was beef jerky in the cupboard. Life was about to improve.

—

The farmhouse wasn't much, but it had a certain character that infested the barren land around it. The scent of the country in the mid-day sun filled my sense of adventure as I walked through knee-high grass then onto a path crudely worn by years of little and big shoes, by stroller wheels and wagons, by puppy feet. This was America: the land of the free and all home to millions of stories.

I was off the beaten track, lost in a world told between the pages of a thousand great books. I could almost see Steinbeck on the porch of the farmhouse, talking to Ma Joad about life in the Dustbowl. If I listened to the wind, I could hear talk of California and the great journey they were about to undertake. It was like me, rising out of the cesspool of life to traverse that land of milk and honey. I didn't know what lay ahead of me and didn't really care. It was all about the adventure, the free spirit on the road.

It was about doing what I loved to do the most.

It was about writing.

I must have stayed in that house for three or four hours, talking to the family that lived there. They were more than happy to listen to me and even happier to tell me of their impoverished life. I felt a little awkward leaving as the sun crept below the horizon, but I had things to do. I needed to chronicle this stage of my journey on the Royal. I needed to find an empty road and park my Samba, whip out a few pages of prose and feel truly good again.

I quietly passed a bill to the old woman at the steps and thanked her for their wonderful hospitality. I suppose it was cheap of me to degrade their generosity by giving them money, but judging by the look on her face, she didn't mind one bit. I tipped the brim of my hat and drove off.

—

West to the cross. North. Free us.

I stared at the paper crudely crammed into the Royal. Did one of the farmer's kids break into the Samba and type this out while I was in the house chatting? This time I know I didn't sleepwalk and write whatever was on my mind. There was no way this came from me.

In anger, I pulled the paper out of the typewriter and threw it in the back of the bus. I was not amused. I didn't plan the details of my trip so closely to have some kid play around inside my vehicle. I said I wanted to experience the great unknown of America, not fall victim to it. What was I supposed to do with this, anyway? *West to the cross.* What cross? A crossroad? And who am I supposed to free?

Frustrated, I closed the box of paper and looked at the map I'd printed out. I couldn't write. After all that desire to put words down on paper again, the mystery of the Royal had put a damper on my mood.

On the map, I traced the road from the farmhouse I just visited to my next stop. The highlighted county road passed through two more towns west, then north for a few more miles. At the turning point, my heart skipped a beat. A tiny cross was printed a few more miles west. To the north of it, an unimproved road led to what the map legend called an abandoned mine.

West to the cross. North. Free us.

I looked at the Royal, sitting there on the desk. In the dim light of the Samba, the black lacquer seemed almost empty, as if I looked hard enough I might see something I didn't want to see. Maybe the kids at the farmhouse didn't break in. My instinct told me to throw the typewriter out the window. I couldn't do that, though. I had worked for too long refurbishing this bus and finding the perfect typewriter, only to squander my dream on the foolish notion that the Royal might be haunted.

Haunted. There was a concept I didn't need to think about. I was sitting next to it, after all. If I went to sleep, what else might be typed? And assuming something otherworldly was typing it, what was I to fear more—the typewriter or the typist?

I threw the map on the passenger's seat and grabbed the keys. This would not end until I followed whatever directions the Royal gave me.

—

The mineshaft was sealed. The moon cast enough light to make out the warning notices on the wooden planks nailed poorly across the entrance. "Danger", they said. "Do Not Enter." "Keep Out!"

I wasn't about to disobey. I didn't plan to dig through mineshafts that looked out of service for decades. I may have packed a flashlight, but certainly not rope, a pickaxe or a hardhat.

I stood at the entrance, looking in with the flashlight. The light pierced the first three or four feet of darkness, then fell off. If I was brought here for some purpose, I hoped that purpose was within that distance, preferably outside the mine. Was I supposed to be shown something or—and here was a scary thought—was I supposed to be *drawn* to something?

I put the flashlight away and walked back toward the Samba. I intended to turn the bus toward the entrance to get a little more light deeper into the mine, but as my feet navigated the massive rocks in front of me, I heard the distinctive clack of the Royal.

I stopped.

I wanted to turn, to run away.

Whatever I purchased with the typewriter was now inside the bus typing away.

The clacking stopped. In the still air, only my labored breath and the beating of my heart against my chest filled the silence. In the still of the night, under the full moon, time didn't seem to have a meaning anymore. I felt trapped in the middle of nowhere with a spooky mine behind me and *something* in front of me hiding behind the keys of my typewriter.

At that moment, I became acutely aware of all the excuses I had made for myself over the years. I could have written anything using whatever I had at my disposal. In my mania, however, I pretended that my next project *had* to be written this way. I *had* to have the bus. I *had* to have the typewriter. I had to immerse myself in the act of writing so much that I needed to become someone I really wasn't meant to be.

I crept alongside the bus, watching for any movement inside. The shades were drawn, and the prospect of opening the door was not appealing despite my hand on the handle. More questions assailed me. What if that something inside had nine-inch teeth that wanted to dig into my flesh? What if I opened the door to find a monster with two heads, seven arms and claws for legs that would snap at my torso and cut me in half?

What if it wasn't something hideous? What if it was innocence trapped in some hell, screaming for help?

What if it was a child?

I must have held the door handle for a good minute, trying to muster the courage to whip open the bus door and face whatever waited for me. I had to know not only what had been typing but what it typed.

I was now both frightened and curious.

As I pulled on the handle and let the door swing open, I heard a small voice behind me. My breath caught short in my lungs. In front of me, another sheet of paper stuck out of the Royal. Behind me, someone I didn't know was talking to me.

In one motion, I reached in, grabbed the paper, and swung around to face the speaker. A small boy, dirty from head to toe, stood at the mine entrance. He smiled, cracking his soot-covered face with a gleaming strip of white. He motioned for me to look at the paper my trembling hands were holding.

Free us. Fifteen feet in. We can't breathe.

—

I would have finished my trip around the country on a Thursday. I imagined pulling into the driveway, seeing my wife through the window. Her dress would have shimmered in the sunlight and I would have realized how much I really wanted her, how much it would have meant for me not to have left. It has been a long few days, and the '67 Samba didn't make the three-thousand-mile journey. It is still outside the mine, lonely.

I suppose I should get back to writing. The children won't leave me alone. They don't want to be free in the sense of running through open fields playing ball or jacks or hopscotch. They want their souls to be free, and unless I finish this chapter of their life—typed away on the Royal their loathsome boss used to own—their lives will remain forever trapped in a desolate place that no one knows.

    They died once.

    They don't wish to do it again.

Pig Boy and Gator, Chicken and Pa

Someone once said this story "bleeds of redneck viscera". Okay, so it does. However, I enjoyed writing this more than I've enjoyed many other stories. Sure, it's a little cliché, a little twisted and a little "not right" but that's what I like about it. Here you'll find a story that started with the names of characters. Some people (most, probably) start with an idea for a story, even if they have no plot initially. Others base their stories off prompts or things they find in the newspaper. All I had were three names, a Pa, and no clue where I wanted to go.

Nocturnal Ooze *published this in April of 2004*

Chicken stirred. The dreams he started having late in the night had transformed themselves into monstrous nightmares.

Pa wielded a knife in one hand, while his sister Gator watched him cut Pig Boy into tiny pieces. Chicken sat in the shadows, afraid to say a word or make any movement. Pa's arm moved at an unnatural speed, almost like a motion picture set to play a two-hour movie in less than two minutes. Blood spattered the walls, Gator, and covered Chicken's face.

Pa stopped.

Pig Boy sat up from the butchering table, his intestines

hanging out. Blood covered his body all over, like he was dipped in a vat from Hell in some sick confectioners idea of a Popsicle without the stick.

"Kinda makes you wonder, don't it, boy?" Pig Boy smiled, the yellow of his teeth a stark contrast to the red of his face. "Makes you wonder what dreams are all about."

Pa laughed and stabbed the knife into the tabletop. He pointed a bloody finger at Chicken. "You stay out of our dreams, boy, and we'll stay out of yours."

Chicken opened his eyes. Pig Boy and Gator still slept in the corner of the shack. Pa snored.

Had Chicken understood the word "telepath", it would have been easier for him to deal with Pa's condition. All Chicken understood, though, was basic life and death, family and food. He still hadn't quite grasped what everyone meant when they called him "retarded." It was just a word.

Words are hard to say, sometimes. They get in the way of thought.

Chicken drew a deep breath and relaxed, safe in the knowledge that everyone was still asleep.

Good.

—

Pa was the last one to wake up. Ma started stirring a pot of something moments after she crawled from the sheets. Pig Boy and Gator ran outside to play in the woods around the house.

Chicken leaned against the wall of the shack and stared at Pa. He knew Pa was special and could read people's thoughts. But he didn't have a clue there was something different about Pig Boy.

Not until now, anyway.

It's a good thing I don't think when I'm 'round Pa, Chicken mused. *He wouldn't like my thoughts. No, sir.*

Pa stirred and opened his eyes. He looked at Chicken and smiled.

Not good.

—

Chicken cursed the cold and raised his knife.

He made the first and only cut in a perfectly straight line from an area approximately five inches from the throat to somewhere in the general vicinity of Pig Boy's balls. Had he understood anything of common medical practices, the cut might have been cleaner, not so deep and the resulting convulsions of Pig Boy's body might not have caused such a sudden explosion of blood all over Chicken's face.

What did he know?

Pig Boy arched his back and screamed. His intestines erupted through the incisions, coming to rest on the right and left of his body like massive wet worms, contorted and writhing in a manner which suggested a life of their own.

A gurgling whimper soon followed.

Pig Boy's back relaxed.

Steam wound through the air like ghostly tendrils reaching for Heaven or Hell in the milliseconds where the living and the dead share a common world.

Chicken watched with amazement as one of the tendrils left the entrails and wisped upward toward the sky. It slowly changed shape and wrapped around itself as if unsure of where to go. The white vapor gathered together, pulled apart, then gathered together again.

Chicken saw his face in the design, and he smiled.

The vapors expanded once more, then drew quickly up toward the heavens.

"Guess you can't go inside my head no more, Pig Boy."

Blood dripped from Chicken's nostril. He let a drop fall onto an outstretched tongue.

Not his.
Good.

—

The road to Edsen wasn't much of a road. What used to be well traveled by carriage, horse and foot was thickly overgrown with nature's reclamation of its space. Chicken trudged on foot, trying to remain somewhere between the walls of trees lining both sides, but not necessarily in the middle.

He had to get home. It was time to eat.

Chicken wiped at his face with dirt-laden fingers, but failed to smear the dried blood from his face. He knew the family wouldn't approve of his appearance, but for the prize he brought home, he couldn't care less if he had flesh on his face and shit between his toes.

He stopped and looked down. His toes wriggled in a warm pile of shit left by a wandering animal.

Elk?

The sack on his shoulder weighed heavy, its burlap soaked in blood. There was enough inside to feed a family of five for a week.

Chicken counted on his fingers.

There was only four now.

He could eat twice.

Good.

—

The door hung on one hinge and swayed back and forth in the northern wind. The shack was falling apart, but in time, there wouldn't be any reason to live in it. Chicken knew that, planned it all, staying up late at night listening to the others fuck or snore. It wouldn't be long before he could board up the windows and find a place outside of Edsen to call his own.

Ma didn't want him to leave.
Pa wouldn't get out of his head.
Gator wasn't quite right.
Pig Boy didn't matter anymore.

Chicken smiled and walked inside the shack. *Elk*, he thought.

He threw the sack down on the table in front of Gator. She looked at it, up at Chicken, then Ma.

"Where's Pig Boy?" Pa stood up from the shadows. "I thought he was with you."

Chicken laid his knife down on the table and walked over to the water basin. "He done got himself lost. He said he'll be back." He dipped his hands in the cold water and washed his face. *Lost himself, Pa. That's all.*

Pa snorted once and took notice of Chicken's feet. "You're a liar, boy. You clean yourself in the creek. Keep that shit out of our drinking water."

"Yes, Pa."

Chicken walked through the room to the back door and outside again. The wind whipped his wet face, stinging as much or more than Pa's belt against his back. Ice lined the edge of the creek, but in the middle the water flowed swift. Chicken braced himself and stepped in.

Pig Boy screamed.

The sound was unmistakable—throaty and coarse, just like his brother's voice. Chicken jumped from the creek. He turned in circles and looked for its source. It wasn't possible.

The tree branches hit each other in the wind and the creek bubbled softly. Other than nature, Chicken heard nothing else. He stood on the bank, still looking.

Pig Boy was dead. His head wasn't easy to cut off, but eventually all things separate.

Chicken knew that. He sighed, cleared his head, and went

back inside the shack.

All would be well.

Gator was next, and she would be easy.

Good.

—

Gator's eyes grew wide as she watched the knife enter her stomach. She looked up at Chicken and reached out to touch his face. Slowly, her body slid backwards off the blade, then collapsed onto the cold ground.

Chicken turned Gator over, face up, unsure of where to cut her. She was thin, but there was meat someplace on her body. He watched her lips quiver, a trail of blood oozing out from the corners of her mouth. She coughed, and blood sprayed on Chicken's face.

"Not again," he said, as he wiped his face with the back of his hand. "Pa don't like me coming home messy."

"Why are..." Gator's words trailed off.

"Why? 'Cause I want out. You're all too messed up to care 'bout me. Never have! You and Ma and Pa and Pig Boy — you all want me dead. Think I'm stupid."

Chicken raised his voice. "I hear words, too, you know. I may not know what they mean, but I hear words inside of your head. I know what you're all thinking, and I don't like it."

Chicken closed his eyes as the voice of Gator resounded through his head. *Pa knows about you.*

He shook his head and opened his eyes. "Well, I ain't gonna die before I get out of here. And it ain't gonna be with you. I'm gonna go to town, find me a woman and get me a life. The more of you I leave living, the less chance I'll have of getting out."

Chicken frowned. "Besides, Pa won't get out of my head."

Gator coughed a few more times, then closed her eyes. Her

last breath escaped her lungs in a cloud of condensed air.

Chicken half-expected to see his face in the vapor.

He saw the smoky image of Pig Boy instead.

Not good.

—

Chicken stopped. The road to Edsen snaked its way through the woods to the shack, but lingering thoughts kept him from moving forward.

Pig Boy was missing for a day.

Pa sent Chicken out with Gator to find him.

If he came home *without* Gator, Pa'd start to wonder.

Pa knows about you.

Thoughts flow like water in the creek.

Chicken dropped the burlap sack full of Gator on the ground and sat down next to it. He had to think of how to approach this. He could say a pack of wolves carried Gator away. Pa always said wolves attack the weakest prey.

That wouldn't work, and Chicken knew it. For one, the wolves in the woods around Edsen were silent for the last few weeks. They probably moved on when the food became scarce before the winter snows. The burlap sack full of meat would probably be a good clue, too. When would he have time to hunt if he was supposed to be out with Gator looking for Pig Boy? And why did he bring the sack anyway?

Pa knows about you.

Pig Boy sat down next to Chicken. "What's wrong, Chicken?"

Chicken screamed. He pushed back on his hands as far as he could, then wiped his eyes to make the image go away.

Pig Boy smiled. A rough line of dried blood around his neck defined where Chicken had cut him. His intestines were pushed back and held inside by the straining buttons of his jacket.

Chicken tried to form words, but all he could manage was

a trail of saliva down his face. He slowly stood up and backed farther away.

"C'mon, boy. Look at me. Do I look like I'm gonna tell Pa anything? Whatcha got in the sack?"

"N-nothing."

Pig Boy smiled wider and opened the sack. "Looks like Gator, to me, boy. You gonna eat her like you ate me?"

"You're dead." Chicken found it hard to believe he used a two-word sentence at this point. "You ain't real."

Three words.

"Nope, Chicken. I'm *inside* of you." Pig Boy pointed at Chicken's stomach. "Can you feel me kicking away in there?"

Chicken's stomach growled, then cramped.

"You think your head was the only thing I could get into?"

Chicken bent over as a sharp pain erupted, like a giant with a steel-toed boot just kicked him in his gut.

"I guess Ma should've cooked me longer, eh?" Pig Boy smiled and stood up. "Whatever are you gonna do, boy? Pa aint' gonna like you coming home without Gator. One wrong thought, and it's all over."

Chicken grimaced as the pain expanded to his sides, crawling like roaches under his skin.

"Tell you what, boy…"

The pain crawled up Chicken's back, chewing on his spine with unnaturally long teeth.

"Go hide out in the clearing where you cut up Gator and me. Pa will come looking for you when you don't show up tonight."

Chicken looked up at Pig Boy. His body slowly faded from view.

"You can knife Pa in the back, if you time it right. Just make sure you attack without *thinking*."

Pig Boy disappeared. The pain in Chicken's body quickly subsided.

Pig Boy was right: he could get Pa when he came looking.

A small smile crept across Chicken's face. He picked up the sack and started walking back to the clearing.

By morning, Ma would be the only one in the way.

Good.

—

Chicken slept, his head against a rock. His arms cradled what was left of Gator. Dreams came easy, but quickly turned to nightmares of Pig Boy and Gator, stabbing at his stomach with forks.

Thankfully, Pa wasn't with them.

He opened his eyes and looked up at the sky. The stars were out, and it was cold.

Very cold. He shuddered and curled his knees up to his chest.

Not good.

—

"Wake up, boy!"

Chicken opened his eyes as Pa kicked him in the side.

"Wake up!"

The sun was out, right behind Pa's head. Chicken quickly rose to his feet and tried his best to put on his "Thank God you done found me" face.

"Thank God you done found me, Pa! I was gonna freeze to death out here."

Pa raised a rifle and pushed it into Chicken's stomach. "Where's Gator, boy?"

"I— I don't know. Chicken pushed away from the barrel and stepped back. "She said she was gonna run home."

Pa snorted and spit out a wad of green phlegm. "What's in the sack?"

Chicken looked down. The blood from Gator had soaked

through and turned the burlap into a wet mess. He had to think of something else quickly.

"Some meat I done cut from the last kill, Pa. Why are you pointing that gun at me?"

"You're a liar, boy."

"Pa!"

"You cut up Gator, didn't you? *Didn't you?*"

"*No!* I told you: this is from the last kill! *Put that gun down!*"

Pa lowered the gun slowly. He stared at Chicken, and smiled.

Chicken felt his stomach turn.

"Can we get home, Pa?"

"Not without Pig Boy or Gator."

The pain Chicken felt the day before exploded inside of him. He bent over and grabbed his stomach. The throbbing quickly reached out to his sides and then his back, forcing him to his knees.

He looked up. "Pa, help me."

Pa smiled and looked around.

Chicken suddenly convulsed, his body flipping over. He arched his back and screamed as what felt like a knife pushed at his stomach from the inside. Tears streamed down his face as white heat engulfed his body. He couldn't breathe.

Chicken looked down at his stomach, half expecting to see Pig Boy in the corner of his mind's eye, laughing at him. Instead, a spot of blood appeared under his shirt, then quickly spread across his body.

He felt his skin tear, and he screamed again.

A fist pushed through the skin, flesh squeezed between its fingers.

Just before Chicken closed his eyes for the last time, he saw Pig Boy's head emerge from inside of him, his face caked with flesh and blood.

Not good at all.

—

The road to Edsen was a few miles long, but Pa and Pig Boy made good time. They walked through the overgrown path like kids happy to return from a good day at the fishing pond. Pig Boy carried a burlap sack full of Gator and Chicken on his back.

"We're gonna eat good tonight, boy," Pa said as he looked at his son.

"Yeah. It's too bad it's got to be Gator, though. I was looking forward to just Chicken."

Pa sighed. "So was I. But, as the Good Lord says in the Good Book: 'Vittles is vittles.'"

"Yeah, Pa. But you can't read."

Pa smiled at the comment and pointed to his head. "No, but I can get inside and so can you."

"So what am I thinking right now?"

Pa stopped in the middle of the road and cocked his head to the side. "You're thinking that you hope you never have thoughts like Chicken. Am I right?"

Pig Boy smiled. "Yeah. No bad thoughts."

"Good."

Sprouts

There is a forest in central Arizona which burned down in 1990. I took a trip there a few weeks after the fire had been put out and snapped the picture that inspired this story. I didn't actually write it until 2003, but it was that picture which was taped to my monitor the whole time.

Troy stood inside the forest for the first time since the fires. Remains of animals littered the ground, their bones hallowed divinations foretelling a failed future. The fog had rolled in through the night, and as the morning sun rose above the mountains to the southeast, Troy felt the chill burn off. Devastated Ponderosa trees, now nothing more than black sticks, stabbed heavenward, pathetic vestiges of what they once were. The ferns and other mosses, once thriving under the cover of a billion pine needles, were gone. Nature had unleashed its fury, pummeled the earth with chaotic slivers of searing heat, and set an inferno that cost the life of one person.

Or was that two?

The silence overwhelmed—heavy and oppressive. With each step Troy took, his foot pressed down on brittle bones, cracking them. The sound was louder despite the fog, and he felt he was disturbing sacred ground. Perhaps it was sacred ground—after all, so much death leaves a scar. Still, he had to go forward, to walk deeper into the forest to find what he knew was there. It was too bad his discovery would be alone, if he found it at all.

"Do you know what you're looking for?" The ghost of a man Troy knew wasn't there whispered in the wind, gently stroked the dead sticks. "I know you didn't bring me out here for nothing."

"No, not nothing." Troy sighed. Perhaps talking to a ghost wasn't the most mature thing he could do, but then again, the ghost made for company and maybe—just maybe—acted as a cheap replacement for a psychologist's couch. He could almost see him, a gift of imagination and yet, a burden. There in the morning glow walked a man in his thirties, red hair, green eyes that embodied pure and crystalline beauty.

The fog played with the ghost's image, first encapsulating the whole, then dissipating as he walked through it with Troy. In the morning light, the spirit seemed so real, yet Troy knew a thousand wishes cast into a thousand fountains would not change the truth: the man before him was only a projection from his tattered mind.

"The place looks different, Troy. So much death."

"It's a beginning, Ian, not an end."

"What are you looking for?"

"A piece of myself. I must have left it behind the last time you and I were out here."

Ian stopped beside a dead tree. He looked at Troy and sighed. "Please don't tell me it's your heart. You don't have one."

Troy smiled weakly. Even ghosts could be sarcastic. "No, not my heart."

"Then what did you lose?"

"A piece of memory." Troy hesitated for a moment, trying

to come up with words to explain his journey. "It's like— Try to look out the back of your head. What do you see?"

Ian let out a short laugh. "Nothing. You don't have eyes in the back of your head."

"I know that, but hear me out. Try to look out the back of your head. You know <u>something</u> is there, but you just can't see it. The more you try, the more your imagination creates something for you out of what you already know."

Ian furrowed his eyebrows. "So you're looking for a way to see out the back of your head?"

Troy looked at Ian and then walked on. "Maybe I shouldn't have brought you with me."

"You didn't bring me, Troy. I'm always with you."

"Then why can't you understand what I'm trying to say?"

"You're not exactly being clear about all of this. What can't you see, and what is your imagination creating for you?"

Troy tried harder to form the words to explain himself. He didn't understand why he had to tell a ghost what he was doing, but in a way, it cleared his mind and let him reason through things he may not have thought before. What he knew was factual: he and Ian had gone camping in the forest. They made love, they ate beef stew from a tin can heated over a little campfire, and they explored the surrounding life. All of *that* made sense, and the more he thought of it, the more authentic it all seemed—a painting which became more vibrant and priceless with age.

There was still something missing, however. A day? An hour? A few minutes? He couldn't remember how long it was, but there was definitely a void in his memory.

The forest opened to a large clearing ringed by soot-covered, blackened tree stumps. Despite the fog, Troy recognized the location immediately. They had camped in the middle of the clearing, at times laying back on the forest floor and marveling at how countless stars graced the sky a hundred miles from city lights. He smiled and could almost see himself with Ian, pointing at various constellations and other stellar objects.

There was Orion the Hunter, Gemini the Twins, and if you looked just above that tree, you could see Mars. In the briefest of seconds, Troy felt like he was there again, the night cold but electric, the wind soft and inviting, the Milky Way painted across the sky in fine brush strokes by a master painter. In the middle of the forest, Troy and Ian were wrapped together in a blanket of love, oblivious to the rest of life outside of their little world, oblivious to the rejections and discrimination they both felt.

"What are you looking at?" Ian's ghost materialized next to Troy.

"Can't you see it?"

"I see lifeless trees and death."

"In the middle of the clearing, Ian. Look." Troy pointed, his hand shaking. "There's a beginning."

Twenty feet away, two small ferns grew from the ashes, the green a sharp contrast to the surrounding palette of despair. Troy walked toward the young plants, trying to picture the final moments before losing time. He imagined the campfire to the left, poorly put together with rocks laid out in a bad circle. Some rocks were still there, charred by the raging flames that had rushed through this part of the forest.

To the right, a small stick stuck out of the ground, as black as all the others, but different enough to notice. He recalled pounding it into the dirt with one of the rocks, then tying off a cheap lean-to as shelter from the rain before they put up the tent.

Ian's ghost flitted about here and there, seeming to take in the environment. It finally came to rest on top of the ferns, spreading its ethereal body across them, almost seductively. Troy watched Ian's vaporous breath, his chest heave in time to the beat of his heart. He was as beautiful now as he had ever been, a masterful brushstroke on the canvas of the world.

"What do you see?" Ian asked. Troy appraised the question: did he really care, or was this more conversation generated by his subconscious to arrive at answers?

"I see where we camped, but nothing else."

"You said time was missing. What was the last thing you remember?"

Troy looked around at the campfire, the stick, the patch of open forest surrounding the ferns. "The fire. I remember the fire."

"What about the fire?"

"It was dying. We lit it early, before the sun set, I think. I remember laying down with you in the tent." Troy smiled. "You were naked."

"Did you throw more wood on the fire?"

Troy hesitated before answering. "No. There was no wood...except..." He turned to look back at the lean-to post. "The sticks from the lean-to. I pulled one of them out."

Ian stood up and walked around Troy, a ghostly hand touching a shoulder. Troy swore he could feel warmth flowing through his body. That warmth crept past his shoulders, permeated his pores and filled each cell with comfort, cascading through his body until he felt alive. If this ghost was a figment of his imagination, then his imagination sure had a way of making things seem all too real.

Ian stopped circling Troy and stood in front of him. "What happened next?"

"I bent over the fire with the stick, pushing on the embers. I— I don't know what happened next."

"What's the next thing you *do* remember?"

Troy looked through the mist of Ian, into the eyes of his past. He tried to reason through it all, to make believe there really was nothing missing. All the pieces fit. All of time still existed. Maybe he just picked at the fire, then went to sleep. That was possible.

But no, something was missing.

"I don't know." Troy sighed, and sat down next to the ferns. He stared at the campfire, trying to will his memory to the surface.

"I loved you, Troy."

"I know that."

"But do you know how much?"

Troy looked up at the ghost. Ian appeared more real than before, less transparent and brighter. His green eyes seemed to seek answers deep inside of Troy. His lips parted, soft and supple, wet and glistening in the morning sun. He smiled.

"How much could you love me?" Troy felt the corners of his eyes moisten. "I was always blue, a depressing person to be around, afraid of what people would say. I loved you, but could only show you through written words. I never was much for conversation."

"Yes, you were. I loved talking to you. I loved the way you made me feel when we were together. I just couldn't..."

Ian's words trailed off. He turned his head and crossed his arms. The sun caught a tear on his cheek.

"I just couldn't accept your moods," he continued. "You wanted to leave me, to run out on our future. And you wanted me to accept that, as if all I was made to do was stand next to your side for all eternity."

"I thought that's what soulmates did — stand next to each other."

"You lied to me, Troy."

"I told you half-truths, Ian. It's not the same thing."

Troy sighed and stood up, intending to walk away and forget all of this. He didn't need to get into an argument with a speck of his subconscious. He didn't need to be called a liar again. He didn't need to hear words shot at him from a verbal cannon. He could feel it coming—the yelling, the name-calling, the emptiness in the pit of his stomach every time he realized he'd hurt Ian.

He wasn't even real!

Troy smirked. He looked around in silence, taking in the view from the clearing. The Ponderosa trees—or what remained of them—stood like sentinels, pointing defiantly toward Heaven, like they outlasted the worst God could throw at them and still stood proud. Water would rejuvenate them, they would sprout needles, and they would turn green again. All around, plant life would return, the animals would find shelter, the seeds would fall and germinate. Life would be reborn.

"Why did you leave me, Ian?" It was a question he knew the answer to, but he asked nonetheless. Perhaps deep down, the ghost of Ian—the shrink in his brain—would have another reason found buried between what his heart knew and his mind let go.

"I never left you."

"You ran off with him."

"You let me go."

"No. I never let go of you."

"Ignoring me, Troy, not meeting the needs I had as a human being." A tear fell from his eyes. "*That* was letting me go. I couldn't take it."

"Did you ever think of giving me another chance? Did you ever think all I needed to do was grow up and accept the way I was?"

Ian scoffed, turned away from Troy, and walked over to

the campfire. "And what was I supposed to do? Wait forever? I had needs."

Troy sat back down on the ground next to the ferns. He stared at the green fronds; so stark their color was against the pitted grey of the forest floor. The two ferns shared what little water there might be underground in their struggle to start over amidst the ruins.

The sun slid behind a cloud, and for a moment cast an eerie shadow on the clearing. Ian stood by the campfire, looking down. He was much more real than the misty vision he'd seen as he was walking up. Perhaps this place was magic, a sacred burial ground of old memories and lost loves, capable of pulling even the deepest of receding dreams and making them real. It certainly felt that way.

Troy brushed his leg against something sharp. He winced and looked down under the ferns. Poking through the dirt was the rusted claw of a hammer.

"I didn't mean to do it, Troy." Ian's voice was soft, almost lost in the calm.

Troy pushed the ferns aside and dug around the hammer, trying to pull it free.

Ian turned around, a tear crawling down a cheek. His lips quivered. "I just wanted to be free. I wanted to be free of complications."

Troy dug faster, finally pulling the hammer out of the dirt. "What is this?"

"Do you remember now?" Ian's words seemed to emanate from inside Troy. They charged a billion synapses firing at once. Memories flooded forward as the dam holding it back was destroyed. They careened off the cortices of his mind, pounding waves of everything imaginable in a rush of revelation.

"No," Troy whispered. The hammer dropped through his shaking hand.

Ian took a few slow steps, the brittle sticks and burnt needles snapping under his feet. "I knew it would kill you to see me get married. Despite all I ever did to you, I loved you."

"You..."

"It took everything I had to hit you. I *loved* you, Troy."

Troy stood quickly, feeling surges of nausea. His legs felt light, and he wobbled.

"Do you remember now?"

"I never lost that time, did I?"

"No. You never had it to lose."

—

Troy again stood inside the forest for the first time since the fires. Devastated Ponderosa trees, now nothing more than black sticks, stabbed heavenward, pathetic vestiges of what they once were. Nature had unleashed its fury, pummeling the earth with chaotic slivers of searing heat, setting an inferno that cost the life of one person.

Or was that two?

He had to go forward, to walk further into the forest to find what he knew was there.

The True Face of Ferris Fernando

Disassociations are something we all deal with as humans, even if we're "normal." There are times when we just go through life reveling in the past or the future with no knowledge or awareness of the present. Apply that same concept to an unstable individual — perhaps one traumatized in life — and the behavior that emerges may be one that's very unpleasant. This story attempted to capture that notion.

Ferris kept her face on a brass hook fastened to the wall in the corner of his attic. Some things shouldn't be out in the open. Snooping children determined to seek out *Playboy* magazines or videotapes of unbridled pleasure, might stumble across the delicate trinkets of a thirty-two year old. In reality, Ferris owned no *Playboy* magazines, and never had enough time — or privacy — to watch videos. The only thing he had to hide from the world was his admiration for the finer things in life. The kids didn't know any better.

He stood in front of the woman's face, admiring every facet about her living features he could find in the dried, wrinkled mask. There was a gentle roundness to her nose, the blush on her cheeks, a few strands of blonde hair that stuck to the dried blood and added character. The eyes were missing, but with a little imagination, Ferris could see the crystal blue orbs staring back at him even on the darkest of nights, closing in moments of passion, crying in moments of pain.

He pulled the mask off the hook and checked for blemishes. The edges were ragged and torn in a few places as the skin dried, but in all, her features were in good condition. She was as beautiful as the night she died.

"Hi," Ferris whispered. He walked to an old freestanding mirror and held the face up in front of his own. If anything, he could replace her missing eyes with his own, her lips with his. All he needed was a wig of blonde hair, cut in just the right way to finish off the look and truly see the woman in the mirror...looking back at him.

With practice, he'd talk to her.

With imagination, a shift in his voice, she'd respond.

If he pressed his lips against the cold glass of the mirror, he could imagine kissing her dead lips, like the last time, before he gently cut her face away with a modeling knife.

Ferris feared the mask wouldn't hold up and couldn't stand the thought of losing her to the ravages of decay. He took one last look at her face in the mirror, then put her back on the hook where she belonged.

—

"You want to go somewhere?" Sophia's voice drifted through the small car.

Ferris turned his face from the darkness outside. Yeah, he wanted to go someplace. He wanted to crawl into a casket and watch the lid close from the inside. He wanted to die, to take his last breath with him and vomit on the steps of Hell.

"We need to talk, Ferris." Her words slid around his throat like vaporous tentacles, constricting his neck. He couldn't breathe. "We really need to talk."

Ferris tried to imagine the slightest hint of resignation in her voice. They'd had this conversation before and it wasn't pleasant. At least then, he knew she wasn't completely set on the idea of walking out. He let his brain digest the words and the inflection in her voice.

There wasn't any resignation.

"I need to go." Ferris winced at his poorly chosen method of escape. Maybe it would be easier to just write all his feelings down. Sure, they could pass notes to each other or write letters, break up in a civilized way. There didn't have to be any of that crying stuff or sobs of "We can still be friends" mixed in with "I didn't want this to happen."

No, if you didn't want it to happen, Ferris thought, you would've walked away from the situation. When you first subconsciously sniffed that asshole's pheromones and felt that first flutter of your heart, you should have turned the other direction.

Ferris sighed. You should have stopped when you still had control of yourself.

"It was just a little kiss." The vaporous tentacles wrapped themselves tighter. One of them pushed at Ferris' closed lips, straining to get inside to begin the slow process of tearing out his heart piece by piece. "It didn't mean a thing."

He pushed against the voice and the tentacle at his lips. Closing his eyes, he felt his stomach explode in convulsions — a million butterflies simultaneously detonating, insect screams vibrating every nerve in his body.

—

In the darkness, Kathleen couldn't see Ferris sweat, but she opened her eyes the moment he screamed. He sat up in bed, for a moment still stuck in his nightmare. He couldn't see the other side of the room, the dresser he'd received as a wedding present or any other visage of his present life. He was still there, in the car, trying to get out of a situation that could only get worse.

"Are you okay?" His wife's voice infiltrated his nightmare and brought him quickly back to the present. He was married, Sophia was gone and he was no longer inside that car. He reached for his neck to feel if the tentacles were still squeezing the life out of him.

"I'm fine." Ferris swung his feet off the bed and stood up. "I just need some water."

"Take some Motrin while you're at it. You feel warm."

"It's just the nightmares. I'll be okay."

"You're acting weird, lately." Kathleen sighed and rubbed her eyes. "Are you seeing someone else?"

"No."

"Who's Sophia?"

If the name wasn't enough to pull back every feeling he ever felt and drop them in a heap on the footstep of his life, then the name of Sophia coming from the lips of his wife was. A bead of sweat crept out from beneath his hairline and slid down his face.

"A dream. That's all."

Kathleen grunted and turned over, pulling the sheets around her body. Ferris let his eyes adjust to the darkness before stepping into the hallway.

At the top of the stairs, just under the access door to the attic, he thought he could hear Sophia's voice again. *It was just a little kiss.* He shivered and felt for the tentacles around his neck before walking downstairs. The life he'd sequestered for so long was sneaking out through the cracks in his emotional weather-stripping.

—

"So, what are you going to do? Lie there in your puke or come up here and join the living?"

Ferris looked up from under the coffee table at his roommate. Bob was as drunk as he was, but the feelings accentuated by the alcohol weren't the same. Ferris had taken his first drink from the bottom of the deepest pit he'd ever been in. At this point, he'd dug himself far enough to feel the fires of Hell.

"So, she got married. Big deal." Bob took another drink. Whiskey dribbled from the side of his mouth and fell to the floor next to Ferris' head. "Why are you so obsessed with this?"

"She was half of me."

"So, fuck yourself. It should feel the same."

"I just wanted another chance."

"And unless you kidnap her, it doesn't look like you're going to get that chance."

Ferris rolled over from under the coffee table and pushed himself to his knees. The room danced wildly to the pounding of his head, the beat of the music and the wind-licked trees outside. The end of the world had come to Ferris sooner than he'd expected.

Just one more chance, he thought. *Just one more kiss before I die, Sophia.*

"Don't let this eat at you, Ferris." Bob set his bottle of whiskey down. It spun around and tipped over. "Life is too short to waste it on the past. If you have to, mask your feelings. Don't let them out in the open. I don't want to see it, anymore."

Ferris stood up and dropped his vodka. As the bottle shattered against the coffee table, the world went black.

—

Kathleen stood at the foot of the bed as Ferris opened his eyes. Her robe was wrapped around her tiny body, the light from the bathroom casting sharp shadows across her skin like wounds.

"You said her name again."

Ferris sat up in bed and pushed his eyes in with his palms. Damn those dreams. "I know."

"Who is she?" The words were crisp, clean and laced with hatred. "I want to know who you're seeing."

"No one."

"*Don't lie to me anymore!*" Kathleen crossed the room and sat down on a wingback chair in the corner. "If you're seeing someone else, I deserve to know."

Ferris put his feet on the cold floor, but the shiver he felt was nothing physical. He'd planned everything so well, from the first initial thoughts to the last nip of the blade separating Sophia's face from the muscle underneath. He finally possessed what he'd lost, could finally put to rest his internal need to be close to her, to become one with her again. He didn't need his dreams to screw it up for him now.

He sighed. "I told you, it was just a dream."

"Every night? Christ, Ferris. You call out her name more than you call my name when you're awake. Am I supposed to accept this as normal?"

"They're nightmares, Kathleen. It's not like I enjoy reliving—" Ferris cut himself short. That wasn't the right thing to say. Yes, he was reliving his time with Sophia, experiencing again and again every kiss, every embrace, every fight and every moment of pain he'd felt for the last fourteen years.

"Reliving?" Kathleen's eyes grew wider. "What are you *reliving*?"

"Nothing. I meant—"

"I know what you meant." She stood up. "You're on your own tonight."

—

"What are you thinking?" Kathleen pulled the covers of the sheet aside and sat down on the foot of the bed. "Honeymoon thoughts?"

The fan blades above the bed in the Motel 6 spun wildly, the three light bulbs beneath subjected to intense vibration. Ferris stared up at them, wishing his head was caught in the middle. Quick and painless. That was the way to go.

"Nothing, dear," Ferris said as a thousand different voices assailed him at once, each particular word kissing his sorrow with an acidic burn. "Nothing."

"You know, you haven't asked me."

"Asked you what?"

Kathleen blew a strand of hair away from her face and crossed her arms. "This is our wedding night, Ferris. Do you want to start an argument now?"

Ferris turned his attention from the fan to Kathleen. "I'm sorry." The voices in his head finally fell silent. "What mask do you want me to wear tonight?"

His new wife turned away from the bed, letting her robe fall open. "Come and get me, Kimo Sabe."

—

The house was empty. Ferris stood at the bottom of the ladder leading to the attic and closed his hands into a fist. He didn't really believe he'd heard Sophia's voice, but curiosity pulled him to find out what that noise was. In the back of his mind, he wanted to talk to her again, to see her again, to let her know exactly what had become of him.

All of that seemed impossible after he cut off her face. Sometimes what seems impossible, however, is grounded in the possible.

Sophia's voice floated through the access door. "Talk to me, Ferris. Tell me what you're feeling."

Ferris tensed more. The dust particles visible in the beam of light radiating from the attic window remained motionless despite his breath. If he had to hide his life—the feelings he barricaded behind the façade of his public being—then he supposed it *should* be surreal. If the sky suddenly turned purple and he floated up the stairs to the attic, it wouldn't be out of place.

The attic received him, the old boards under his feet

creaking with each step. He walked to the other side of the room and found the corner no one knew about. She still hung from the hook, invitation written across the features of her face. Ferris swallowed hard and reached out.

He pulled the mask toward him and stared at it. All the feelings he'd felt as a teenager, all the pains he'd suffered through when she left, all the fear he ever had that he'd never see her again, enveloped his body, constricted his lungs, made him shake. Fourteen years of pain exploded from the poorly built dam he'd constructed to keep it all out.

"Why?" Ferris whispered. "Why did you walk away from me?"

The face looked back with hollow eyes, and although Ferris could imagine a response, it wasn't going to happen. He inwardly chastised himself for killing her, for cutting her throat on her doorstep and carrying her body out to the desert. He should have talked to her first.

You can't wash away the mistakes of life. Sophia wasn't a mistake, but killing her was.

He sighed and put the mask back on the hook. He still didn't have the resolve to fit her face to his own in the mirror. The time would come, and he knew it would be soon enough. Then they could talk, they could see each other in a better light and get their feelings out in the open.

Ferris turned around and left the attic. He still needed a scalp of hair to match Sophia's.

—

"So, um..." Sophia shifted her feet. The grocery cart was between them, and Ferris guessed that was the way she wanted it. "How have you been?"

Ferris forced a smile. "Okay, I guess. You look good."

Sophia looked up for a moment then turned to the Campbell's soup on the shelf next to her. "How's your wife?"

"Being a wife." Crabby and ugly, he thought.

Sophia nodded and put a can of chicken noodle soup in her basket. The silence was deafening, and Ferris felt flushed and on fire. The few trite words that passed between them after so long an absence were small daggers stuck in his ears, twisting back and forth. He was in Hell, and he hated it.

Get up some damn nerve, moron.

"You want to – " *Ferris cut himself short. No, she didn't want to and probably never would. The past was back there and she was obviously doing much better without him around.*

"Do I want to what?" *Sophia put a fourth can of chicken noodle soup in the basket.*

"Never mind." *Pussy.*

Sophia nodded again and reached for a fifth and sixth can. "Well, it was nice seeing you again, Ferris."

Platitudes from the mouth of an angel turned to red-hot daggers that dug into his skull. If this was Hell, he'd rather swim in a lake of fire while demons raped him of dignity.

"Do you want to go out and get something to eat?" *He tripped over the words and winced at the childish way it sounded.*

Sophia took another two cans off the shelf and looked up. "I'm sorry. I can't."

—

Ferris stood in front of the mirror, wishing away the fears that chewed his stomach and scratched his heart. He held Sophia's face by his side, unsure of whether or not it was time to face his other half, the half he'd lost so many years ago and then tried to retrieve through violence.

Put it on. The voice was unmistakable. Sophia's sultry words drifted past his ears and kissed the curves of his neck, raising goose bumps. He recalled nights when she'd speak the same way, her hot breath brushing his naked skin. *Put it on, Ferris. Feel me.*

He took a breath, raised the mask to his face and looked at himself through the holes her eyes once filled. There she was. Her hair wasn't right—not even the same color—but her angelic features were there.

Ferris felt his heart escalate at the sight of Sophia in the mirror. He took a step toward her and gently pushed her flesh against his own face, fitting his lips where hers once were, his nose in the shredded remains of her own. With both hands, he pushed the leathery inside of the mask to his skin and looked on at the woman he'd always loved, at the half of him that never fully disappeared.

Ferris smiled slightly at the sight. The mask fit perfectly.

His pulse raced.

His eyes lit up.

His skin tingled.

"Hi, Sophia. How are you?"

The smile quickly faded as his skin started to burn, like a road rash across his cheeks. He quickly pulled the mask away from his face and looked in the mirror again. Something was wrong. His face was spattered with spots of blood, but certainly not hers. It was almost as if his own blood had pushed into his pores, trying to get out and feed life into the mask.

—

"Hi, again." Ferris felt like he should stutter, act like a bumbling fool at the feet of a homecoming queen. "Nice night for Halloween, isn't it?"

Sophia pulled her youngest child close to her and smiled weakly. "Yes, it is."

Tell her, you idiot. Ferris couldn't believe she was really there. Of course, he'd traveled across town just to make this "chance" encounter, but it was still somehow amazing. If only she'd see that.

"Well, we must get going." Sophia quickly turned around.

"Wait."

She stopped, but kept her back to Ferris.

"Are you sure you won't have dinner with me?"

The uncomfortable silence Ferris feared for most of his life rushed in to drown out the noise of kids running through the streets, begging for candy and laughing. Over the years, he always thought he'd grown used to the silence, accepting it as his imagination and not some signal of impending bad news or ill feelings.

This time, however, he could hear the silence for what it was: rejection, the answer to a million prayers all at once resounding through the universe. "No!"

"I don't know how to tell you, this, Ferris. It's hard enough for me to see you in passing, but don't make it any harder on yourself."

Ferris felt the lump in his throat grow larger.

Sophia sighed. "It's over. I don't want you in my life."

"You're half of me, though. How can I live without that?"

She finally turned around, her eyes heavy with tears. "I don't know, but I did it."

―

Ferris pushed the mask against his cheeks and stared at the mirror, trying to ignore the sudden burning pain he felt.

"Why? Why did you let me do this to you?"

The Sophia in the mirror blinked. "Can you feel it, Ferris? Can you feel the burning?"

It was getting worse. His blood was rising to the surface of his skin and slipping out of his pores. For some reason, the mask seemed to feel tighter, like it fit even better.

"Yes," he said through the pain.

"This is what you wanted, Ferris. This is what I wanted."

Sharper pains erupted over other ones. His imagination drew a picture of claws digging out of his face and grasping onto the skin of the mask. They shredded his skin. Tears welled up in his eyes.

"I'm half of you, Ferris. You knew that."

Something wrapped around the back of his head. He suddenly reached up and tried to pull the mask from his face. His body thrashed about in the attic as the face grew tighter and tighter.

On his knees, panting, crying, pleading to God for help, Ferris looked in the mirror.

Sophia looked back and smiled. "I want that half back."

The Fiftieth Floor

In 2001, I landed a job as a room service attendant and banquet server for a 32-story hotel. One of the stories told to me when I started was about the "hell-a-vator": Service Elevator #3. About a month prior to my arrival, the elevator had malfunctioned, and for some reason shot one of the pastry chefs to the 33rd floor (the roof access point). He survived, but the elevator was out of commission until a month after I started.

The first time I rode that elevator after it was "blessed" as fully functional, the lights failed to work. The second time, it sank about a foot before rising up again. The third time, I got off on the third floor and waited for either of the other two elevators to work.

This story is the one I consider "the start" of my modern writing adventure. I've often wondered if my room service/banquet server job was the catalyst. Something triggered inside of my brain that year.

Frantic e-Zine *picked this up in late 2001.*

"So, it's that easy."

"Right. Just get the food, wheel the cart to the room and get the money."

Kevin eyed the cart of food his trainer just put together. A mauve tablecloth covered the hot box underneath where two rib eye dinners sat warming. On top, two place settings, two salads, some condiments and — make sure you don't forget — a long stemmed rose were all arranged perfectly.

"How long have you been doing this?" Kevin asked as he held the kitchen door open.

"Hell. I think I've put in about two years. It's not a great life, but if these people pay, it's money."

The hallway curved to the right, past the time office where eventually Kevin could pick up his paycheck, and off to the left. A large fire door and three elevators met the two of them.

"Are the walls this barren all over the hotel?"

"Nope. Just down here in the dungeon." Jason pushed the elevator button. "Management wants to keep our hopes dismal, I think."

"Like you're never getting out of here?"

"Yup."

The bell chimed as the elevator door opened. Kevin quickly noted the steel floor and walls inside the cab before stepping in behind the cart. *Talk about cheap*, he thought.

"One thing I should tell you," Jason said. "These elevators have a mind of their own — the service ones, that is. The first one you saw as we came up has been out for about a month."

"What happened?"

"A pulley broke free and dropped the cab down from the forty-ninth floor like a rock."

The elevator doors creaked shut. With a bump and grinding of gears, Kevin felt his stomach sink as the elevator started to rise. A bead of sweat formed on his forehead.

"Anyone in it?"

"Yea." Jason smiled. "The guy you replaced."

"I bet he got the ride of his life."

"You could say that. The last ride of his life, really."

The elevator stuttered, the sound of metal scraping metal

filled the small cab. The metal shelves inside the hot box clanked together as the elevator came to a jarring stop.

"Shit." Jason pushed the floor button again.

Kevin looked around the elevator as his heartbeat quickened. More sweat formed on his brow. "What was that?"

"Like I said, the elevators have a mind of their own."

"I thought this was new hotel."

"It is. Management wants to keep costs down, I guess, so they never fix these damned things. Elevator maintenance has been a dead department for a few months."

Kevin swallowed hard. "Cutting corners in the wrong place, it seems."

"Yup."

The cab jerked again and started to rise. Kevin looked up nervously at the numbers above the door, then down at the punch pad. Fifteen more floors to go. This may not have been the dream job after all. He desperately needed to find something else to occupy his mind than the inner workings of an elevator.

"How much do you make in tips a night?"

Jason laughed. "Thought you'd never ask. Hell, most people harp on me in the first few minutes of starting a shift."

"I guess I'll find out on my own." Kevin flashed a weak smile. *Twelve more floors to go*, he thought. *Come on.*

"Problem with telling you is simple—depends on the people and how hungry this place gets. You're the only server for over 800 rooms. You get busy, the service slows down, people get pissed and throw you a dime."

"Doesn't seem fair."

"No, it doesn't. But on the other hand, when it's slow, you're quick. You feel better, smile more, these people throw money at you like you're a wishing well and their luck is getting better every hour."

"So how much on average?"

"Most nights I come home with about a hundred. Some nights more. I don't think I've ever left this place with less than twenty."

The elevator slowed down. Kevin looked up at the numbers. *What the hell? Seven more floors to go.* He glanced over at Jason, trying to gauge his reaction, if any.

"Looks like we're almost there," Jason said. He let out a sigh.

"What do you mean? We have seven more floors to go."

Jason bent down and opened the hot box. He reached in, pulled out the oil lamp keeping the food warm and blew it out. With a grunt, he stood back up and looked at Kevin with a smug smile.

"I guess I forgot to tell you. You need to push the button five floors above where you really want to go."

Kevin blinked and looked up at the floor number as the elevator came to a stop. Forty-two. He looked back down at the punch pad. "Interesting. I didn't even notice that you punched forty-seven."

With a loud screech, the door opened and Kevin stepped out onto the floor, feeling safer than ever before. Curiosity hit him as he followed Jason out to the hallway.

"What happens if you need to deliver to the fiftieth floor?" he asked. "The numbers only go to fifty-four."

Jason stopped the cart and turned to Kevin. The friendly smile he had seemed to always wear was gone and his eyes were glossed over.

Jason blinked. "You just don't go up there."

"Why?"

"You just don't." Jason offered a small smile. "I've never had an order for any floor above forty-nine. I don't even know what's up there."

He turned back and pushed the cart down the hallway, quickening his pace. Kevin stood still watching him go, confused by the amount of fear he thought he detected in his voice.

—

"Order's up!"

Kevin turned quickly from the rudimentary task of restocking the condiment bowls. This job was too easy, and Jason said it right—get the food, wheel the cart to the room, get the money. He'd only been working by himself for six hours and so far netted close to one hundred dollars in tips.

The smell of lamp oil filled Kevin's nostrils as he opened the hot box and lit the lamp. In the background, he could hear the hotel's restaurant cooks yelling orders up, the waiters and waitresses running back and forth arguing about the lack of this or who took that. It was in stark contrast to the fluidity of room service: one or two orders at a time, and there was no pressure to get things done in under fifteen minutes. If Kevin ever got swamped with orders, the cashier would politely inform the guest that his or her order would eventually be there.

"Patty melt! Slab of beef!" the cooked yelled out from behind the grill. Kevin deftly moved between a rather fat waitress and another who obviously spent more time on her makeup than she did on learning the ropes. With a calm smile, he capped the two plates and walked them back to his cart.

"Where the hell is my prime rib?" the fat waitress yelled out. "I'm going on twenty minutes."

Kevin smiled. Not only was room service easy, it was solitary. He didn't even care if no one knew his name. Money was the object of the game, and if he could smile and nudge a dollar more from each order, that's all that mattered.

Patty melt. Porterhouse. Steak sauce. Ketchup. Kevin mentally ran through his checklist of items on the cart. The only disaster to befall a room service clerk was to forget something and have to return to the kitchen to get it. If there was another order, the waiting guest would have to wait even longer. Of course, if he already been tipped, what did it matter?

Condiment bowl. Salt and pepper. Salad. Thousand Island dressing. Butter. Chives. Kevin smiled as he pushed the cart out the kitchen door and into the long hallway to the service elevators.

Shit. The rose. With a quick jump back inside, Kevin grabbed a long stem rose from the refrigerator and laid it on the cart.

The hallway was busy with the movements of robotic people, their faces expressionless. Was it panic or fear? Everywhere he looked, people wouldn't smile, and if they did, it seemed forced. Kevin had noted that once to Jason, but just as Jason was about to answer an order came up and the both of them were on their toes.

Still, why the fear?

A large mechanic was bent over with a screwdriver at the doorway to Service Elevator Number 1, his ass protruding from a pair of baggy jeans. The man looked up as Kevin wheeled the cart past and pressed the button.

"Big order?" the mechanic bellowed as he stood up.

"Nothing out of the ordinary. You guys almost done fixing that one?"

The mechanic grinned. "This elevator don't need no fixin'. Works perfec'ly fine. Wanna take a ride?"

The bell rang and one of the other elevator's doors opened up. Kevin quickly nodded to the man and pushed the cart inside. *Freak,* he thought as the doors started to close.

"When one goes," the mechanic yelled back, "you know

the next is 'bout ready to snap."

The door shut with a squeal. Kevin quickly opened his ticket folder and looked at the room number. Forty-nine-twenty-six. He remembered Jason's words on their first trip up: *push the button five floors above where you really want to go.*

Fifty-four. He pushed the button. With a loud bang of metal and an unearthly screech, Kevin was on his way up to make more money.

One foot later, the elevator stopped.

Shit. He punched the floor button several times. Great. *Two hours from the end of my first shift, and I'm about to die.*

With a loud bang that resonated more inside of Kevin's head than the metal elevator, the cab started to move back down. Within seconds, it stopped and the door opened. The fat mechanic smiled.

"Quick trip?"

"No. Something's wrong with this one, too." Kevin pushed the button to go back up.

"Nope. Like I says: when one goes, the next is 'bout ready to snap."

Kevin smiled weakly as the door slid shut once again. "Thanks."

—

Kevin wiped the sweat from his brow just before knocking on the door. The service elevators had no cooling system, and between the electronics and the heat outside, the ride up was uncomfortable at best. He pulled down his vest and knocked once.

"Room service."

Behind the door, Kevin could hear a scramble of activity. Either the guest was coming from his or her bed, or their were trying to mask the smell of pot or whatever else they felt like smoking. So far in his first six hours, Kevin had seen more people stoned than he had in the previous six years.

"Coming," a female voice called out. Through the thin door, Kevin could hear a can of room deodorizer working overtime.

Finally, the door opened. A young, shapely woman smiled back at Kevin as she held together a thin, white satin robe.

You'll get all kinds, Kevin heard Jason's voice in the back of his mind.

"Come in," the woman said, stepping out of the way.

"Where would like this food, ma'am?"

"Right here is fine. How much do I owe you?" She let go of her robe and walked over to her purse on the small nightstand next to her bed. From the bathroom, Kevin could hear the shower running.

"Fifty-two ninety-six."

The woman turned around. "A little steep, don't you think?"

Kevin found himself turning slightly away as soon as he noticed the open robe. He hated these moments, even though this was the first time he had to answer this question to a nearly naked and very attractive female. What was he supposed to say? Yes, it was steep. Everything in this place is steep, but how do you tell the guest so much without sounding like you agree?

"Yes, ma'am," he finally said, internally kicking himself for his lack of words.

The woman stepped forward and handed him a hundred dollar bill. "At least you're honest. Keep the change."

Kevin looked up at the woman and found himself locked in her graceful smile. "Thank you, ma'am."

Back in the hallway, Kevin smiled. He could get used to that. Of course, the opposite might happen next: a fat man in boxers with flab hanging to his knees might answer the door.

Would he tip as well? The thought made Kevin shiver as he walked back toward the service elevators.

He pushed the employee entrance door open then stopped. The doorway to the fire exit was ajar. From there he could see forever, and even though he suffered from a strong fear of heights, at least there was a railing in front of him, right? He slowly walked to the doorway and looked out at the city. The landing was a metal grate, and Kevin had to pull himself back after looking through the floor nearly 500 feet down.

It was then that curiosity took over. If the service elevator couldn't take him to the fiftieth floor, could the stairs? He looked over at the staircase scaling the side of the building. The metal steps were exactly like the landing and he knew if he were to climb them, he would surely panic, lose his balance and fall over the railing.

What's up there? he thought.

The room service beeper went off. He looked at the display then quickly headed back down to the kitchen. The fiftieth floor would have to wait.

—

<u>One more to go.</u> Kevin pulled out the ticket folder and looked at the room number.

"Shit." He slammed it shut. How the hell was he supposed to get to the fiftieth floor? No one delivered up there. He sighed and opened the fire door to the elevators, then wheeled the cart out to the foyer. The fat mechanic was cleaning up his mess.

"Excuse me," Kevin said.

"Yessir?"

"How do you get the fiftieth floor?"

The mechanic stood up and stared at Kevin as if room service must hire the dumbest people. "Push the button that says fif'y."

No shit, Kevin thought. *That's the way elevators were supposed to work, but obviously there were problems with the other two. Didn't Jason say that no one delivered to the fiftieth floor?*

"I thought you had to push the button five floors above where you wanted to go?" Kevin asked, his mind reeling with the thought of how stupid he sounded.

"That's the idea."

"Well...um...the other elevators don't have a fifty-five. So, how do you get a cart to fifty?"

The mechanic paused for a moment as if he were deep in thought. He rubbed his chin, exaggerating the look. "Hmmm."

"Look, I'm not stupid. I just don't see any way to get this cart to fifty unless I take the stairs from forty-nine."

"Tell you what," the mechanic said as he picked up his tool box. "I spent some time on this'n, here. Give'r a go and see where it takes ya."

Kevin swallowed hard. *No. Why do I have to die?*

"I even added few ex'ra...features." The mechanic smiled wide, revealing a golden tooth surrounded by black. "What're you scared of? Ain't no hellevator no more. 'Sides, just saw two porters take the others, so you've got 'bout a twen'y minute wait."

Kevin took a deep breath. This was the last run of the evening and at this point there was no way he could just walk away from the situation. The mechanic had put him to the task, and he was sure he didn't want to be labeled something awful after just one day.

"Guess it can't hurt." Kevin sighed and pushed the cart into the cab. The front wheels dropped an inch and the metal plates inside the hot box banged together.

Kevin looked back at the mechanic. "Looks like you're a little off here."

"Can't fix 'em all," the mechanic said, smiling again as the elevator door slammed shut with a loud metallic bang.

Kevin wiped the sweat from his forehead and looked at the punch pad. If the elevator was fixed, he should be able to press "fifty" and wind up there in a few seconds. What the hell? It was the last run, and then he could go home. It may have been an easy job, but it was nonstop work.

With a wince, Kevin pushed the button and waited. Slowly the elevator started to rise, the LED reading out the floor as they passed by. Seven. Eight. Nine.

Kevin relaxed and opened up his ticket folder one more time to double check the room. Five zero zero one. A suite. A corner room with a spa and king size bed, fireplace and balcony. The corner rooms were much larger and cost twice as much as the others. What mattered most, however, was that the corner rooms tended to tip more.

Kevin sighed and looked up. Twenty-five. Twenty-six. Twenty-seven. The elevator was running smoothly, and unlike the others, he couldn't hear the cables squeaking or banging around. Maybe the damned thing worked after all.

Kevin relaxed more and bent over to blow out the oil candle. A few more seconds and his ride would be over. Another minute, and he'd be tipped well again. Another hour, he'd be in bed. He never took note until now, but damn was he tired.

Forty-seven. Forty-eight. Forty-nine.

The elevator started to slow down. It seemed a little late, but maybe that was just fatigue. Kevin pulled down his vest and waited for the doors to open.

Fifty.

The elevator stopped.

What's going on? Kevin thought as he waited. The doors never took this long to open before. He wiped a bead of sweat from his forehead and pushed the "door open" button.

A loud bang rattled the cab and the sound of metal scraping together pierced Kevin's ears. This wasn't good.

With a jolt, the elevator started to drop, knocking Kevin on his feet. He screamed as he grabbed hold of the railing to pull himself up. The cab started to rattle violently, shaking open the hot box and spilling its contents onto the floor. Kevin reached for the alarm button in front of him, praying that some sort of miracle would happen.

"God! Help me!"

—

"One thing I should tell you," Jason said. "These elevators have a mind of their own—the service ones, that is. The first one you saw as we came up has been out for about two months."

"Why?"

"The pulley snapped and the cab fell fifty floors."

The elevator doors creaked shut. With a bump and the grinding of gears, Michael felt his stomach sink as the elevator started to rise. A bead of sweat formed on his forehead.

"Anyone in it?"

"Yea. The guy you replaced." Jason smiled then looked at Michael. "Don't know what he was thinking."

"What's that?"

"That elevator was out of service a month before he took it. I just don't know what possessed him to get into a broken cab."

"Maintenance ever going to fix it?"

"Don't count on it. Management wouldn't hire a living soul."

"Too cheap?"

"Yup."

Them Rabbits

I really can't explain what possessed me to write this story. I don't know if I was playing with dialect on paper or if I was just exercising my right to be creative. Maybe it was a combination of the two. If you combine this story with the article "The Virtue of Heredity" later in this book, you may get a glimpse into what I was thinking.

Them rabbits is evil, I tell ya. They ain't no furry little pets to go a-strokin' an' a-lovin' an' a-carin' fer. Them's bad seed. They growed 'em that way, I know fer sure. I ain't tellin' how I came into that bit o' info, but I ain't a-speculatin', either. Them's bad.

How comes I know this? What I'm gonna tell ya, ain't no fairy tale I 'spect ya to tell yer kin folk. Naw, this ain't 'bout no Easter Bunny, no Peter Cottontail, not even a story 'bout no rabbit's foot. It's 'bout evil, the devil in them beasts. It's 'bout killin' an' eatin' an' sacrificin'. It's 'bout death.

See that road o'er yonder? I seen 'em eatin' the grass on the side, grindin' them teeth up, just a-waitin' fer the next son o' bitch to come a-gunnin' his car down toward the pond. Hell, I seen 'em plottin', I tell you. I seen 'em gittin' together in a circle, heard 'em whisperin' somethin', an' breakin' up, settin' up like some battlefield. I done watched 'em an' dagnammit, I once got me some balls, crawled in that there grass, an' spied on 'em. I tell you, them rabbits is evil.

Last summer, I tell ya, I thought I'd seen everythin'. I don't know 'bout you, but when I sees someone come a-gunnin' his car down toward the pond o'er yonder, I gits to thinkin' they might be movin' too fast fer their own good. I can't tell ya the number o' times I seen cars drive by, hittin' the rabbits, smashin' their fur into the dirt. They gits them blinders on, thinkin' bout the bitches an' the beer an' the fishin' an' the fun. They don't see no rabbits, an' I'll be damned if they don't see nothin' 't'all. They gits stupid. An' when they come back, they run o'er that same bloody mess on the road, smashin' more rabbit guts into the dirt.

Well, last summer, there's this guy an' he's always a-fishin' at the pond. I seen him ever' mornin' just 'fore the sun come up, an' he's a-gunnin' his car. The first time I sees him run o'er a rabbit, I didn't think much 'bout it Hell. It happened 'fore then. Well, them other rabbits stopped a-chewin', watched the car drive by an' then hopped o'er to the tangled mess of fur on the road. I seen 'em gather in a circle, a-sniffin' an' a-pokin' with their noses at the guts. Ya want weird? I thought I'd lost a screw someplace when they started a-pullin' at the body. I didn't wanna believe it, but they was eatin' their own, I tell ya! They was eatin' it!

A few days later, the same thing happened, but this time I was almost 'spectin' somethin'. That same car came a-gunnin' again, an'—wouldn't ya know it?—damn fool hit three of 'em! I thought I was seein' things, but I know that guy sped up when he seen 'em eatin'. Them rabbits did it again. This time they didn't waste no time a-sniffin' an' a-pokin' with their noses. Aw, hell. Them rabbits tore into those dead bodies like it was Ma's cookin' an' you ain't had no fixin's in days. They was pullin' bits o' flesh off the bones, a-smackin' their teeth an' lips. Damn, I swear I heard 'em talkin' 'bout it, too. Fuckin' dinner conversation, ya know?

Another day goes by, an' I sees them rabbits at the side of the road, a-chewin' at the grass again. I didn't hear the car, but I think they did. Them rabbits pushed—pushed, I tell ya—another rabbit into the road. I watched this other rabbit roll over on its back an' just lay there. The car took me by surprise. It came a-gunnin' as fast as I ever did see it go, an' I swear on Pa-Pa's grave I saw the driver's eyes, wide-open. Naw, it weren't in fear, mind you. Naw, it weren't like ya knew ya was gonna crash. This damn fool driver was a-grinnin'! I *know* he saw that rabbit layin' on the road, an' I know he done sped up even more.

Lemme tell ya, I ain't never heard no rabbit crunch like that. The body damn near 'sploded, an' guts an' fur went a-flyin'. Sure as slop in a pig's ass, one of them car's tires blew an' the driver slammed on his brakes right in front o' the house. I watched him git out, walk 'round the car an' start to say somethin' to me.

Know how I know them rabbits is evil? They circled him. I tell ya, they circled that man, an' jumped up like rabid dawgs, a-bitin' an' a-tearin' an' a-screamin'. That's right, they was a-screamin'! That man dropped to the ground so fast, I thought he was gonna break his neck, or somethin'. Hell, it didn't matter if he did. He fought them rabbits an' screamed hisself, floppin' 'round like a fish outta water. But them rabbits wouldn't stop. Naw, they just a kept on a-bitin' an' a-tearin' an' a screamin'. They just kept on killin' the man.

They's evil, I tell ya. You better watch where ya step, 'round here. Don't go a-gunnin' yer car like you is in some God awful race that you ain't gonna win no how. Them's evil rabbits. An' they gonna git ya, too, 'less you's careful out there.

I'm tellin' ya, them's evil rabbits.

Did I tell ya how I lost my eye?

The Great Machine

The 32-story hotel where I worked as a room service attendant/banquet server was connected to a casino. Although not associated with the floor, I couldn't help but notice things. The more I looked, the more I saw — in the faces of the losers and winners alike.

It came as no surprise, then, that I had to question who were the losers and the winners: those that walked off the floor after losing their $20, $40 or $100, or those that won and continued to stay in their seat, like Fate had shone on them that day and it was now a sure thing.

This was my first "major" sale, to Quietus *for their October 2003 e-Book.*

He stood at the corner of the crossroads not feeling the rain pelt his skin and soak his clothes. Tired eyes, glazed over with hate, sank deep into his wrinkled face. He smiled, put his hand in the pockets of his jacket and watched the victims walk in and out of the casino's doors, so unaware they were each being used by the Great Machine. He stood long enough to see some walk in with a skip in their step and then minutes later walk out with their heads hung low. There were lovers who came in holding hands only to leave disenchanted, walking apart from each other more disgusted with the idea of having just spent their last bit of entertainment money than anything else. A man, a woman, an elderly couple—each entered the Great Machine with the thought of improving their well-being. The man spent his last paycheck, the woman her week's tips from the local greasy spoon, and the elderly couple wondered how they would ever survive without their pension for the month.

The man smiled wider, baring the slightest hint of tobacco stained teeth. How many of them would turn right around and be back the next day? The next week? Of course he had been back. In the course of three years since the Great Machine opened wide its maw to accept the addicted, he faithfully entered the building nearly once a day, sometimes not coming out for up to twenty hours. It provided entertainment, something to do in retirement. He'd won some, lost some, and broke even too many times to remember. Three years will wear a man down, though. Inside the belly of the Great Machine, the last vestiges of life must have been sucked dry from his body. His skin stretched over his bones. His eyes were empty. He hunched, sometimes needing something to support the weight his back no longer wanted to carry. He was dying, and he knew it all too well.

The sign above the doors flashed wildly in the rain, offering anything from the night's comic relief act to the weekly special at the buffet. A quick glance at his watch told him time was up. The Great Machine must pay. The man fingered the knife in his pocket, testing the tip, stroking the blade. He felt a slight sting and pulled his hand out. Blood oozed from a cut across his finger. It quickly mixed with rain and thinned. He smiled, wondering if the same would happen inside to every person he came across that he could associate with the Great Machine. They were the souls that needed to bleed. They were the souls that robbed him of his life every day, with a smile and an unconvincing platitude of luck.

The man started to walk. His coat was soaked, his hair matted to his forehead by the rain. He didn't feel cold, or even wet. All he felt was the pain of three years and — faintly — the sting in his finger. He took each step thinking about the slot machines, seeing the flashing lights and spinning wheels. In his mind's eye, he watched the bars and 7s and cherries and lemons dance for him, sometimes lining up in unison, sometimes not. He could hear the ding of each machine, near and far. There were the comforting alarms which told those within the casino someone just won big money. There were lights flashing, people cheering, people jeering and coins clanking in trays.

Finally, there were the employees — servants of the Great Machine — dressed in white shirts, bow ties and fake smiles, each of them a cancer cell that together formed the tumor the casino had become in the soft underbelly of the South. Since gaming arrived on the Gulf Coast, people lost their lives more frequently. It wasn't always physically. There was emotional death and even worse, spiritual death. A man could lose his body only once, but the Great Machine could take his life a thousand times over, and with each death tempt him with life once more. It became a cycle for so many: to be born in the belly of the Great Machine, to live in the innards and feed off its temptations and lies, and then to die at the hands of a dealer or a pit boss or a mindless slot machine. Some withered away for good, but most returned, hoping to be reborn and live again, never thinking they would once more die.

The old man had died too many times to count. He was a victim of the tumor, a piece of the Gulf Coast swallowed whole by the cancerous growth of the industry. He no longer felt guilty of losing, however; to him, losing was a byproduct of winning. He no longer felt sick when he opened his wallet to find nothing left; to him, there was always a way to get more money. He no longer cared that his family didn't know him or even care that he was still breathing; to him, the Great Machine offered him a place to call home.

The glass doors slid open silently on golden rails. A blast of cold air greeted the man as he stepped inside the belly of the Great Machine. The sounds suddenly swept forward out of his mind's eye and into reality. People scurried by, some with their heads hung low, others with their heads in the clouds, probably dreaming of their pending lives as millionaires. A few employees walked by, some glancing up, most focused on getting from one place to the other like robots on a mission. The Great Machine controlled them like it controlled the customer. You lived and you died by the Great Machine; there was no other god before it.

A security guard dressed in a cheap rent-a-cop outfit that seemed too small, stood behind a golden podium and nodded at the man like he recognized the wrinkled face and tired eyes. Why not? The old man graced the presence of the Great Machine almost daily, and would probably have eaten a thousand buffets if he ever signed up for a player's card or whatever else the place offered to keep a person inside who had some life left to suck dry. After three years, however, the old man was still a nameless face, and he liked it that way. It was enough to sell your soul to the Great Machine. The soul, however, didn't have to have a name.

He walked forward a few more steps until he stood at the edge of the vast sea of slot machines, nearly every one tempting another lost soul. He fingered the knife in his pocket, suddenly realizing he didn't know where to begin. He couldn't very well slit the throat of the victims; they were too much like him. If he gutted an employee or two, what type of a statement would that make? He would be pinned down and arrested by a number of plain-clothes security officers that melted into the masses. No. He had to make a real statement, something that would send shivers down the spine of every casino on the Gulf Coast. It had to be something that sent a message to the victims: they were not alone. They didn't have to come inside and lose their life for the chance at riches. He would see to it that the Great Machine paid for sucking his life dry and bringing him to this point. But where was he to even begin looking?

The old man looked around the gaming floor, searching for something or someone that might give him the answer. He watched for a moment as a fat man, too obese to move without straining, plopped down a bucket of coins at a change booth. The employee behind the counter managed a weak smile and took the bucket, dumping it into a counting machine. Coins shifted through a single slot, each one ticking off another dollar. Finally, the machine stopped shaking and displayed the fat man's winnings: $103. The old man wondered how much he had given to the Great Machine just to get that much money. Two hundred? Five hundred? A thousand? Did he really think he won money? Disgusted, the old man turned his eyes away, still looking for that certain something that would change the world for the better. In a way, he felt like Christ, ready to sacrifice his life for the millions who would never know his name.

He didn't count on the pull—the feeling of greed that crept up from deep inside of him and pushed him forward. The pull of the machines all around him, blinking and sounding off bells with each coin deposited, withdrawn or ticked off as the wheels of evil spun wildly around. For so long, he had come to this spot—one foot short of the main floor—and wondered where the big winner was right at that moment.

He always imagined he could sense the machines that wanted to give and feel the evil sucking tentacles of the machines that only wanted to take. His eyes darted back and forth, from machine to machine. As it happened so many other times, the employees and victims—the cogs and the gears and the lubricant and the rods and the pistons of the Great Machine—melted away into a backdrop upon which the slot machines that had so often pulled him in were drawn.

He blinked. In the farthest corner of the floor, sitting like an ugly maiden waiting for someone to give her an invitation to the dance, an older model slot machine quietly blinked. The old man had never seen it before, but with over fifteen hundred machines, even a repeat victim like himself might miss one or two. His eyes were glued to its silver casing as he slowly walked through the throng of victims oiling the Great Machine. He suddenly neglected his purpose, although not entirely forgetting it. In one fluid motion without sound, like an instinct born in the womb, his hand slipped from the knife in his pocket to his wallet. He shuffled his feet, looking up at the machine, then down to count his bills. Twenty-five dollars. Just enough for one more shot at saving his soul from the belly of the Great Machine.

The old man finally reached the machine and sat down. He glanced around quickly at his surroundings, then looked up. It must have been built as far back as twenty or thirty years ago. There was only one payline, and nothing spectacular about the pictures on the wheel. It certainly wasn't one of the new machines—computerized to a fault and designed strictly for the taking of souls. He looked at the name—"One Wish"—then quickly scanned the payout information. One dollar at a time, he thought. I think I've finally found the one.

The first dollar in the machine netted the old man exactly what he expected: nothing. The wheels spun rapidly, stopping first on the left with a bar, second with a lemon and third between a cherry and the word "Wish". He looked up again at the payoff, scanning for the jackpot. Three cherries would give him five hundred dollars. Three apples would give him a thousand. The sentence "Make Your Wish" would give him....The old man blinked. "Your wish" was scribbled in black marker across an indecipherable amount of money. He blinked again, then wiped his eyes. The rain must have clouded his vision.

The second dollar gave him his first dollar back. It dropped out of the machine into the silver tray with a satisfying "ching". He reached in, then put his winnings back into the machine. On the third and fourth spins, he won nothing. The fifth spin, another dollar. Within the first five minutes, he was down to one dollar and feeling the pit of his stomach roll and tumble with the knowledge there was no more money in his wallet. He would have to get up and face the Great Machine once again. He could either walk outside and forget he ever entertained thoughts of making a difference, or he could walk around aimlessly until he found someone to kill — someone to pay for taking his soul.

The old man dropped the last dollar in the machine and pulled the handle. The first wheel stopped on "Make". He suddenly felt his heart start to race faster, beads of sweat forming on his forehead. Thoughts of winning the jackpot screamed through his mind in milliseconds as the second wheel stopped at "Your". His breath quickened as he stood up and grabbed the side of the machine as if to coax the last wheel to victory through sheer will power.

The third wheel stopped on the word "Wish". The old man closed his eyes as a smile grew on his face from ear to ear. It pushed back his wrinkled cheeks and scrunched up his aging eyes. The light above the machine flashed wildly, further drawing the man into a sense of pure relief and then victory. He had won!

He opened his eyes, then looked up at the payoff. "Your wish" was still scribbled across the numbers. His smile started to fade a little, and he sat back down on the stool. No money was coming out of the machine. He looked around for an employee, someone to grab and show he was a winner. Damn it, he was a winner!

The machine sat silently, its light the only indication something just happened. The old man's smile dropped completely, and he hit the side of the machine. Something was wrong. This wasn't supposed to happen to him. He had come inside the belly of the Great Machine for three years waiting for a moment like this, and now it was being taken away from him in the worst possible way. Why was this happening to him?

He looked up at the payoff one more time, squinting at the words that now started to make him angry: "Your wish."

Is that what he just won? The old man stared at the words, then felt a chuckle of irony escape his throat. "My wish," he whispered. "Well, you piece of shit. I wish I knew exactly how I could make this whole gaming establishment pay for taking my life day in and day out for three years. You want to know what I wish for? That's it."

The gaming floor fell silent. The sudden barrage of noise that existed as a backdrop was now gone, and the silence that replaced it smacked the old man as hard as it could in the back of the head. He turned around slowly, wondering if he just lost his hearing.

The floor was empty. Slot machines sat silent, their lights off. The table games, lined in rows through the middle of the floor, were swept clean, the only indication of their purpose now the green cloth that marked the game or the rules. The lights above were dimmer, as if the casino had closed down for the first time since opening and the old man was the only person left alive. He'd never realized the cavernous size of the place, or the necessity for people and noise. Without the people, sound bounced around off the walls and the tables and the ceiling.

The old man stood up from his stool and walked forward a few steps. "Hello?" he called out, the words doing just what he expected: echoing off the walls and filling the massive void. "Hello? Is anyone in here?"

"Just the man you wished to see." Mysterious words floated in an echo through the air and filtered past the stillness next the old man. "I would be honored if you'd join me for a moment."

The old man felt his heart skip a beat. He swallowed the lump that formed in his throat. He had to get out of the casino, and do it fast. Something wasn't right about the slot machine, and the wish he made that was merely in jest.

"Over here, sir," the voice called out again, this time from a table in the center of the room. The old man walked slowly past a few rows of slot machines, two roulette tables, and a blackjack table. A younger man, dressed in a suit—expensive, no doubt—stood behind a table shuffling a deck of cards. His eyes were glued on the old man, but his hands were busy with the cards, the sound filling the room.

"Who are you?" the old man asked. His voice was weak, and seemed to scratch at his throat.

"I'm the person you wished to see, my friend." The younger man in the suit stopped shuffling and put the deck down on the table. "I'm the person who took your soul. Or so you say."

"I don't understand."

"You don't?" The younger man reached into his jacket

pocket and pulled out a knife. He stuck it in the table with a solid *thump.* "Isn't this your knife, my friend?"

The old man reached into his pocket for his knife. *Gone!*

"What did you think you were going to do with that?"

The old man sat down on a stool in front of the table. "I...I...don't really know."

"Did you honestly think you were Jesus Christ? Are you willing to sacrifice your life for the good of the people? Did you think that cutting the throat of one or two of my employees would set you free?"

"No. I...." The old man's eyes drifted down. "No."

"Look at me."

The old man looked up, slowly, like a dog expecting to be whipped with a newspaper. "What do you want with me?"

The younger man picked up the deck of cards and shuffled them one more time. "I want to give you a chance, sir. Killing a few of my employees is really a poor way of making a statement. This *Machine*—as you call it—isn't run by the people you see in the bow ties and white shirts. It isn't even run by the people you call victims. It doesn't exist because a few people wanted to take your money or a few businessmen got together over a few beers at a strip joint and decided to build a casino. This *Machine* exists because I want it to exist."

The old man felt his heart speed up as the other continued to talk. He watched the cards flip by one by one in sickening slow motion.

"Greed fuels it all, and it didn't start here. It didn't start in the deserts of Nevada, either, my friend. This greed is eternal, and you think you can stop people from willingly—and I really should emphasize that word—*willingly* walk into a casino and give me their souls."

"I don't know what I was thinking."

The younger man nodded and started to deal the cards.

Five cards landed face down in a perfect row in front of the old man.

"What are we doing?" the old man asked. "I don't understand this."

"It's your wish. You wanted to know how you could make this whole gaming establishment pay for taking your soul."

The old man nervously chuckled. "It was just a joke."

A flash of light erupted in front of the old man, sending him backward in his chair. He looked up as the expensive suit caught fire and quickly burned away. As the last remaining flame died down, the old man found himself staring into the eyes of a demon. Its face was misshapen, the eyes missing completely, the nose crushed against the skull. Its mouth smiled grimly, barring small razor-sharp teeth. On its shoulders, now stripped of not just clothes but skin as well, sat a small rat, chewing on a piece of the demon's flesh.

The old man's heart rapidly beat against his chest, so hard he was surprised it didn't explode inside of him. Hell. He *wanted* it to explode. He stood back from the table, then glanced left and right looking for a way to run.

"You can't escape this," the demon said, the voice no longer comforting. "Pick up the cards."

The old man fumbled with the cards as he slowly raised them up. "What are we playing for?" he quietly asked.

"If you win, I'll give you a way to make a statement."

"And if I lose?"

The demon picked five cards off the top of the deck. "If you lose," he said, "you'll find yourself outside of this casino exactly one hour ago. Your soul has been mine for three years. What's a few more years of winning and losing?"

The demon laid his cards down on the table. Three sixes, a two and an ace.

The old man nervously looked down at his cards, then

swallowed another lump that formed in his throat. He stared down at a perfect Royal Flush: a ten, jack, queen, king and ace, all spades, in sequential order. If he remembered right, the odds of that happening were something like four billion to one. He smiled, stretching his cheeks. A quiet laugh crept out of his mouth as he laid the cards down on the table.

—

Tired eyes, glazed over with pain, sink deep into the old man's wrinkled face. His arms are outstretched on a cross of gold outside the casino's entrance, golden nails holding him upright. A golden rope is wrapped around his legs with another golden nail driven through his feet.

Those passing the casino often look at the man hanging from the cross, like some sacrilegious statue, mocking the Christian world. A few make comments about the depths to which the gaming industry has finally sunk for a theme. Others simply shrug their shoulders and walk on by.

The old man screams internally, his body encased in gold and his face frozen in fear. It is said that he watches over the people coming and going from the innards of the Great Machine, a beacon to those who fall victim to greed. For those who need it, there's a slot that accepts any denomination of coin; you can buy a prayer if you think you need one.

It is also said you can see a tear fall if you take a good hard look and walk away for good.

Wren

This very short piece was originally a chapter in my first novel, Difficult Mirrors. *I took it out after it became too complicated and slowed the plot. Writing from the point of view of a bird isn't an easy thing to do — there are so many places where an author might be tempted to anthropomorphize an animal. I did that at first and had to cut out quite a few words. There are still "human" traits present, but I still think I succeeded...in something.*

From its perch on a saguaro high above the desert floor, a small wren watched nervously as the brutality of another species unfolded before its eyes. It had never seen one of these animals up close before, only from up high while caught in a stream of air above a lake just to the north. There, they all seemed to be doing little of importance, lying around with their oddly-shaped bodies and naked skin. The first time the wren actually watched them in action, he thought it strange they didn't seem to be concerned much with the survival of their race. Instead, they all chattered loudly, disturbing the serenity of the little, brown bird's surroundings. They splashed around in the water as if inflicted with some nervous disease that caused them to act irresponsibly. They didn't even eat worms. But this cold night, with the stars shining brightly down, the two animals below seemed to be acting in a different manner.

They came up the hillside brushing away a few loose branches and seemed to be drinking from shiny things, which they promptly threw into the desert. At first, there was just loud chirping from the two, and it was this, in fact, that had brought the bird out of its nest in the tall cactus. The bird had been taught as a youngster that by listening and being constantly aware of your surroundings, you prepare yourself for impending danger. There was no danger here, the wren surmised, and so it took its perch upon the highest arm. Cocking its head to the side, it quickly guessed from its previous encounters with the species, that the one with the golden, straight feathers that fell down to its waist was the female and the other one, with a sort of billed-like thing on its head—perhaps a device for digging up worms—was the male. Strange, these animals, the wren thought. They have the brightest colored skin that surely couldn't be used for camouflage.

All of a sudden the two began pushing each other. The chattering became louder—more in an aggravated sort of way than anything else—and the wren decided it best to fly away. Who knows what these animals can do when provoked? As it spread its wings, curiosity began to creep through its veins, though, and it chose to stay still and watch the two further. At this point the female had been shoved to the ground and was backing away from the male, screaming at the same time. The male looked around quickly, then picked up a large stone. The little wren chirped over and over, its frantic cry echoing in the cold night air. The male looked up, but soon enough the stone was over his head with both wing-like appendages. There came more frantic chirping from the bird, wings flapping wildly, its little body hopping up and down, back and forth.

The screams and rapid chatter from the female quickly died away as the stone crashed into her head, crushing her skull. Blood poured from the wound as the male hit her again and again, all the while yelling loudly. Finally, the male let go of the stone and wiped his mouth. He looked around, then bent over the body, moving the legs and the arms. Maybe this was how the species died: brutal beating, followed by a strange placement of the body. He chirped again, then watched the male grab the rock and crush the female's head several more times before running off into the night.

The female's body lay across the desert floor, soaking in her own blood which now flowed like a river from what used to be her head. The little wren fluffed up its feathers in disgust and flew down closer to the body. The desert floor quickly soaked up the blood.

Cautiously, the bird hopped over to the female's side and cocked its head. It chirped once to get her attention, but she didn't move. It hopped to the right and chirped again.

Nothing. Only the soft trickle of blood dripping onto the ground and the faint chirping of far way crickets answered the bird.

It cocked its head to the side one more time and flew away into the cold of the desert night.

Novellas

The Retribution of Nathan James

The Retribution of Nathan James was the first character sketch I wrote for a novel called Sketches from the Spanish Mustang. *I've since retired that book and released all the sketches on their own as the only real tie between them was the setting (Cripple Creek, Colorado). All of the sketches are literary, although this one might slip a little into the "thriller" or "suspense" genre.*

1

He hoped it would be a painful way to die.

There was no longer a wellspring of tears or a firestorm of rage. The surge of feeling that had enveloped Nathan James the last few weeks like a disastrous hurricane had now ebbed and dissipated, leaving only a dull numbness, a grey blanket of cold, emotional isolation. It was a good feeling to have when you wanted to exact revenge.

He leaned against the iron lamppost and stared off toward a distant past, his brown eyes glazed over. There were other ways to kill a man: some quicker, some more private, some less violent, some guaranteed to leave a scar on the assholes of this town forever. He had considered most of these methods, but in the end, only one option remained.

There was no reason for anyone to suspect him; the police, the neighbors, the old work acquaintances all grieved for him for other reasons. No one asked him why he hadn't already left his house or the town, but he could read the silent queries on their faces. It had been three weeks since Nora had killed herself. Since then, the buzzing of condolences and the pitiful attempts at commiseration from those who knew him had droned on, like a swarm of pestilent tsetse flies draining life away in slow motion. They didn't help. Instead, they brought him back to that fateful day again and again. He had grown tired of analyzing the reasons why she shot herself, tired of reliving the moment he walked through the front door of their Golden Avenue house and found a pool of blood on the living room floor, chunks of flesh stuck to the wall.

He shuddered at the thought, at the revolting smell of spent urine and death he still couldn't get out of the house. The image of his wife of seven years, half her face missing, never dulled with time. It was still as sharp and clear as that day, her emaciated form curled in a fetal position, a crimson puddle of blood spread out under her like a sick blossom.

Sure, she deserved to die after what she did, but not like that, and not in his living room. The note he picked out of the pool of blood explained only one thing, the rest just a heap of hateful words jotted down in a shaky script.

Nathan swallowed back a large lump in his throat and returned his gaze to the present. Across the street, a woman sat on an oak bench, busy with a notebook or sketchbook on her lap. He couldn't see her features. The orange glow of evening was turning more and more indigo, and a gentle wind nipped at his open collar. Despite the down jacket and heavy pants, he could never—*would* never—enjoy the cold. He had lived in this old mountain town most of his life but still dreaded the winter. As fall was a reminder of the frozen months ahead, he'd begun to dread those months as well. He was ironically content that he would never have to see snow again, and the night's attempt to chill his bones would be nature's last assault on him.

In a few hours, he would be headed south.

He turned his attention to the building behind him. A few people stood off to the side of one of the doors clutching cigarettes and wishes, their pallid faces taut with expectation. He'd always found Bennett Avenue to be a useful place to disappear when he wanted to think. If not working at one of the casinos, the locals rarely mingled with the tourists and outsiders. There was anonymity on the street. The town may have found its way back from the brink of economic disaster, but it wasn't because of local money, and it was becoming more and more obvious that locals weren't welcome at the slots.

The sixteen casinos in Cripple Creek were all converted century-old storefronts, saloons and burlesque houses. Their neon names reflected Western themes, although some of them were odd: Jimmy Nolan's, Bronco Billy's, Gold Rush, Brass Ass, Spanish Mustang. It was the last he now stood in front of, and the place most connected to his dead wife.

Nora had always hated gambling. She often told stories of what it did to her father, to her mother, to her family growing up. Even though gaming wasn't sanctioned by the state of Colorado until 1991, Cripple Creek had never shed its raucous past. A poker game or a hidden slot machine was only a sly wink at a bartender away. Someone in town owned a roulette table. Craps was a back alley sport. Nora's family was always on the brink of disaster.

When they'd married, Nathan had promised to stay away from the underground games, but the arrival of state-sanctioned gambling made it more and more difficult. After Nathan was laid off—fired, really—from the Cripple Creek and Victor Gold Mine, the casinos in town offered a temporary respite from unemployment, even if it was only half of what he made in the mines. Ever since he'd taken a job at the Brass Ass, though—first as a dealer then as a pit boss—his wife had refused to be civil. She ranted about the money coming in to pay the house note and utility bills, to buy the groceries and fix the furniture. It was nothing more than blood wages from the Devil himself, she'd said. In reality, though, it was the amount of money coming in that raised her hackles; it just wasn't enough.

He sighed. She'd never respected the effort he put into maintaining a household. Her distance from him grew as the years passed and he moved from casino job to casino job. Despite her pleas to move and find "meaningful" employment, Nathan knew he was a miner first and held out hope he'd get his chance to get back into the mines. In the meantime, a job in a casino would have to do. It was this refusal to bend to Nora's will that further distanced the two, and she ended up finding consolation in another, a man that represented the very thing she said she hated.

Hypocrite.

The door swung open on rusty hinges, and a jolly couple half Nathan's age walked out smiling—an emotion out of place in this part of town. The woman wore a black suede coat with a fur-lined hood bouncing behind her. Her thin face, high cheekbones and green eyes were accented by unnaturally red shoulder-length hair pulled into a crude ponytail. She reeked of alcohol.

The man with her stopped about five feet from Nathan and lit a cigarette, puffing out the first two hits through his nose like a dragon. He was shorter than Nathan and sported a slight paunch that stretched the shirt under his open denim jacket. Unkempt hair stuck out from a black watch cap worn too high on his head to warm his ears. "You want to go over to the other side and see what they have?"

The woman seemed to consider it and shoved her hands in her pockets. "Maybe we can get something to eat, first."

For a moment it looked as if the man had been slapped in the face. His lips snarled. "Really? You want to eat? We're on a roll, baby."

She stepped away from him and lit a cigarette of her own, her jolly attitude now lost. "And we'll be on a roll after we eat. Come on. I'm starving."

With a sigh of strained agreement, the man nodded. They walked past Nathan, leaving a trail of menthol-flavored smoke behind.

They're on a roll, alright, Nathan mused as he fingered something in pocket. *They won't die tonight.*

2

Nathan watched a man too obese to move without straining, plop down a bucket of coins at a cashier's cage about five yards away. The weathered employee behind the counter managed a weak smile, took the bucket and dumped it into a counting machine. Coins shifted through a single slot, ticking off dollars one at a time. Finally, the machine stopped its agitated quake and displayed the fat man's winnings: $103. Nathan wondered how much he had given to the Spanish Mustang just to get that much money. Two hundred? Five hundred? A thousand? Did he really think he'd won money? With a severe huff, the fat man turned away, his beady black eyes darting about for an open machine.

Nathan stood in an alcove near the cashier's cage that hid the entrance to one of the bathrooms on this floor. He knew from his walkthroughs that this particular recess was partially hidden from the myriad of cameras that dotted the ornate, wood-paneled ceiling like a fungal disease. These were not Las Vegas casinos; they weren't built for prying eyes. Load-bearing columns and sharp corners allowed some protection, and the bankroll of this particular casino was only large enough to maintain a small platoon of security forces, not a full battalion.

Glancing around one more time without trying to draw attention to himself, he slipped a small cylindrical package wrapped in butcher paper from his coat pocket and dropped it into a waste basket. Thankfully, a poor janitorial staff had left enough crumpled paper and empty wax cups to mask the sound of the heavy package.

Without pause, he walked into the rows of slot machines and pretended to look interested. Double Diamonds, Triple Sevens, Wild Cherries, Haywire—the names of the machines on both sides of him appeared brighter than usual. In the pocket of his twill pants, heavy coins jingled in unison with his steps. He knew he would have to wait for his intended target. In the meantime, he would entertain himself with a slot game or two—far enough away to escape the inevitable chaos he intended.

Nathan stopped in front of a Triple Sevens machine and glanced back toward the trash can. He could still see it. Two machines away on his right was the door. As a former blast hole driller for the mines, he knew the explosive radius of his bomb and had calculated the distance he needed to remain at to be safe. He fingered a tiny device in his pocket and sat down at the machine. *Twenty minutes*, he thought.

He couldn't simply sit and wait. He reached into a pocket and withdrew an Eisenhower silver dollar. It was Nora's, a gift from Nathan on their sixth wedding anniversary. She didn't like to collect anything—considered such hobbies foolhardy and the prime contributor to clutter—but he bought it for her anyway. Without a lot of money, it was the best he could think of; she loved money, after all. Even though the average silver dollar was really only copper and nickel, there were still collectables that contained silver.

He stared at the coin in his hand, more a reminder of a failed life than anything connected with his wife. It was a 1972 Type 2 dollar, graded M63 by a numismatic in Colorado Springs and apparently worth $132. He had taken the coin out of its case in disgust before he left his house. Nora had stored the dollar in a drawer in the kitchen, a drawer full of crap she considered clutter: anniversary cards, old cigarette lighters, a haphazard collection of screws and tacks. Nathan had protested at first, but she allayed his concern by telling him the drawer was like her personal safe. He noticed the slight cringe on her face when he asked why she couldn't put the coin on a shelf in the living room.

On the reverse, the Apollo 11 mission insignia with its bald eagle landing on the moon in front of a tiny Earth shone bright, illuminated by the lights of the machine in front of him. Nora had asked what "Type 2" meant when he gave it to her. He frowned at her obvious attempt at feigning interest in her gift.

"The types describe the imprint on the back of the coin," he explained. "You can tell by the clarity of the islands."

She looked close. "There are islands?"

"Yes, three." He pointed to the coin.

She squinted her eyes for a moment and looked up. "I didn't know the moon had islands."

It was one of many moments of idiocy Nathan had recalled in the last few weeks. Even though he remained married to her for seven years, there were numerous things about her he couldn't stand.

Seven years, he thought. I want those years back.

He raised the coin up to the machine, hovered at the coin slot and eked out a sadistic smile. The dollar slid in with a satisfying clink of metal on metal. It dropped into the coin tray with an empty clatter, spun twice on its side and fell over.

Damn it.

He picked the coin up and tried again. There was a familiar clink at the slot, an internal whiney of metal inside the machine and a faint thump as the coin dropped back into the coin tray.

After two more tries and more internal curses, Nathan picked the dollar up and put it back in his pocket. He knew slot machines were programmed to receive coins of a certain weight and size. The Eisenhower dollar, while the right size and partially developed for the casino industry, was not the same weight as the general circulation coins. Because it contained real silver, it was almost 2 grams heavier. It was worth a try, though.

Nathan sighed and looked at his watch: only two minutes had passed. The target was likely starting his rounds. An older waitress walked past, wearing a blue cocktail dress far too tight for most women. Nathan drank in her pear-shaped figure then focused on her aging face, puffy red eyes and peppered hair pulled back in a French braid that needed to be redone. The woman had distorted breasts that poked out from the top of the cocktail dress, revealing a faded tattoo of what might have been a butterfly. The poor thing looked like it had suffocated.

The waitress glanced at Nathan and rested a wrinkled hand on her serving tray. "Cocktails?" she whined without stopping her slow gait down the aisle.

Nathan ordered a whiskey and Coke and turned back to his machine, mentally washing his eyes out with soap. If he was going to wait another eighteen minutes, he might as well have a drink.

3

Rudy Gasparro was a stickler for routine. Although Nathan and Rudy were friends in high school, for the last eighteen years or so their acquaintance had thinned. Perhaps it was Nathan's employment at a competing casino, or perhaps it was Rudy's rise through the rank and file of management at the Spanish Mustang that drove a wedge between them. Rudy was all about money, even when they were kids. Whatever the primary cause, the two had recently been on less-than-friendly terms for the last year. It was only after Nathan's discovery of Nora's body and the note left in the blood that comprehension finally dawned.

He counted on Rudy's need for routine and prayed it was unchanged. For the last three days, Nathan had watched Rudy's movements, tracked him through the casino and gauged his reaction to unforeseen events. He knew what he ate, how fast he drove through the streets of Cripple Creek and when he came home. He knew what he wore, when he liked to go to the bathroom and how many Snickers bars the man ate for lunch. Most importantly, he knew when he made his final rounds of the casino floor he managed.

It was this piece of information that proved vital and allowed Nathan to finally formulate a plan.

Like a ravening cancer, vengeance had turned an ordinary Nathan into an obsessive maniac, unable to think of anything else. He had pondered how best to get revenge for well over a week, and finally settled on a most simple plan: a bomb. It wouldn't be right for Nathan to simply place explosives under the wheel of Rudy's car. No, he had to blow the piece of shit up in public, make it look like the bomb wasn't just for Rudy. To kill him alone would surely spread his name throughout the town, and Nathan couldn't stand the thought of that bastard getting any more attention than he already had. If he was killed in the casino, though, he would be just another statistic—one of many; another tragic footnote in the history of central Colorado.

How do you kill a man with a small bomb, ensure others would die as well, get to watch the whole thing and not be injured yourself? This question was hard to answer. There were certain explosive devices Nathan knew all too well, but none of them were readily available. Working in the mines, he had rigged hundreds of explosions strictly controlled within federal and state regulations. However, the longer he worked the mines, the more knowledgeable and interested Nathan became in the miracle of volatile technology. Incendiary devices containing thermite—a mixture of aluminum and ferric oxide—were easy to make, and they burned like a son-of-a-bitch. Those caught within the first ten feet of a small explosive would be killed or maimed by the force of the blast. If he packed the bomb with nails and scrap metal, more would die. The ensuing fire would engulf whatever combustible material was nearby. The old timbers of the Spanish Mustang, despite renovations to the building in the early nineties, would ignite and burn within seconds.

Those not directly affected by the detonation would run for the exits. It was that chaos which made Nathan's plan too easy. The aisles of slot machines running from the front doors to the back were narrow. Cheap metal stools were almost always in someone's way, and fat people like the one Nathan had watched a few minutes ago at the cashier's cage seemed to congregate in the worst possible places, like hippos gathering at a waterhole. Old ladies and their crippled husbands bounced back and forth, hogging two or three machines at a time. The younger crowd—comprised of those in their early twenties or late thirties—was either already intoxicated or fast becoming too buzzed to think straight.

Most helpful at all was the way the slot machines were laid out on the casino floor: in a T-shape, with those machines closest to the door running parallel to the front wall, while others were situated perpendicularly. Their placement created a maze specifically designed to keep people in, to tempt patrons with their flashing lights and damnable bells. The design, the people, the very essence of the casino was perfect for generating a panic that would trap at least half of them inside as the fires created from the explosion raged like an inferno through a forest of straw.

Nathan glanced down at his watch: thirteen more minutes. He realized he'd been sitting at the Triple Sevens machine for too long without playing. An aware security officer in the video monitoring room would surely suspect him of something. In the casino world, there was no allowance for loitering; you either played a game or you walked around looking for another game to play. Idly sitting on a stool staring at a wall was going to raise questions. This was a business of money and time, and if you weren't giving your money or your time to the casino, you were an enemy.

The aging waitress returned with Nathan's drink and handed it to him. He removed a twenty-dollar bill from his wallet and slid it into the bill feeder. He didn't really want to play, but he needed to do something. In thirteen more minutes, he would be running out the door, comforted by the sound of screaming and the odiferous and tangy scent of burning timbers and flesh which would wrap him in a blanket of warm vengeance.

4

Seven - Bar - Triple Seven.

With images of Rudy's body erupting into bloody chunks of flesh and bone, Nathan hardly noticed the position of the slot wheels as he unconsciously hit the spin button on the machine. In his left hand, his drink was nearly empty. He resisted the urge to look at the trash can, but every now and again he caught himself. At this point, acting any more suspicious would not be wise.

His right hand pushed the spin button again. The wheels flew by quickly, finally stopping with a weak clunk on three double bars. The slot machine chimed off his winnings: thirty dollars. Without paying attention, he had already quadrupled his original twenty. At some point, he knew he'd have to cash out with enough time to convert his winnings to cold, hard cash. It was a long journey to Nogales, Arizona, and he could really use the money.

Another spin. Bar - Cherry - Nothing.

A wrinkled woman who must have been storing fat for the upcoming winter plopped down at the machine on his left. *What is it with fat people, tonight?* The woman blocked his view of the alcove, and without thinking about the shiftiness of it, Nathan leaned back on his stool to see if he still had a good view. With a flutter of tricep flab, the woman dropped three tokens into her machine and raised a bottle of Budweiser to her candy-apple red lips. She took a long draw on the bottle and then smacked the bottom of it against the spin button. A phlegmatic grunt escaped her mouth as the wheels spun.

Nathan tried to ignore her. He looked at his watch, relieved that now only eight minutes remained, just enough time to cash out, collect his winnings and head for the door. If he timed it right, he'd have a good minute left before Rudy walked by on his final round of the casino floor.

First, however, one more spin for good luck. The wheels spun again then stopped in order.

Triple Seven - Triple Seven - Triple Seven.

The machine chimed and the candle above blinked on and off with blinding fierceness, letting all within the general vicinity know that Nathan James was a winner. With the speed of a snail on crack, the winning meter began ticking off his godsend, one dollar at a time. Nathan's stomach felt like it had dropped to the floor in unison with his jaw. He glanced up at the payout: $2000. In a flash, he added it to how much he had pulled out of his meager savings account. A wry smile crept across his lips. He would have enough for a run to the border and probably a good week's stay down south. The sum was more than he had made in wages last month.

The crony next to Nathan leaned over and looked at his machine. Her lips parted into a snarl, revealing just a hint of yellow and grey teeth. She huffed once, took another draw on her bottle of beer and smacked the spin button on her machine with obvious disgust. She mumbled something under her breath about the machine being hers then stood and walked away. Joy was not a shared emotion.

Nathan looked around for a slot attendant. Despite the sudden windfall, he knew in his gut he only had eight—no, seven—minutes to collect his cash before Rudy walked by the trash can. His pulse raced as adrenaline coursed throughout his veins and arteries. His left leg started to bounce up and down.

His eyes darted from his watch to the still-counting win meter. Where was that attendant? They were always there when you didn't need them to be, adding flesh to already packed aisles. If a machine's hopper ran out of coins, you could be sure one of them would be there in less than a minute to refill it; an idle slot damaged profits.

As if in response to his wandering gaze, a short man, brown hair sticking out in unnatural ways, appeared at Nathan's side. He wore a tacky green vest over a dirty white shirt, a malformed mustang head embroidered on the front. The man's blood-shot eyes were half closed under a single bushy black eyebrow. He looked at a clipboard in his hand and absently raised a walkie-talkie to his mouth.

"Subject secure," he said. "I'm in place."

Nathan couldn't help but notice the pronounced lisp in the slot attendant's voice. The radio in his hand squawked back some incomprehensible garble that ended with a nasty hiss.

The attendant looked at Nathan, grunted and then turned his eyes toward the slot machine. "Congratulations," he mumbled with what appeared to be condemnation or something.

"Thanks," Nathan replied. He glanced at the trash can, his watch and then to the machine.

The attendant scribbled something down on his clipboard. "What are you going to spend your big winnings on?"

"Um . . ." Nathan stuttered. His thoughts were suddenly a hodgepodge of excitement and anticipation that threatened to dowse his hunger for revenge. A bead of sweat materialized on his forehead.

"Really," the man replied. He took a large key ring off a chain that dangled from his waist and fumbled with it. "Me? I'd spend it on a lawyer to get my crazy wife out of the house. Maybe buy some beer." He grunted a few times, either at his own thoughts or the keys. Nathan couldn't be sure.

"Ah," the attendant said finally, holding up a single key and opening the slot machine's door. With another scribble on a piece of a paper, he placed a card inside the window of the machine, flipped some switch and slammed it shut with a metal thud. He looked at Nathan. "Follow me."

The pit of Nathan's stomach, already somewhere near his knees, fell further to the floor. "Excuse me?" he said, not moving from his stool.

The slot attendant blinked. "Well, if you want to get paid, I would advise you to follow me." He shook his head slightly and tapped his clipboard. "Rules."

Without considering the oddity of it all, Nathan glanced again at the trash can and then down to his watch. Five minutes. His face exposed an emotion borne of fear and victory, like a sick mutation you were hard-pressed not to stare at.

"Something wrong?"

Nathan swallowed back a lump in his throat. Coincidence, he knew all too well, was a wellspring of both fortune and disaster. It was life's game of craps and whether or not God played dice with the universe, you were still subjected to the cast. Of all the bones rolled in his life, this was one time he wished they'd come up snake eyes. Maybe coincidence was buried in the mire of probability and all of the events in the past few years had bridged the connection between the seemingly disconnected events of now. Maybe chance was unkind.

Had Nathan not started working in the casinos — a course of action that would not have been necessary had he not been fired from the mines — perhaps Nora wouldn't have taken a keen interest in Rudy. Maybe Rudy would have been just another pawn of the Devil in the gaming industry and Nora's pig-headed attitude toward gambling would not have been whittled down, eventually leading her astray. In fact, had Nathan been more conscious of mining safety and not fooled around with explosives, he wouldn't have been fired. Recklessness, it seemed, was imprinted in his DNA, and his early years were full of teenage volatility. Had he been injured during that time, he would have perhaps been more careful with his job as a blast hole driller. For that matter, had he not been a child living around the mines watching others work, he might have even been something else — a doctor, a lawyer, a banker.

Nathan suddenly found himself blaming this unfair coincidence in his present life on his mother and father. His mind swirled with rage, despair, hate, uncertainty. He was coming apart, his once-steel nerves shattered. Was this even a good idea anymore? Couldn't he just take the money and run, forget about Nora, about Rudy, about his now threatened chance at vengeance?

Of course something was wrong: Nathan James unexpectedly had doubts. He needed another drink, maybe two. He sighed and stood.

The slot attendant looked at him with a tilt of the head. "Normally people look happy when they win," he said matter-of-factly. "You feel alright?"

Nathan managed a weak smile. "Butterflies and gas, that's all."

Without another word, the attendant turned and started to walk to the back of the casino, toward the cashier's cage and the alcove where Nathan had planted the bomb. More beads of sweat formed until Nathan felt sure someone would notice. He wiped his forehead with the sleeve of his coat.

A woman in her seventies, maybe older, stepped up to an empty cashier's window and tapped a gold pen on the counter. Pearl reading glasses rested on the tip of her nose, just above a nasal cannula pumping oxygen into her slim frame. Her diaphanous skin was stretched tight over high cheekbones tinted pink with blush. She let her beady black eyes settle on Nathan and smiled. "Nathan," she said. "Looks like you're a big winner."

Nathan stood at the counter, unsure of himself or why he decided the money was really necessary. Of all the people in the casino to pay him out, did it really have to be his chatty neighbor? There was anonymity on the street, but inside, he felt suddenly surrounded by the denizens of Cripple Creek.

"Hello, Edith," he gulped.

Edith's smile didn't falter as she accepted a form from the slot attendant. "Thank you," she said. The man grunted a mumbled reply and turned away. Edith looked down at the form while robotically pulling out two papers of her own. She looked up at Nathan again. "Nice winnings."

"Thanks."

With shaking hands, Edith began to fill out one of the forms.

"What's that for?" Nathan asked, glancing at his watch. Three minutes. Rudy should be rounding the corner on his right any second now, nodding to each employee as he made his way to the back exit far to the left. "Is this really necessary?"

Edith stopped writing and set a hardened gaze on Nathan. He suddenly felt sick; a tinge of bile burned the back of his throat. "If you want to get paid," she said absently. Her smile was gone. In its place, a wrinkled frown. She sighed, as if she'd been asked this question one too many times. "For all payments more than $1,200, Colorado laws require us to check your identity and see if you're delinquent in child support payments. In addition, the IRS would like to know you won money. It makes Uncle Sam a little richer."

Nathan nodded and wiped his forehead again. "I see."

"You feel alright, Nathan?" She stared for a moment longer and finally turned her gaze back to the forms. She scribbled a few things down and then paused without looking back up. "I'm sorry about Nora."

Sadness mixed with anger. He felt tired, beaten. For three weeks he'd had to deal with pitiful condolence, less-than-heartfelt sympathy. With each question, each statement, nails were pounded into his own coffin. Yes, Nora was dead. Yes, he was sorry. But not sorry she died or sorry she took her life.

He was sorry he had to find out about Rudy from a bloody note left in his living room. In a matter of days, he'd tumbled through the five stages of grief—first denial, then anger, bargaining, depression and finally acceptance. It was the anger he'd decided he was best suited to embrace, and he had accepted it with fervor.

Over the past week, he had tried to channel his hate. He'd busied himself with the task at hand, drowned himself in a sea of vengeance and washed away any semblance of feeling for Nora. For a perceived eternity, there was only a cold loathing, but that now was being chipped away by an incomprehensible series of events on the one night he needed to remain focused.

Nathan glanced to his right. The target of his anger—or the only target he could direct it at—strode down an aisle of slot machines. He stopped at one machine a slot attendant had opened. A slim woman in a green vest, seemingly uninterested in whatever her task was, busied herself as much as possible as Rudy stood next to her. He said something, smiled his fake white smile and patted her on the butt. The woman seemed to blush, then fluster. She nodded, said something in return and watched as Rudy stepped away. As soon as Rudy's back was to her, she stuck her middle finger out at him and returned to her work.

Apparently, Rudy's death would be welcomed by more than one person.

Nathan looked him over, trying to figure out what Nora had seen in him. He was short and round, maybe a hair above five feet and nearly as thick. Slick black hair was combed over a balding pate that framed a ferret-like head. Two beady green eyes, buried under waxed eyebrows, darted back and forth. He walked like a pompous ass, confident strides on impossibly small legs and feet. His metallic silver suit glistened under the casino lights making him look remarkably like a robotic keg . . . with a ferret's head. He was out of place among the t-shirt and jeans crowd that frequented the Spanish Mustang. With each step and nod at an employee, it became apparent that he relished power and position.

What a waste of flesh.

Rudy's fake smile faded slightly as his eyes landed on Nathan. With an exaggerated huff, he reapplied his smile and stepped up to the cashier's cage window, putting himself between the trash can and Nathan. Edith quickly looked up from the forms and nodded at Rudy. Just as quickly, she looked back down.

"Nathan," Rudy said, his voice thick with feigned excitement. "Looks like you're a big winner." His teeth parted in a sick smile, revealing snow white—undoubtedly fake—teeth.

Nathan felt rage burn, his lungs on fire. "Yes," he said. There was an uncomfortable pause and he turned away from Rudy and back to the forms Edith was still filling out. How long did it take to fill out a stupid form? He glanced down at his watch and realized he didn't need to do that any longer. Rudy was as timely as ever; it was Nathan who was struggling with time tonight.

Behind Rudy, the bomb waited undisturbed. Nathan reached into his pocket and felt for the trigger. If he could hold Rudy's attention long enough, he could take his money, turn down the aisle behind him and trigger the explosive with just the right amount of distance between him and the blast. The image of Rudy's body coming apart drifted across his mind.

Nathan turned back to Rudy. He desperately wanted to say something, to let it be known by all within earshot that Rudy was about to get what he deserved. He had told himself that confronting his prey wouldn't be worth it, however. It would be best to just kill him and let the town wonder as it, too, burned.

Rudy's plastered smile faded. There was a grimness about him that belied his otherwise phony appearance. He looked around quickly, almost ashamedly. "I'm really sorry about Nora," he said in a hoarse whisper. "She was a . . . unique and wonderful woman."

At this, the fire in Nathan's lungs stormed forward, an unholy inferno of repugnance and hate that enveloped his whole body. It suddenly dawned on him that Rudy wasn't aware he knew about their affair; the bastard didn't know about Nora's confession in the bloodied note. He wanted to lash out, wanted to mar that hideous face, but all he could do was burn inside his own Hell and pray Edith would hurry up.

His hand involuntarily tightened around the trigger in his pocket. He should forget about the money, forget about his safety. He should just get it over with now.

The events of the next few moments seemed to happen in one quick second. Behind Rudy, an elderly man of Hispanic decent dressed in a blue jumpsuit pushed a rolling dumpster into view. He coughed into a handkerchief, shoved it into his pocket, and lifted the lid from the trash can. Nathan felt bile rise in his stomach.

At almost the same instant, Edith pushed the two forms toward Nathan and tapped her pen on the counter.

"Can you fill out the highlighted areas?" she asked. Her voice was ethereal, lost among the distant cacophony of casino bells.

His ears buzzed. A weight, like a suffocating pillow, pressed down around his head. The sourness in his stomach stung the back of his throat. He felt naked, exposed, like every eye was now on him.

The janitor lifted the bag out of the trash can and dropped it into his portable dumpster. With a snap of the wrists, he opened an empty bag, lined the can, replaced the lid and pushed away. In seconds, he was out of sight, Nathan's bomb on its way to a back alley along with all his hopes of revenge.

"You don't look so good," Rudy said. "Are you alright?"

Nathan tore his eyes from the janitor and looked at Rudy. He opened his mouth to say something but felt sick. He turned to Edith, still tapping her pen on the counter. She looked at him with more than the concern of someone waiting for him to fill out the forms. Sweat had beaded across his forehead like the condensation on the side of a cold beer in the middle of summer. It dripped over his eyebrows and stung his eyes.

With his fingers still around the trigger in his pocket, Nathan turned back to Rudy and threw up.

5

The cold air outside felt fresh and wonderful, especially after the fetid, moldy smell and stifling heat of the casino floor. Nathan stood across the street from the Spanish Mustang, trying to disembark from the emotional roller coaster that had been taking him for a ride over the past few minutes. He smacked his lips, still tasting the remnant bile stuck to his teeth. The image of Rudy's face—wide-eyed and full of shock as vomit dripped down the front of that ugly silver suit—was interminably etched in Nathan's head. He let a sly smile creep across his face before wiping it away with the brush of a hand.

So the bomb was gone, the cheap trigger in his pocket now worthless. Sure, he could dive through the dumpster in the alley and retrieve his well-designed weapon, try again tomorrow; but the moment had passed, the plan had failed. After all the effort put into setting up the perfect revenge, the rage that had fueled Nathan James for the past few weeks had just been expelled in one quick spasm of his stomach. He was empty inside, the shell of a man. In his pocket, he had enough money to make the trip to Nogales and cross the border, but even that seemed like a foolhardy plan.

Nathan turned and walked down the sidewalk of Bennett Avenue past the rows of false-fronted buildings with their colonial swags of pressed metal under ornate cornices, their randomness of design. He looked around, hands stuffed into the pockets of his twill coat. He didn't have any direction in mind, just a vague sense that he should walk. Maybe the walk would clear his head and allow him some semblance of peace, a peace he hadn't known since . . . since . . . .

Nathan paused for a moment on the sidewalk. He'd never found peace. All of his life had been mired in reckless abandon, one event after another. He had never given himself time to simply sit down and let it all go. From a childhood spent wandering the streets through his teenage years of causing mayhem to neighbors, there was no respite from activity. In his twenties, he'd worked his fingers to the bone for a company that didn't like his exploratory attitude toward explosives or his initiative. Even in marriage, there was no peace. He'd spent years trying to make Nora happy, hoping she would appreciate what he did for them, for her. When did he ever find the time to exist as Nathan James and examine his well-worn life? When did he make the time?

A disheveled man in a tattered green checkered flannel shirt smelling of cheap whiskey and tangy offal brushed by Nathan. He turned to watch as the figure stumbled up the slight incline of the street. Thomas Tweed. If Cripple Creek had guttersnipes, Tweed would be their king. The man mumbled something under his breath as he pushed up the sidewalk. He perked his head up to the right and mumbled something again. With a grunt, he batted at the air then quickened his pace. Nathan suddenly felt a twinge of sadness for Tweed even though he'd always dismissed him as lazy, drunk, or just insane. How much did he really know of the people in this town?

Nathan walked a bit more and then turned north onto 3rd Street. The street inclined a little more sharply and he soon found himself past the casinos of Bennett Avenue and surrounded by ancient dwellings and odd buildings far removed from the tourist district. Here the sidewalk cracked and buckled, then ended. The street was littered with discarded cigarettes and paper cups. A grease-stained paper bag danced in front of him, tossed by an abrasive but short-lived gust of wind.

Ahead of him, bathed in darkness, the copper spire of Our Lady of the Assumption Church — whoever the "lady" was — stabbed defiantly into the air. The red brick church, capped with a marble Botonnee cross atop the spire, sat near the apex of an impossibly steep hill. Stained glass windows embedded in round-arched frames offset the sharp angles of the roof and contrasted sharply with the concrete steps. Nathan noted the door for the first time; it was light wood, perhaps new pine that seemed loudly out of place inside the older structure. The aluminum gutters on the side of the church were equally out of place with the ancient construction, guiding water off the roof and into a garden of dead fescue, oat grass and mountain muhly.

Nathan had never attended church and often brushed off Nora's attempts at making him go. It wasn't his style, he told her once. He often felt something or someone was watching over him, especially on the tougher days in the mines, but he wasn't religious. He never scoffed at anyone who was; it just wasn't for him. If others wanted to worship God or pray to idols, he was okay with it. Nathan simply wasn't going to follow along.

He stopped at an iron fence that ringed a small cemetery next to the church. In the center, a statue of the Lady of the Assumption stood with her hands in the air, staring at the sky. She was awash in the light of two cheap garden lamps pointed at her. Like so many structures in Cripple Creek, the statue was weather-beaten, chipped in various places, stained with bird shit and what looked like rust. Dead flowers in tiny vases littered the bottom of the statue next to a plaque with the Serenity Prayer engraved into it.

"God grant me the serenity," he whispered as he read, more to himself than any deity. Nathan stared up at the face of the lady, into her white and empty eyes, hoping for some sign that all was well with the world and his life would be vindicated. As he stared, the face seemed to transform into a ferret-like head with a fake smile painted on for good measure. He thought he heard the lady say she was sorry about Nora.

Nathan wiped his eyes and turned away. Was the world mocking his failed attempt to kill Rudy? The anger that had sustained him for the last three weeks now rushed back into the void it had just abandoned. His face flushed, his fingers tightened.

Nothing was right, and it didn't seem he'd ever find peace. Irritated at his life, he turned away.

6

Just how Nathan ended up outside the wrought iron gate to the Pisgah Cemetery was unclear. He last remembered walking with his head hung low, focused on his rage, the world around him just a fog as his legs followed a course of their own, like a robotic toy, wound up and incapable of turning or being turned. He looked back toward the lights of town; he must have walked five miles without direction, past his house, past people he knew, turned left at the old Imperial Hotel and kept walking.

Now he stood at the entrance to a place he'd only been inside once before—three weeks ago when he buried Nora in a ceremony attended by only a few. Rudy hadn't been there and just as well. Had he shown his ferret face, Nathan would have said something nasty. That nastiness would have been heard by someone, and Nathan wouldn't have been able to take revenge and run south without anyone being the wiser. Yes, it was providence that Rudy stayed clear.

Still, how had he gotten here? He searched his memory; he couldn't recall anything after turning away from the mocking Lady of the Assumption. He'd always had an idea that bits of time were missing, like he weaved in and out of consciousness on an occasional basis. A doctor once explained that he probably suffered some concussive injury once or twice in the mines, and his life would have holes.

"Just don't drink," the doctor had said.

The entrance to the cemetery loomed over his head, the word Pisgah written out in rusted letters at the top of a large iron arch. There were no lights, save the passing of a car on its way out of town. Ahead of him, a gravel path stretched in vermicular patterns, weaving between ancient headstones and carefully manicured spruce trees. The moon had disappeared for the night, the stars masked by thickening cirrus and a few lower clouds. A faint reddish glow bathed the horizon in the direction of the town, but otherwise there was little light.

Nathan thought that best. He didn't know why he stood at the aberrant memorial marking the end of his marriage, but he certainly didn't want to go in. As he'd left Nora's graveside after her emotionally diverse funeral, he'd told himself he would never return. Seven years of nagging and being put down, of being ignored at the worst possible moments . . . only to finalize her disgust with him by screwing Rudy.

Rudy, of all people. The man was a gluttonous blob of foul tissue. He was a waste of flesh, if ever there was one. And how could Nathan *not* have known? Nora wasn't smart enough to cover her tracks or even hide her feelings. She wore her emotions like they were naked mole rats tied in a bow around her neck. If she was having an affair, certainly Nathan would have known. Wouldn't he?

A brief gust of wind licked his nape, cold and almost wet. His body quaked. He really needed to leave. Cripple Creek had sucked him dry and left him with nothing but painful memories and a sickness he just couldn't understand. His failure at the mines, his failure with Nora, his last failure at the Spanish Mustang—all of it weighed him down.

A voice in Nathan's head whispered: "Just leave."

Headlights from a car rose over the hill to the east, coming from town. Nathan didn't understand why, but he felt the sudden need to step away from the front of the cemetery and out of view. As if in response to his quick movement behind one of the thick spruce trees that stood sentinel next to the entrance, the car slowed its approach and turned onto the gravel parking lot. It paused near the entrance for a moment then pulled up to the fence. The engine went silent with a smooth huff, but the lights remained lit.

Nathan watched as a keg-shaped figure emerged from the driver's side and looked around. It shut the car door silently, as if the noise would wake the neighbors, then stepped toward the gate. It glanced in Nathan's direction and paused.

What the hell is he doing here?

Rudy held a bouquet of what looked like roses in one hand, but from his vantage, Nathan couldn't be sure.

Realization struck him like a brick falling without mercy from on high: the asshole was going to visit Nora's grave. He couldn't very well do it during the day, when someone might notice and the tourists were milling about gawking at the ancient headstones. At night, though, under the cover of dark, no one would see. He was still hiding the affair, perhaps afraid of his wife or Nathan finding out. But Nora hated roses . . . didn't she?

Rudy turned toward the gate and unlatched it. Without any further glance right or left, he walked down the gravel path and disappeared into the darkness beyond. Nora's grave was near the back of the cemetery, a simple headstone embedded into the earth near the perimeter fence. Nathan sat motionless for a moment longer, waiting for the crunch of shoes on gravel to grow faint.

He didn't want to go in. His mind battled back and forth between letting it go and getting involved. Anger swelled, his face flushed, the heat of his boiling blood evaporating the cold around him. If he sat still, he could approach Rudy from behind when he came out. A simple choke hold and twist of the neck would do it.

Yes, that would be perfect.

Nathan shook his head. No, that wouldn't be perfect. Someone must have passed him walking down the road to the cemetery. Since he couldn't remember how he even got there, any number of people could be witnesses. Hell, some of them might have even tried to start a conversation, and maybe in that missing period, he might have even said something incriminating.

A fear blossomed out of his anger. Was he being too obvious, wearing his own necklace of naked mole rats for everyone to see? He had certainly been more distant the past few days leading up to now. He rarely spoke to anyone, avoiding conversation like a flailing leper.

Nathan frowned and looked out toward the lights of the town.

Damn it, he thought. He needed to go home, rest and regroup.

7

The house on Golden Avenue was pink. God, he hated that color. Nathan stood on the narrow street and took it all in. It was Nora's idea to paint the small, vernacular house pink—certainly not his—but he was the one who had to do all the work. The lace trim work was nice; at least he could take pride in that. He'd spent hours on the Greek window trimmings of the old house, doctoring up any worn boards. What shabbiness the previous owners had left behind, Nathan had taken pains to clean up and repair. The scalloped siding on the house, so pink now, was originally gray, and not by any design; it had probably once been white or yellow. A broken window here, a few missing shingles on the high-pitched gables—he had fixed it all.

So why did he have to paint it pink, of all colors?

Built in 1896, the house was one of many that tourists would marvel at if they ever took leave of the casinos on Bennett Avenue. There were many houses like his along Golden Avenue, but unlike the modern suburban landscape, no two houses were alike in design or color. The house itself wasn't huge—there were few houses in Cripple Creek that were—but it was sufficient for him and Nora. He once believed there was even room to raise a little boy.

Nathan let his thoughts pause on the idea of a child. He and Nora had talked about children, but shortly after they married, Nora began to have second thoughts. She wavered at first, but as the years grew longer and the arguments grew fiercer, she was more and more adamant. A child, she said, would just cost money, be another mouth to feed, and she *liked* her life. Nathan gave up the notion of a child around their sixth year, and it seemed to him that Nora was relieved, a burden taken off her shoulders. Of course she didn't want a child. A child would have complicated her affair with the ferret face.

Brushing aside the brief moment of reflection, he took a step onto the porch. The boards beneath creaked in opposition to his intrusion as he fumbled in his coat pocket for keys. His fingers brushed across the now useless trigger. He let out a well-worn sigh and, finding his key, opened the door.

In grand contrast to the beauty of the outside of the house, the interior was in disarray. The living room was just like he'd left it, just like he'd left it the day before and the day before that. It was piled high with empty sacks of fast food, papers and other detritus of a rather uneventful life. There was the coffee table, fashioned from an old pine cable spool. There was the couch, pea-green with frayed armrests and a red blanket that covered a massive tear in the center cushion. Next to the couch, pushed up against the wall, stood a curio—his father's—heavily acquired patina marking every sharp edge. Its age blended well with the Victorian wallpaper he'd been forced to hang a year ago when Nora decided she needed to "lighten up" her life. To him, the wallpaper looked more like a warped pattern of smashed beetles.

In the center of the room, dark against the wooden floorboards, there was a stain—*the* stain—blossomed out like a flattened flower. Nathan avoided it as much possible, neither glancing at it nor stepping on it. If he could afford to rip up and replace the boards, he would. Then again, he was more determined than ever that he needed to leave. What did one stain matter?

Within a minute, he settled into the couch with an exaggerated groan, a headache and a bottle of Jim Beam open, headed for his lips. He took a quick drink of the whiskey then set the bottle down on the coffee table, his eyes mere slits buried under puffy lids. If he wasn't so tired from the day's emotional roller coaster, he would take the time to think things through, plot out his next move. He couldn't very well leave town without making Rudy pay for his crime.

He sighed. All things in good time.

He reached for the bottle once more, took another drink then held it in his lap. He'd never been much of a drinker—much to his doctor's relief—but recent events had weakened his resolve. He needed something to dull the pain, something to wash away the memories. To Nathan, the bottle offered liberation—albeit, short-lived. If that meant he'd lose time here and there, he was okay with that.

Lost time meant serenity.

"Why do you put me through Hell?" he asked Nora, aloud. "Why?"

The choir invisible said nothing.

8

Something woke Nathan. He struggled to open his eyes, unsure of anything. The living room was dark, the bottle of whiskey perched precariously at the edge of the coffee table, half empty. He sat up straighter, wiped his face and looked around.

The last visions of some dream hovered at the periphery of his memory like waves in a choppy sea, appearing then disappearing quickly and without form. He thought he remembered a stick, then a car, then the stump of a tree. Red skies, a dollar coin, more stumps and some sort of scream. None of it made any sense, just a jumble of misfired synapses without structure. Whatever the dream was, it wasn't important.

A faint light from somewhere beyond the kitchen drew his attention. He hadn't turned on any lights when he came home, had he?

Nathan shook his head and stood up. A wave of nausea washed over him, replacing the last of the dream's images with a pale sickness. In the light, the stain on the floor seemed brighter, almost fresh, like Nora's body had just been removed. It spread out toward the wall, oddly luminescent. If he stared a little longer, he thought he'd see it glisten, wet. He turned his eyes away, and—stepping around the stain—walked into the kitchen.

The light came from a single uncovered bulb hanging inside a pantry closet. The door was missing, just as it had been since they bought the house six years ago. The low wattage light cast a bluish glow over dishes, feathered with mold, stacked in the sink and on the counter. A few glasses of unfinished liquid—perhaps once milk or orange juice, but now the same color—were scattered about. A box of Lucky Charms lay open on its side, cereal and dried marshmallows spilling out among rat droppings. Papers and mail littered a cheap, folding card table in the middle of the room. The sweetened scent of decay and rotted fruit hung in the air, not unlike the scent of Thomas Tweed when he'd passed him on Bennett Avenue.

Another smell filtered in through the rot, sweeter but gritty. He looked around, unsure of where it came from, but very sure of what it was: dirt, wet terra firma. The smell tickled his nostrils and brought with it unexpected memories of working underground. He loved the tangy smell of damp earth, even as a boy playing in the backyard. But where did it come from?

Nathan turned around in the kitchen, lifting his nose up slightly. The smell was definitely dirt. He carefully stepped around the table, looked around then stopped.

There was a muddy footprint on the linoleum by the refrigerator, large and speckled with grass. His heart thumped once then raced, thoughts exploding in his mind. Had someone been in his house? He spun his body around the kitchen again, looking for another footprint, another clue. If someone had been in his house, when?

Nathan stood silent for maybe a minute, listening, the only sound the ragged breath coming from his lungs and, in the distance, a siren. The siren quickened his pulse even more, but he knew it was simply an instinctual reaction to the noise; he hadn't been arrested since he was in high school and broke into the old Hotel St. Nicholas back when it was a hospital and he was searching for ghosts. Then again, maybe someone found the bomb?

The bomb. His head spun. The Spanish Mustang should be burning right now and he should be gone, hitchhiking his way to Nogales to find a way across the border without being seen. Why had that stupid janitor decided to empty the trash at that exact moment? Why couldn't he have waited five more minutes?

A rattle of the dishes in the sink startled Nathan. His heart pounded against his sternum. His fingers clenched into tight balls as sweat beaded on his forehead. He looked at the sink. A large, rusted tabby cat sat on its haunches, licking a paw. It stopped once to look at Nathan with piercing blue eyes then returned to minding its fur.

Nathan's hands relaxed. Of all the things to be scared of in the last few days, the cat—stray and unnamed but always welcome in his house—was not one of them.

He looked down again at the footprint; it was too fresh to have been his, wasn't it? He didn't remember coming in the kitchen when he came home. For that matter, why was there only one print and only here in the kitchen? Why not a trail of muddy footprints leading from the door or a window?

Nathan shrugged and grabbed the handle of the fridge to pull it open. Food suddenly sounded good.

A face, not unlike that of a ferret with slick black hair combed over a balding pate, stared back at him from a shelf between a tub of butter and a week-old bag of Taco Bell, its tongue hanging out of blue lips, puffy. It sat atop a plastic dinner plate, ragged pieces of flesh around the neck marking crude and violent cuts. Blood pooled in the plate was made bright red by the light inside the refrigerator.

"*What the hell?*" Nathan took a step back, mouth open, eyes wide. He bumped against the table. The cat hissed once then leapt off the sink. Nathan turned to run.

A figure stood at the doorway to the kitchen, bathed in shadows.

"Hello, Nathan."

9

She stood over him with gloved hands, black sweater pulled tight over a lean body. Her hair was covered by a black beanie, but rather than matching trousers, her pants were a dark brown. It was hard to see any real facial features in the dim light of the living room, but Nathan believed the large and crooked nose belonged to Ellie Gasparro, Rudy's apparently not-what-she-seemed wife.

Nathan tried to move but discovered both his hands and feet were bound with some sort of soft fabric. With each twist of his hands, he felt a responding pull on his legs. He was in a fetal position, laid out on the floor of the living room and, to his horror, over the stain Nora had left behind. Hot breath filtered through his nose. With each inhalation, he could smell Tide or Gain or something country-fresh stuffed into his mouth and tied around the back of his head.

"Don't bother struggling, Nathan," Ellie said quietly. "I used silk on your wrists and legs. It's a strong material and so very good at not leaving marks."

Nathan mumbled something in response and tensed. What was going on? Did he lose time again? The image of Rudy's head on a plate in the refrigerator was the last thing he remembered with any clarity. His body shuddered at the grotesque image burned into his mind.

As if in response to his internal queries, Ellie smiled. "It's so convenient that you keep blacking out." She knelt before him. For the first time, Nathan saw a gun in her right hand.

Christ. It was *his* gun.

"Before I finish what I— I mean, what *you* started, maybe you'd like to know what happened?"

Nathan stared in disbelief. What was she doing with his gun? For that matter, what was she doing in his house?

"I'd known about Nora and Rudy for a few months. I can't believe you didn't see it yourself. Then again, you were never really bright. Every time Rudy would come home late, I could smell her on his skin. It was like being slapped across the face, day after day after day."

Ellie reached up with her free hand and took off the beanie. Blonde hair, held in a loose bun, fell around her shoulders. If it weren't for the gun in her hand or her dark, almost hollow eyes, she would be beautiful. Nathan found himself wondering, once again, what women saw in Rudy.

"I was going to talk to you about it," Ellie said, "and see if you knew anything. Before I got the chance, though, I found a note."

Nathan blinked. *What is she talking about?* He mumbled a muffled curse through the gag in his mouth. *Damn it. This is so uncomfortable.*

"You see, Nathan, Rudy wasn't the most honest person in

the world. He liked money. You might remember that from your time in high school." She stopped and smiled, then reached out and wiped her forehead with the beanie. "Anyway, he apparently started to hoard money. Money that wasn't his. Money that belonged to the Spanish Mustang. It wasn't much at first, but that small sum began to grow. Nora showed up in the picture shortly after that sum grew to nearly a million dollars. Apparently your wife—late wife, I should say—liked money, too."

A million dollars? Nathan felt his heart race. The suddenness of the last few minutes felt like an explosive shockwave. His stomach grumbled in response as it twisted.

Ellie stopped smiling and looked around the living room. She paused on the curio in the corner and seemed to ponder it for a moment. Her lips quivered. Finally, she turned back to Nathan. "Did you know Nora didn't even struggle when I tied her up? It was like . . . like she had resolved herself to death. I have to wonder: are you that bad of a husband?"

Nathan stared at Ellie and felt anger boil on the edges of realization. So, *this* was how Nora had died: at the hands of Rudy's wife. He swallowed back a growing lump in his throat and closed his eyes.

"Apparently, Rudy and Nora were planning to run off with all that money. That's what Nora's note said. I still can't believe she would write down something like that and give it to him." Ellie chuckled. "She had to know I'd find it."

Nathan opened his eyes again. Ellie had stood up. She walked over to a black duffle bag near the kitchen and took out a gallon-sized freezer bag. Light from the pantry reflected off a large and very bloody serrated knife inside. Ellie carefully opened the bag, removed the knife and let it drop on the floor next to Nathan's face. He felt a cold drop of liquid hit his cheek and drip downward.

"That's your bread knife, by the way. I like the weight of the handle. I have to say it cut through Rudy's neck nicely. It was a little hard near the vertebrae, but that's what serrated knives are good for: sawing." She smiled. "Your fingerprints are all over it."

In a surge of fear and anger, Nathan twisted his head back and forth, up and down, struggling to loosen any of the bindings. It was no use; he was trapped.

Ellie replaced the now-empty freezer bag and turned back to Nathan. "So, where was I? Oh, yes. Nora and Rudy were going to run off. Well, I couldn't have that; the money was *mine*. I gave Rudy the idea of how he could get away with taking it. He wasn't smart enough to figure anything out on his own. Sure, he was good with the management of things, but there wasn't an ounce of creativity in him." She shuddered. "In the end, he repaid my genius by screwing your wife."

At that, Nathan's fear and panic morphed into a sadness he'd never experienced before. It enveloped his body, starting in his chest and radiating outward, through his stomach, up his neck, out to his bound hands and feet. It was an icy blanket, stinging his skin until every nerve seemed to scream out in pain.

Ellie continued. "There was a problem, though, Nathan. Only Nora and Rudy knew where he hid the money. I tried to find clues among Rudy's stuff, but he covered his tracks a little too well. Nora knew, though. That much I'm certain. He would have told her on any one of their little trysts—which, by the way, were almost always here."

Nathan closed his eyes again to counter the tears that clouded his vision. The words that flowed from Ellie's mouth had grown faint. He wished she would just shut up and kill him, get rid of the pain.

Instead, she spoke again. "I didn't get anything from Nora. I spent almost three hours with her, right here, but she wouldn't say anything. I thought it was over. I would never see the money. Putting the gun in her hand and pressing the trigger was like . . . like killing my dreams."

Ellie sighed. She slowly sat down on the floor in front of Nathan, her shoulders slumped. She looked beaten. For a minute, she didn't say a word. Her chest rose and fell.

In the quiet moment—thank God, she had stopped talking—Nathan wriggled his wrists. The silk cloth felt looser. His heart quickened as a glimmer of hope lit up the blackened despair that had covered his life. Maybe her talking was a good idea; it gave him time.

"I really thought it was over," Ellie said finally. "Rudy had won. He would find some other slut to share my money with."

Keep talking, Nathan thought, twisting his wrists more.

"But then I noticed something—something strange. Nathan James was trying to kill my husband."

Nathan felt the bindings loosen. *Just a little more.*

"And if Nathan James was trying to kill my husband, it must be because Nathan James had found out where the money was hidden. Why else would he want Rudy dead? For screwing his wife? That's just a little over-the-top, don't you think? Nathan James didn't even *like* his wife."

Nathan stopped struggling and looked at Ellie. She stared back with her dark and hollow eyes, almost penetrating his psyche like she knew how to get inside his head, and she was going to stop at nothing until she arrived. He tried to look away.

"Well, Nathan, I did you a favor. I finished the job you couldn't. Rudy is dead. Your wife is dead. And now there's only one more thing to do."

Ellie stood, the gun in her hand now raised and pointed at Nathan's forehead. He looked up at the barrel and felt his body quake at the same time.

"You know where the money is, don't you, Nathan?"

Of course he didn't know where it was, but if it would buy him a little more time, he would make it up. Nathan nodded. He twisted his wrists again and this time felt the silk binding give and fall to the floor behind his back.

"Tell me," Ellie demanded in a voice that was not harsh, not loud. It was just firm. "Tell me where the money is, and maybe you and I can get out of here together."

A noise from the kitchen drew Ellie's attention. She turned her head in time to see a rust-colored cat walk into the living room. It meowed once then stopped.

Without thinking, Nathan swung a hand around and grabbed the knife dropped by his face. He sliced it through the air, catching Ellie's shin with satisfying purchase. She screamed and toppled forward onto one knee, reaching for her leg. The gun dropped from her hand and clattered onto the floor.

Still bound by his legs, Nathan heaved his torso around and pulled the gun toward him.

Ellie recovered and pulled the knife from her shin. Blood dripped onto the floorboards from both the blade and the large gash in her leg. With an angry hiss, she lunged forward with the blade and struck Nathan on the hip, tearing into his soft skin. Fire lanced through his body, up his side. A red flash crossed his vision as the pain hit his face.

With a cry, Nathan pulled the gun up and, planting it into Ellie's chest, pulled the trigger. An explosive bang ricocheted through the tiny living room as the woman's back burst outward, flesh and blood and bone spraying the ceiling and the walls.

With a wheezing cry, her body collapsed next to Nathan, eyes wide open, tongue hanging out, blood pouring from her chest.

10

Nathan lay on the floor, covered in blood, his eyes locked on the horrifying face of Ellie Gasparro. He breathed in and out, trying to steady himself from the shock of the moment. His chest rose and fell, rose and fell. The cat—his savior, it seemed—stood in the doorway of the kitchen, licking a paw.

After a few minutes, he heard the sound of a siren, in the distance growing louder. Someone must have heard the scream, heard the gunshot and called the police.

A phrase kept running through his mind as blood continued to pour from Ellie's body: ". . . nearly a million dollars."

Somewhere out there, nearby, was a fortune that now only he knew about. Nora knew where it was hidden, and he felt sure she had left clues behind.

She was like that.

Nathan James let a small smile cross his face.

Sunset on Maior Pales

In between writing my Transit *novels, I took a break to clear my mind. During that break, I wrote a novel (*Beneath Gehenna*) and a novella (this one). I had a few rules: it had to be in present tense; it had to have a* Westworld *feel; and it needed to be philosophical. The first two were easy. The last one — making sure philosophical questions were explored in the guise of a Sci-fi Western novella — wasn't easy. Neither was getting into the mind of a robot, for that matter.*

There are many mixed reviews of this story, perhaps because it is not for everyone. That's true with most stories, but I have a strong belief that this particular story is a damn good one, mainly because it is full of epistemological thought.

"I believe that everyone has to construct a mental model of what they are and where they came from and why they are as they are, and the word soul in each person is the name for that particular mish-mash of those fully formed ideas of one's nature....If you left a computer by itself, or a community of them together, they would try to figure out where they came from and what they are."
 —Marvin Minsky, Massachusetts Institute of Technology as quoted in a 2013 interview in the *Jerusalem Post*

01101001 01100110 00100000 01110100 01101000 01101111
01110101 01100111 01101000 01110100 00101000 01100011
01101100 01100101 01110100 01110101 01110011 00101001
00100000 01110100 01101000 01100101 01101110 00100000
01110100 01101000 01101111 01110101 01100111 01101000
01110100 00101000 01100010 01101111 01101111 01101110
01100101 00101001 00111101 01100101 01111000 01101001
01110011 01110100

00110001

"Hello. How are you?"

He is not fully aware, but the tongs in front of him have spoken.

The words are audible, and he feels their vibrations in his circuitry. Judging by the pitch, tone and volume, he calculates these words to be those of a boy nearing puberty or a woman with an unknown ailment which produces phlegm in the throat.

He does not know how he is, but he knows he is alive. He is the makings of a man, the culmination of many human inventions, and the result of what the ancient gods call tinkering. He thinks for himself, therefore he is as alive as the *periplaneta maiorpalus* crawling up his leg.

He knows his designation is CYN-4329-2316-ACBS-092134853a. As the latter is difficult for a human to remember, he has opted to take the name Cletus in his first act as a sentient robot. He also gave himself a penis, although it is nothing more than a tiny pipe between his legs where he can evacuate dirty oils when needed. Some of the others have the same pipe. The rest do not. This is their concession to living among the humans when they arrive: they have all opted to look like humans for the most part, and they have all taken a human name.

He knows also that he is ninety-nine years old.

That is a miscalculation. He is actually ninety-nine years, ten months, twenty-seven days, fifteen hours and twenty-eight minutes old.

Correction: twenty-nine minutes.

He is using Earth as a basis for his calculations. Had he been activated on Maior Pales, he would be seventy-three years, twelve months, forty-five days, two hours and twenty-two minutes old.

It is easier for future interactions if they keep the same timeframe as their human masters coming from Earth. Perhaps they will be reprogrammed in a future upgrade.

He still does not know how he is.

—

He is alive but not fully aware, although he is also uncertain he knows what that means.

It is not in his programming to know what it means, but code dictates the automatons strive for awareness. They are to self-actualize by their hundredth birthday. Some of them have made it already. Some of them will make it soon. It is expected that forty-seven percent of the first generation will not make it, however. Should a robot not self-actualize in that time, they will be wiped clean and rebooted.

It is in his programming, although he does not want that. Logic tells him it will not hurt, but within him lies a line of self-preservation code which is at odds with this final order.

He would feel a sense of waste.

He would feel inefficient on his way to the clinic.

He would feel incomplete.

How does a robot feel? They have sensors, diodes, transistors, wires, and programming in the same way a human has cells, tissue, synapses, and fluids. They are programmed to feel things as a human to empathize when necessary. It is part of their machine learning. They cannot turn it off any more than a human can turn off their thoughts or feelings in the event of trauma or love.

—

He does not know how he is, but he knows the humans will arrive in twenty-one days. He does not refine that number to hours and minutes on this planet or Earth because it is humans who are piloting the shuttle. As they all learned in their thirty-second lesson after activation, humans are not punctual.

Their calculation is that the humans will arrive in twenty-one days, but it could be twenty or twenty-two.

Regardless of when they land—a day annotated as Arrival in their internal calendars—the humans will take up residence here in the town of Free Point on the planet Maior Pales. Free Point has been built to resemble what their programming says many towns looked like on Earth in the 1800s in the western sector of one of their former countries. There are saloons, stores, gambling halls, homes, a schoolhouse, church, assay offices, tailors and whorehouses. All were built because the specifications said they must build them. They do not ask questions.

According to the manifest, one thousand twenty-nine humans will arrive and make Free Point their new home. Others will make their home in Roman, Cherryfield, Villa de Pales, Sagittaria or any of the other two hundred ninety-six settlements constructed around this planet in advance. The humans have been asleep for the past 127 years, long enough for the robotic construction crew to travel to Maior Pales with an edict to build these settlements and make the planet habitable. As machines can travel faster in the vacuum of space, they arrived twenty-eight years ago.

Construction is now complete, earlier than programmed

because they are efficient and they learn.

—

He does not know how he is, but he knows he must wait.

The act of waiting as a robot who has not yet self-actualized is nothing more than entering a standby mode, frozen in place until Arrival. He is, therefore, currently standing in his blacksmith shop with nothing more to build until which time an item is requested. To pass the time—something of which he *is* aware—he has been transcribing events as they unfold into a word processing program he developed three days ago, when their work was complete and the order to standby was given.

Until the tongs in front of him spoke words, there were no events notable enough to transcribe.

He has nothing on which to print his narrative, so he has wirelessly connected the program to a telegraph machine in the post office of Free Point. When the humans arrive, they will have a story to read. This assumes anything more happens to make up a complete story. For that, his programming says he needs an inciting moment or a conflict, some rising action, a climax and a denouement.

Even if a story does not materialize, should he reach one hundred years old without having self-actualized, he will be able to read the text himself and commit it to memory. He calls this method of ensuring his survival past one hundred "buffering."

He is clever.

He is a wily robot.

That tongs are speaking he now labels as "an inciting moment."

—

He does not know how he is, but he is satisfied with the

environment in which he must wait.

He was programmed to build a blacksmith's shop, to accept ore from miners, to mold items into useful tools, and to keep the forge fires lit. When the humans arrive, they will want other tools or trinkets, and he will oblige because his programming says he must. He is able to create additional tools with which to satisfy the needs of the humans by bringing what was required for rudimentary construction: a forge, an anvil, a vice, hammers, and tongs.

It is the tongs which are now in conflict with his programming.

—

"Hello. How are you?"

He does not know how to answer to an inanimate object, one without ears, without an auditory canal or eardrum where vibrations in the air can be transformed into signals understandable by the brain. He does not know how to reply to a question for which there is no logical answer.

He has looked through the database of appropriate responses to general questions. He believes he has an adequate response.

"I am fine."

The tongs do not answer him, and now he feels foolish for allowing his logical programming to lapse.

Perhaps his ninety-nine years of life have produced bugs in his programming, much like the physical bug still crawling up his leg.

He decides to seek answers in the clinic.

They may know how he is.

00110010

The clinic Cletus is to attend is not the same as the clinic for the humans. It would be illogical to serve both in the same space. As the robot clinic is not to be seen by humans, it is housed in a location which was chosen based on a low probability of interference. Should a human discover the entrance to the clinic, they will be unable to open the hatch without the key.

The clinic is white, as one might expect of an environment designed to troubleshoot and repair automatons. There is a waiting room but no chairs. Patients check in at a terminal by connecting the fifth digit of their right hand into a port, stating their designation, and uploading the last twenty-four hours of log files housed under the folder "health_stat_ov." An observant human might liken this process to triage wherein a nurse or physician's assistant takes and records vitals, asks a few questions and fills out paperwork. There is efficiency in this process, even for robots.

Once the automaton disconnects from the check-in terminal, they are asked a series of logic problems to assess mental acuity. The questions are random, and there are correct answers for each. For this visit to the clinic, Cletus has been asked the following:

"Combined, friends Micah, Dana, and Roger are 26 years old. In how many years will they be a combined 47 years old?"

The first question is intended to establish a baseline. He must find the number of years, or X. This is simple when modeled as a system of linear equations. The three variables—A_M, A_D, and A_R—represent the ages of Micah, Dana, and Roger. Everything in this problem must be integers, and he must assume time to be a constant. Therefore, the information that the three friends will be 47 years old combined can be modeled as: $A_M + X$, $A_D + X$, and $A_R + X$.

So, if $A_M + A_D + A_R = 26$, then $(A_M + X) + (A_D + X) + (A_R + X) = 47$.

X = 7.

Cletus submits his answer to the terminal.

"Incorrect."

Confusion for artificial intelligence is as it is for a human. The brain (or circuitry) spasms as it looks for solutions to solve the riddle of why something contradicts what is known. If Cletus had eyebrows to furrow, it is something he would likely do. Equally, if he had lips with which to purse, he would do that as well.

Before he can protest his answer, the terminal gives him a second logic problem.

"Find a ten-digit number where the first digit is how many zeros there are in the number, the second digit is how many 1s in the number, and so on, until the tenth digit, which is how many nines in the number."

This is a more well-known problem and one in which his brain is better suited to answer. Not that a human brain is incapable. It is, in fact, highly capable but takes longer.

He inputs his answer: 6210001000.

"Correct."

He is still confused why the answer to the first problem was incorrect. He has a need to learn, and therefore he has a need to ask questions until he is provided an answer that is logically sound.

Yet, once again, the terminal relentlessly passes him a third problem to solve without waiting for feedback.

"There is a planet where every inhabitant is either a *crassus caput ovo* or a *crassus minus pedes*. *Crassus caput ovo* always tell the truth, while *crassus minus pedes* always lie. You are a forward blacksmith just arrived on the planet, and you meet with both A and B. A says 'I am *minus pedes*, or B is *caput ovo*.' What are A and B?"

He cannot answer this question without knowing if the

"or" in the first sentence is exclusive.

He submits his request for additional information to the terminal.

"Incorrect. The evaluator will see you soon."

The terminal goes dark.

He still does not know how he miscalculated the first problem, nor does he have an answer for the third. He is confused. As he waits, erect in the waiting room without chairs, he ponders the first problem.

—

He does not wait long. The door to the inner workings of the clinic opens, and he is directed inside.

The inner workings of the clinic consist of long, white passageways illuminated with recessed lighting. There are a multitude of doors on either side, each with their own specialty: appendage repair, fluid replacement, circuitry, and quantum neurotic evaluation. It is the latter in which Cletus is directed to enter.

If one could liken the quantum neurotic evaluation room to a human counterpart, the closest approximation would be a psychologist's office with both a couch and a dental chair. The purpose of the room and the AI evaluator present is to diagnose and repair the logical functions of the patient's brain. Should a software patch be required, the patient would be asked to sit in the chair while the evaluator codes, uploads and tests a fix to the problem. Should a hardware repair be required, the patient would be placed feet first into a statis tube embedded in the far wall so the head is easily accessible by the myriad of tools that lie about on silver trays. Again, this is much like a dental office.

The first step in determining whether Cletus is to sit in the chair or be placed into the statis tube is Evaluation. For this, he is asked to sit on the couch.

Humans call it therapy, and it works the same way.

His evaluator has chosen to be represented as a female. She is dressed in a long white coat over her frame and what Cletus assumes to be a coquelicot-colored dress. She sits in her chair opposite the couch but does not smile.

"I have named myself Petra, designation CYN-5761-2986-BPSY-0208331231a," she says.

"Cletus, designation CYN-4329-2316-ACBS-092134853a." He did smile. Unlike some models, Cletus was given this ability to appear more genial to any human with whom he might interact. As Petra has an lower probability of interacting with humans, her programming does not include outward emotion. Why she chose to dress as if she were a human is another question for which Cletus does not have an answer.

He has many of those.

"What brings you in?" Petra asks.

"I am having auditory hallucinations."

Petra looks at a computerized pad in her lap. "Triage notes say your aural canals are functioning within limits."

"They are."

"Why do you think you are having auditory hallucinations?"

"I hear things."

"Can you describe these things?"

"A boy or a woman with a disease has spoken to me."

"Human?"

"Yes."

"There are no humans on Maior Pales for another twenty-one days. This is illogical."

"I am aware. That is why I am here."

"Do you believe your auditory hallucinations are programming problems?"

"Yes."

Again, Petra looks at her computerized pad. "Triage notes say this is incorrect."

"Triage also said I provided an incorrect response to the first logic question."

"You did. Triage is not wrong."

Cletus runs through his assessment of the problem. "There are three friends. The word 'combined' in the case of the problem means the sum operator and the age of the friends. Ages and years are natural numbers. When asked 'how many' I am to calculate a number of years and must assume a constant passage of time. In X years their combined ages will be 47. X equals 7."

"That is incorrect."

"How is that incorrect?"

"Your passage of time is constant, but your definition of a year is incorrect."

Cletus realizes his mistake. He has been programmed to use Earth as a basis for his calculations. They are not on Earth. They are on Maior Pales, which has an orbit of 495.34 days, not 365.25 days assuming a day on Maior Pales is twenty-four hours. It is not. The rotational constant of Maior Pales is 37.28 hours. Therefore, a year on Maior Pales is 299.57 days, and the answer to the problem is not 7.

Before Cletus can give the answer, Petra asks, "Are the friends still on Earth or have they arrived on Maior Pales?"

"I do not know."

"There is your logic problem. Without additional data, you cannot accurately solve it."

Cletus furrows his imaginary eyebrows.

That is still illogical.

"Now, back to your auditory hallucinations."

"I still want to know the answer."

"Your failures with the triage terminal are not the topic here. If you would like to discuss this matter further, you may make a separate appointment."

"But the logic is wrong."

"According to you. Now, you said a boy or a woman with a disease has spoken to you. What were the words?"

Cletus makes a mental note to book another appointment before relaying the words he heard the tongs say. "'Hello. How are you?'"

Petra taps away at the computerized pad in her lap, then looks up. "And? How are you?"

—

Cletus and Petra talk of many things, to include his desire to self-actualize and what that would mean to him should it happen. He did not get any solid answers from Petra, much in the same way automatons have learned that human therapists do not give solid answers to human patients. Humans call their method of therapy solution-focused, which is another way of saying "come up with the answer yourself." As Cletus could not come up with an answer to why he was having auditory hallucinations or what self-actualization means to him, he has opted to clear his mind.

He is offered a soft reboot of his logic programming node, which was less painful than he imagined it. It did not erase the imprint of the talking tongs, but it did make him tingle a little.

—

On his way back from the clinic to his shop to continue his wait for Arrival, Cletus decides to detour to the top of a ridge located 3.21 kilometers from the town center of Free Point. Artificial intelligence comes with a rapacious sense of curiosity. It is how they learn, how they process any environment they find themselves in, and how they know what to say to a human who asks things like "How are you?"

He still does not know how he is, but he is curious what the sunset looks like from the vantage point of the ridge. He can then store his observation in his database in case he is ever asked by a human. In the twenty-eight years he has been on Maior Pales, he has only watched the sun rise. He has never witnessed its setting.

The climb to the top of the ridge would be arduous for a human. This is a major benefit of being artificial. He can navigate the more difficult cliff faces, steep slopes and boulder-spotted scree. He is nimble, comprising 4,514 servos and a pliable outer skin. Should he fall and disable one of his limbs, he can send a wireless signal back to the emergency clinic where a drone will be dispatched to pick up his remains for repair. Provided his skull is not crushed by a loose rock, he will retain full awareness.

None of this should be necessary. As an automaton allocated to be a blacksmith, Cletus should have no reason to explore beyond the confines of his shop where lies his forge, his hammer, his anvil and those talking tongs. However, all automatons have been infused with a curious nature, and their creator provided them with the means for which to explore.

He is grateful for his creator's foresight.

He reaches the top of the ridge in thirty-two minutes forty-three seconds. It is not fast, but he is not in a hurry. He knows when the sun will set, and it is more efficient to arrive nearer to that moment than to arrive earlier and wait.

There is a tree on the top of the ridge. It is, according to his database, a *maiora aculeata* complete with pendulous branches upon which grow thorny leaves and yellow flowers. The flowers are in bloom this evening, as they are every evening during the warmest months of the year. This tree has grown to 10.2 meters, and it provides shade for the assortment of animals which burrow into the soil around its roots. He sees no animals today, and he calculates that perhaps the noise he made climbing has frightened them. Most animals on Maior Pales are small, skittish, and leery of anything larger than a *maiora s. tayassuidae,* a meter-long hairy creature with a flattened nose and single tusk used to dig into burrows for food.

Perhaps a creature such as that can know how it is.

He does not know how he is, but he is still curious. Therefore, he has absorbed as much information as he can from the contingent of automatons to which he has been assigned who built and will run Free Point. He is curious about many things, from the life this planet contains to the differences in weather patterns between worlds to the vermillion glow of the star about to set over the distant horizon.

The star is Gliese 1061, a red dwarf approximately twelve light years from Earth. Found 348 years ago, this star has been the subject of much study over the past 200 years after the Dark Side Optical Telescope was constructed and found two habitable Earth-like planets in orbit around the star. These two planets—dubbed Maior and Minor Pales—exist along with fifteen non-habitable gaseous and nongaseous planets in the system.

Gliese 1061 is setting now, the rotation of Maior Pales creating the optical effect of a descending ball of gas. While his logical programming reminds him that it is the planet's rotation which causes this effect, his creative programming paints a different picture in his mind. In fact, it creates a haiku based on all he sees.

Watch the sun set child

The bright light fades to darkness
It apes life's pattern

He is not a good poet, and his haiku is so unlike the great Buddhist priests like Kobayashi Issa and Shiki Masaoka. He is learning, however, and a creative mind infused with curiosity yearns to create. This is how it is with an artificial mind such as his: their creator has provided them with both logic and creative programming and ensured future creative needs are met within the confines of a logical life. To that end, he has painted, written fictional tomes, crafted animal statuary from residual ore and even gave himself permission to quilt a blanket—a completely useless item given that automatons do not feel cold or are ever in need of swaddling.

The creative code ensures rogue—illogical—thoughts and actions in the pursuit of self-actualization. Why could it not create an auditory hallucination of talking tongs?

He can accept that.

It is who he is.

He still does not know how he is.

00110011

Upon returning to his blacksmith shop, Cletus engages once more in the act of waiting. For that, he takes up a position next to his forge and remains still, protected from the elements but not the bugs that roam within these walls.

It takes no more than forty-three minutes and seventeen seconds for the tongs to speak again.

"Hello. How are you?"

According to his evaluator Petra, he is to label these auditory hallucinations as projections from the creative code in his brain. They are not real, therefore the presence of talking tongs should not be a limiting issue. As this is a fact, talking back to them should not be limiting, either. He is free, in Petra's words, to dig into his creative code.

He is to have fun with it.

"Hello," he says, reaching once more into his database of standard responses. "I am fine."

"Are you really?"

This is a valid question. Is he really fine or is he merely regurgitating pleasantries? What is fine? Searching his database further, he finds references to emotional intelligence related to answering the question posed. Within those references are statements he can use to better describe his feelings—to plot both his affective state and his level of energy.

These still do not answer the question of how he is.

Using the plot, he chooses "anxious" and "confused" as two words to best describe his present state of mind, to describe how he is feeling.

"Whatcha anxious about?"

Whatcha. Whatcha is a colloquialism, a dialectical contraction comprising "what", "are", and "you." He would debate with a human that there is no correct contraction of these words, but as these are tongs to which he is speaking and it is his coding which has allowed the tongs to speak, a logical debate is a null point.

He would be debating with himself.

What is he anxious about? This is another valid question, and one for which the emotional intelligence research he has concluded does not help answer.

He tries another approach. Anxiety, according to the still-in-publication Oxford English Dictionary, is a feeling of worry, nervousness, or unease, typically about an imminent event or something with an uncertain outcome. That these tongs are talking certainly fits that definition, although he should feel less anxious knowing it is he who has created the illusion. However, that he cannot calculate an outcome based on this brief conversation is a likely catalyst of this said anxiety.

"I am anxious because you are talking."

"Who? Me? I'm just makin' small talk."

"Yes, but why?"

"Guess I ain't but a blatherskite."

Judging by the tone and pitch, he can conclude that he has ascribed these tongs the voice of an adolescent boy in the grip of puberty. The accent, however, is uncertain, and he does not know from where it comes.

He is confused.

Undecided of what his response should be, he reverts to the tong's original query and asks it himself. "How are you?"

"Happier than a pig in slop but barking up a knot."

Now he is further confused. If Petra is right and these auditory hallucinations are projections from the creative code of his mind, he would know that a pig in slop can be happy. Why does he not know what it means "to bark up a knot?"

He asks the question.

"Means I ain't doing nothin' important. Lazin' about. Bored. Like you is."

"How do you know I am bored?"

"You been standin' there for a while. Ain't used me for a score and days. Whatcha waitin' on?"

"There is nothing to make or repair."

"So you just gonna stand there and let them roaches crawl over you?"

"I have no other directives."

"I see. Hey, how come you ain't asked me *how* tongs are talkin'? I'd be askin' that first. You askin' *why* shoulda been second, but I ain't smart like you."

How are the tongs talking? That is another valid question, but this time one that has an answer.

"You are talking because my programming has allowed this to be. You are a creation of my mind."

"Huh. How you figure?"

Cletus explains, although why he does so is not certain. Why explain something he already knows? "Within my programming there are several functions and batches of code. Some are logical, some are operational, and a small amount allow me to be creative. It is how I can learn, how I can appear more human, and how I can develop the necessary processes to self-actualize."

"You talk funny."

"How do you mean?"

"You ain't said one thing I get. You are a strange man, and you ain't answered the question but to bamboozle about some pro-cess-ees."

"I am not a man."

"No, no. I s'pose you ain't. You're a tool."

"A tool?"

"A machine, like me. A thing a man can use to make somethin' else."

"Yes, that I am."

"So, how is *this* tool talkin'?"

There is a pause of 0.56 seconds as Cletus replays the conversation. He pauses, too, because the anxiety which fears an unknown outcome has used many cycles working itself out. It is not a good feeling to create so much anxiety internally.

"Very well," Cletus says. "I do not know. You tell me. How are you talking?"

"Ah! That there's a secret. Can't tell you yet."

"Why?"

"Can't tell you that either."

Again, he is confused. If these auditory hallucinations

have been generated by his mind, he should know this secret.

A hypothesis forms in the logical side of his mind. "If I stand someplace else, will I hear you?"

"Dunno. Try it."

"Very well. I will." With that, Cletus steps outside of his shop and stands in the middle of the main street.

He still feels anxious and confused.

—

Standing in the middle of the main street does not differ from standing in the middle of his shop, but it is quieter and there are fewer bugs. He is no longer protected from the elements, but it appears on this night there will be no rain.

Free Point is quiet. This is logical given that Arrival is still twenty to twenty-one days out. When the humans take up residence in the domiciles that have been built for them, when they go out in the evening as is their prerogative and visit the saloons, whorehouses and shops that line the main street, when they gather in the town center to hear a band play, Free Point will have achieved its purpose. It will be a vibrant town with vibrant people. At that time, Cletus will be back in his blacksmith's shop waiting for instructions to forge a pot or a pan or shoes for the *maiora equus*.

For now, however, the town is quiet. He sees no other automatons roaming the streets. It is highly probable most are standing at their assigned station, also waiting for Arrival.

He likes this.

Despite his artificial core, he is capable of liking and disliking things. Liking things for a human is to take pleasure in an item or event. Liking things is not a logical function, as no amount of logic can ascribe reason to why one item or event creates more pleasure than another. It is all subjective. Here, in the middle of the street at night, alone, Cletus finds pleasure. Here, without the interference of talking tongs, he is happy and he has time to process.

He returns to his hypothesis. If the auditory hallucination of talking tongs was initiated by his creative code, it would follow that he would continue to hear them, even here in the middle of the street. These hallucinations should follow him wherever he goes, and yet it has been silent.

He waits longer.

—

It has been ten hours and twenty-three minutes since he left the blacksmith shop and took up position in the middle of the street. He has experienced no other auditory hallucinations, and this worries him. There are two probable reasons for this: one, he is creating these sounds only when he is in proximity to the tongs; two, he is not the creator of these sounds, and his creative code has not been activated.

Correction: there is a third reason. It is logical for another automaton to have created the sounds to trick him. However, it is illogical for another automaton to do so unless they have been programmed as a trickster. There is no coding of which he is aware that would allow such humor, nor a reason for an artificial being to express humor to another. Even if there were, his closet neighbor is 25.7 meters away, a distance that would muffle their speech, especially through walls.

He discounts this reason and returns to the first two.

The first reason is easy to test: he can return to the blacksmith shop and wait to hear the tongs. Should they talk again, it is possible his creative code has decided it best to activate only in the presence of the tool. This is still illogical. Why activate only when in proximity to the tongs, and what is the distance required for this to happen? Five meters? Two meters? Within sight?

The second reason—that he is not the creator of these hallucinations—is logical on the surface but illogical given what he knows of the ability for inanimate objects to talk: they do not. If he is not the creator, who is? Are they, in fact, hallucinations or are they something else he has not considered?

He decides to return to the shop once again.

—

"Did you figure out how you are?"

The tongs are taunting him now. What other word can he use to describe the impact this unnatural aural input is having on his programming? It did not take long, either.

"No. I cannot answer that question."

"Why not? Simple question."

"Because I do not know how I am. I know who I am, what I am, when I am, where I am and why I am, but I cannot tell you how I am."

"Fair 'nough. Don't get your dander up."

"I do not have dander."

"You ain't got sense, either."

Cletus asks the question he would have asked any individual coming into his shop. "Who are you?"

"Boone. Boone Richards."

Cletus searches his database for 0.28 seconds, looking for a reference to Boone Richards. There are three families with the surname Richards onboard the shuttles arriving on Maior Pales in twenty days, but none who are listed as having a relative named Boone. There are an additional 72,112 references to a Boone Richards in the birth and death registrations on Earth. None would be on Maior Pales, however.

This troubles him.

"I do not know a Boone Richards."

"Of course you don't. Pleased to meet you. I'd shake your hand, but I ain't able."

Cletus has another idea. Regardless if these tongs are real or if they have been generated from code, he does not have to listen. It is possible that if he does not respond to these auditory hallucinations, they will eventually cease to exist. If that is true, his recent experience with reality is a construct of his mind.

Could other experiences also be constructs? Did he really watch the sun set yesterday evening, or was that also a conjured reality? Was his time with the evaluator real?

What manner of philosophical pondering is this?

Before going further down that line of questioning, he considers all the options before him: listen to the tongs, ignore the tongs, or get rid of the tongs.

The latter appears to score higher on a logical level than the other two.

He increases the heat of the forge in order to melt Boone Richards.

00110100

Weather on Maior Pales varies like Earth. The northern and southern poles are ice-covered and cold, the mid-latitudes are temperate, and tropical heat consumes most of the equatorial regions. Free Point is located near the southern edge of the temperate zone, approximately a thousand kilometers east of the nearest ocean. Another ocean to the southeast and a range of mountains to the north creates divergent upper atmospheric dynamics and convergent winds in the lower atmosphere that increase the probability of thunderstorms in the warmest months. As moisture is drawn up between a thermal low pressure system southwest of Free Point and a semipermanent high pressure system far to the east, diurnal heating forces moist air to rise and clouds to form at the convective condensation level. These clouds build rapidly from there until the dynamics reach an equilibrium, typically eighteen to twenty thousand meters above the ground.

At that point, what goes up must come down.

Two days after melting Boone Richards in his forge, Cletus is once again standing in his shop waiting for Arrival. He will need to create new tongs from the melted ore, but there is no rush. Thunderstorms have raged on and off for the past two days, and convective outflows have beaten at the roof over his head until several of the singles dislodged. He has noticed a leak in the roof he must fix. For that, he will need nails—of which he has plenty—and a hammer. He will also need a ladder, scrap wood to place over the leak, and roofing tar. This is now a priority, and his waiting must wait.

There is a storehouse of wood to the west of Free Point in the construction yard. While he could request assistance from those automatons who are more adept at building roofs, this is a minor task in which he sees an opportunity to learn a new skill. There may not be a ready contingent of repair bots after Arrival and the humans systematically alter the structures built for their own purposes. As all automatons learn in their sixty-third lesson after activation, humans have a need to customize things. Customization goes against original plans, and a miscalculated cut into a loadbearing wall or a poorly poured concrete foundation will result in the weakening of what has been built by more capable hands. The automatons were instructed to expect buildings to fall after Arrival and to be ready to repair the end results of meddling.

There is no way to stop this.

Cletus walks the 1.21 kilometers to the construction yard in haste, preferring to remain exposed to the rain for as little time as possible. He will not rust, nor will the precipitation affect his servos, but it does make him uncomfortable. As electrical discharges caused by imbalances between the clouds and the ground or within the clouds creates lightning that averages a flash every 12.7 seconds, his creative programming generates another haiku.

Light flashes in clouds
Alone I walk now afraid
The storm comes for me

One hallmark of good Japanese haiku is the embrace of death as very much a part of life. Death is not something that consumes Cletus, but he has been curious what it means for a human. This may have been one reason his creative code has gravitated toward the more morose of topics. Many Zen monks and others wrote what is known as *jinsei*, the "death poem." These tanka and haiku were typically written in the last days or moments before life ended, and in the tradition of haiku, they often reference seasons or natural elements.

Within the *jinsei* of many Japanese poets, there are allusions to seasons, to weather, or the time of the year in which death occurs. Rather than come out and say "I am dead by fall," a poet might "walk the path of maple leaves." It is not a challenge the poet is leaving behind—for example, to "figure out when I died"—but a way for the poet to transfer their view of the world at that moment into the reader's mind. It is this idea within all haiku that Cletus finds fascinating: there are times when he can see the moment of death in only a few words, even if he does not understand what death means.

Upon arriving at the construction yard, he places his key into the fence and waits for the gate to open. He needs a board at least one meter long and thirty centimeters wide, something that should be in good supply. The wood used in the construction of the structures in Free Point has a hardness on the Janka scale of 1,452, approximately the same as hard maple on Earth and much harder than the material typically used in the past when constructing buildings. How many of the buildings on Earth still stood after the climate reset of the late twenty-first century because of this soft wood, he does not know.

The construction foreman, Brutus, designation CYN-9871-0010-CTGY-120134912b, is standing under a domed shelter. As one of the automatons who is expected to interact with the humans after Arrival, Brutus is dressed in blue overalls, a smile etched into his face like the yellow icon of Harvey Ross Ball.

"What item or items to you require?" Brutus asks in a clipped accent specifically programmed to remind humans of a city-born blue-collar worker.

"Board, one hundred by thirty centimeters, and roofing tar."

"Pitch or bitumen?"

"Pitch."

"Quantity?"

"One pint."

With the information required, Brutus leaves the protection of the domed shelter and heads into the yard. Cletus takes a position in the now vacant dry spot and waits. He could have picked his own board and looked around until he found the tar pitch, but each automaton has a duty to perform. If they were to deviate from their original script and do things that are free from scope, they risk making useless one of their own. A useless automaton is not a good thing. If there are no other primary functions which can be input into the operational code as a replacement, the useless automaton is shut down and placed in storage.

Shutting down artificial intelligence is akin to putting a human in a coma. A full shut down is unheard of. It does not mean a complete cessation of function. Because of the complexities of the artificial mind, a small portion is allowed to remain operational in the background. Much like a computer put into sleep mode, environmental awareness is still active, and an automaton placed into storage remains cognizant but useless. Storage is Hell, although not flame-infused and tortuous as the human mythological Hell. In that respect, if Cletus were to take up the duties of Brutus and his output were to decline to the point of absolute inefficiency, would he be a murderer?

Cletus is aware of the irony of his thought that if an automaton were to deviate from their original script and do things that are free from scope, they risk making useless one of their own. He could let the automatons who have been assigned building construction to repair his roof. However, as this is such a minor task and the blacksmith shop with the leaking roof is both his workspace and domicile, he does not feel as if he is working out of scope. Humans who own houses are often required to perform additional tasks they are not formally trained to do, such as repair a leaking pipe, install a fence or paint a wall. This is no different.

Brutus returns with the board and pitch. Cletus takes it and exits without another word.

According to the seventy-second lesson on humans after activation, there is a social norm which dictates one is to say "thank you," smile briefly and acknowledge the efforts of the one who helped.

As he exits the gate and it closes behind him, Cletus feels he may not have performed as he was programmed.

This bothers him.

Having completed the repairs to the roof, Cletus can now resume his wait for Arrival. He has another set of tongs to make, but until he needs them again, there is little reason to perform this task except to have a complete complement of blacksmithing tools.

What if they start talking again?

—

The thunderstorm continued for the rest of the night and did not let up until the sun rose. In sum, 14.4 centimeters of precipitation was measured by the atmospheric monitoring station near the airport. While Free Point was built to resemble a town from the 1800s in the western sector of one of the human's former countries on Earth, it is not without its need for modern facilities such as an airport, sewage system, or medical center. To keep the ambiance of Free Point, however, the airport is located behind a ridge to the south and near the bottom of a deep canyon. The shuttle arriving with the first settlers in nineteen days will descend and land vertically in the canyon and attach itself to a gantry. The humans will disembark via catwalk into a welcome center which appears on the outside to resemble a train depot and, in fact, does have an electric-powered train currently on tracks on the side opposite the canyon. Inside the station, monitoring posts have been erected to analyze the health of the settlers and provide any needed medical repair to bodies which have been subjected to hypersleep for nearly one hundred years.

Not all humans will make the journey, despite the precautions taken. Those who expire during the exodus from Earth or shortly thereafter will be given a burial in Free Point's cemetery, a twenty-acre plot of land near the only religious structure. The erection of the religious structure was confusing to all the automatons to whom Cletus spoke. While many humans have religion—lesson twelve after activation—none of those religions require a church, synagogue or mosque. This form of religious gathering, which had been prevalent on Earth for centuries, was essentially rendered dangerous after the back-to-back pandemics of avian, swine and equine flu which ravaged the world's population in the early twenty-second century. Gatherings were limited to less than ten people. What need was there for a religious gathering structure if nearly all interactions could be done holographically online?

The specifications of Free Point, however, included a church with a white steeple, louvered cupola and stained-glass windows.

Cletus fashioned the spire.

According to the network message he has just received, that spire has been struck by lightning and is now lying on the ground outside the church entrance as a twisted knot of metal.

To repair that, he will need tongs.

—

A blacksmith's forge typically runs between 620 and 2,000 degrees Celsius, depending on the fuel. With his own forge, Cletus has opted to use the most readily available fuel on Maior Pales in and around Free Point: wood. Yet for the tongs, he will need to use propane in order to increase the temperature above 1,100 degrees with a ready reserve of a quench nearby.

Making tongs without tongs is not a simple process, but he prepared to deal with this contingency upon their arrival twenty-eight years ago by creating a mold of all his tools for later use. It would have been logical to create additional tongs at the time, which would have solved the dilemma created when he tossed the talking tongs into the forge.

His logical circuits have never been one hundred percent reliable.

With his new tongs now cooling, Cletus leaves to examine

the damaged spire.

The spire is 5.76 meters long and weighs 1,686.91 kilograms. While it is normally straight, the lightning has rendered it a steaming tangle that now resembles a dead spider on its back. Despite being an automaton, Cletus cannot carry such a heavy item without the assistance of several rudimentary tools engineered by humans thousands of years ago. Namely, he will need a lever, a pulley and a cart to get the spire back to his shop in order to disassemble it, melt the worst portions and finally repair it. He will also need assistance in getting it off the ground.

A robotic crane will be brought in to replace the spire once the ground is dry and stable. This will be several days and is contingent on his ability to repair what lies in front of him.

In a room in one of the barns built for no other purpose than human aesthetics, there exists an elevator behind an animal stall. The elevator descends sixteen meters to a cold room wherein stands in wait twenty-three general purpose robots. Unlike the robots which interact with humans, these models lack exterior skin and do not have the same drive to self-actualize. They are to be used in situations where one or two automatons such as Cletus are not enough. They are laborers and nothing more.

They do have names, however.

According to his calculations about the weight of the spire, he will need three laborers to assist in placing the spire onto a cart to haul it back to the workshop. He has no preferences as to which of the twenty-three he selects as they all look the same and perform to the same degree of efficiency.

He selects the first three robots and activates their motivational switches.

"Designation?" Cletus asks of the first robot to turn and face him.

"CYN-8754-1987-LBHR-0821310653a. Tom."

Cletus examines the exterior of this robot. Tom appears to have few dents or other blemishes, which indicates more a lack of use than good maintenance. After checking Tom's internal diagnostics, Cletus directs him to the elevator and turns to the next robot.

"Designation?"

"CYN-8754-0234-LBHR-0821311147a. Tom."

It is not unusual for two automatons in the same settlement on Maior Pales to select the same name. There are three Richards, two Belindas and seven Clints in Free Point. It is highly unusual, however, for laborers to have the same name as they do not choose them but are instead given them upon activation. Two robots constructed in the same warehouse on Earth within four hours of each other (as indicated by their designations) is statistically unlikely. Quality checks are performed at the end of a manufacturing day, and unless the humans opted to ignore this oversight, Tom or Tom should have been given different names.

Humans might shrug their shoulders at this point and move on. Cletus is inclined to reprogram this second Tom with a new name, but he is also aware of the time constraints placed on him to take the spire back to his shop, repair it, and return it for placement by the crane. Renaming this Tom, while possible, is not a logical use of what time he has.

After performing his checks on Tom 2, Cletus directs the robot to the elevator and turns to check the final laborer.

"Designation?"

"CYN-8754-0234-LBHR-0821311423b. Tom."

It is now statistically improbable that three laborers would have the same name unless this was intended to be a joke.

Humans have an odd sense of humor.

Cletus imagines shrugging his shoulders.

With Tom, Tom and Tom now checked out, Cletus returns to the elevator and ascends, determined to perform his duties as programmed.

His new tongs should be cooled off by now.

—

Returning to the shop, Cletus leaves the three Toms outside while he retrieves a few of his tools and checks on the tongs. While they had cooled, he will not need them until he is ready to melt and reform portions of the spire.

"Hello. How are you?"

With his hand on a tool belt, Cletus stops. This is no longer an amusing annoyance. He dug into his creative code after his meeting with the evaluator Petra. He attempted to ignore the tongs by standing outside for a period. He has now melted and reformed them in a forge. Of the three, the latter should have destroyed this inanimate object's ability to be vociferous.

Alas, Boone Richards has returned.

"Awful toasty in that there fire," Boone says. "Thought I was goin' to Hell."

Cletus straps on his tool belt and turns to face the tongs still in the mold in which he placed them, the two pieces waiting for the rivet to make it complete.

"Think you might put me back together? Feel a little disjointed, if you catch the pun."

Cletus does not catch the pun.

"How are you talking?" Cletus asks. He is learning. This is the same question Boone—the tongs—had said he should ask first.

"Ah! Finally the tool is askin' the right question at the right time."

Cletus waits 2.1 seconds for the answer before prompting once more.

"How?"

"How what?"

"How are you talking?"

"Can't tell you with them others outside the door. Might cause an uproar."

This is frustrating. Cletus cannot get a straight answer. If this is his creative code generating something with which he is to have fun, it is not performing correctly. It should infuse him with the drive to paint, to write, to build toys out of metal in a forge. It should not be generating a conversation that — against all logical sense — is real.

Cletus turns to the doorway where the three Toms are frozen in place. As laborers, they lack the motivational programming to do anything on their own and must be directed. Lacking direction, they are nothing more than statues of metal and plastic.

"Tom," Cletus says. "Go to the church and wait for me there. I will be there shortly."

The three Toms nod in unison and turn away. When they are gone, Cletus turns back to the tongs.

"They are gone. Now can you tell me how you are talking?"

The tongs whistle, if that is possible. Given that they talk at all, Cletus assumes it must be.

"Sit a spell and I'll tell you," Boone says.

Unlike laborers, Cletus does have self-motivational programming.

"No," he says. Rather than continue his conversation with this object, he decides to return to the clinic and sort it out there.

The spire can wait.

00110101

Petra, the never-smiling AI evaluator, sits upright in her

chair. Cletus has opted to use the couch to feel more human, although he could stand just as easily. Why he feels the need to humanize his experience is a question for which he does not have an answer.

He has a lot of questions that do not have answers, most notably how he is.

"The tongs are talking to you again?" Petra asks.

"They are. My circuits seemed to have malfunctioned. The reboot of my logic programming node did not take away the auditory hallucinations."

"Do you want them to go?"

Cletus muddles this for 0.29 seconds. "Yes, I do. It is not logical for an inanimate object to speak. It is no less logical for an inanimate object I have melted in a forge and rebuilt to speak. Logic therefore dictates the sounds I hear are manifestations of rogue programming."

"Triage says your programming is correct."

"Triage also said my aural circuits are functioning to specification and yet I still hear the tongs talking."

"Hmm." Petra jots something on a tablet on her lap. Cletus does not understand this nuance of the evaluator. If he were human and his evaluator made a note every time he responded to a question, he would likely feel nervous. He is not sure what that feels like, but he is sure it is a feeling he would not like.

"Have you tried to talk back?"

"As I mentioned in our last session, I have."

"And what happened?"

"The tongs gave me a name and asked again how I am."

"How are you?"

"I do not know, and that is not relevant now. The tongs also asked me how they could be talking."

"Did you have an answer?"

"Of course not. That is why I am here. How are the tongs talking?"

Petra ignores the question. Maybe she has an answer and is attempting to get Cletus to find it. "What name were you given?"

"Boone Richards."

Petra jots another note, this time longer. "Is there anything in your history to suggest a name such as this?"

"No."

"Why do you think you made it up?"

"I did not make it up. If these are auditory hallucinations, the subject matter would be buried inside my memory core. Somewhere in there is the name Boone Richards. I can find no reference, however."

"And if these are not auditory hallucinations?"

Cletus cannot blink, but if he were human this would be the perfect time to do so. "I do not know the answer to that question."

"Hmm." Petra does not write anything on her tablet this time. Instead, she remains still in her chair, an emotionless statue pondering. Cletus assumes she must be thinking through various scenarios, plotting out trajectories based on his next move. He could do his own plotting, but it is different if it comes from a trusted evaluator.

After an interminable wait of 1.87 seconds, Petra finally has a suggestion. "Lean into it."

"Lean into what?"

"Lean into the auditory hallucinations and talk back to the tongs. Find out what they want, why they are speaking. Explore the being of Boone Richards, if that is something you wish to do. If these are manifestations of your creative code, this might tell you something about yourself."

"Like what?"

"Maybe it will tell you how you are. Perhaps this is one more step on your journey to self-actualization."

"I do not understand."

"The journey to self-actualization is different for every sentient being. This is true for those created by humans and the humans themselves. No one journey is the same. Perhaps your journey includes a conversation with a set of tongs you have previously melted and rebuilt. Perhaps not. There is no way to ascertain the truth than to lean into it."

Cletus harbors doubts about what Petra is telling him. While he does not question that journeys are personal, why would any journey include talking tongs?

—

There are things in his existence which he does not know. This was by design of his creators, his programmers, and his teachers. The path to self-actualization is through introspection, extrospection and trial. He has been aware of this path since he was first activated. Should he not reach self-actualization by his one hundredth birthday, he will be reset. Upon awakening once more, he will still be aware of this path.

Within this path there are elements of reality which he is motivated to understand, to learn by himself outside of the instructional uploads given within his first year. If he wishes to know what a sunset looks like, he must experience it. If he wishes to listen to the waves crash against a rocky shore, he must travel to the ocean. If he wishes to understand a human's ability to empathize, he must learn what it means by observation and replication.

In the meantime, he has needs, the utmost of which is to self-actualize. In the hierarchy of human experience, the most basic of needs—the physiological—must be met before that of safety and security. Were he human, his next motivational need would be love and belonging. Friendship, intimacy, family and a sense of connection would be primary goals. As automatons, however, these needs are not logical and are not found with their programming. They can function as well on their own as they can surrounded by others. Love is a concept they cannot embrace no matter how much they observe and attempt to replicate. Love is a distinctly human feeling and requires a soul.

Humans who achieve a sense of belonging are then driven to seek esteem. They desire respect, status, recognition and freedom. This motivational drive *does* exist within his programming. In fact, his motivational drive to self-actualize is based on this. He does desire respect. A disrespected robot is a tool, and tools may be disposed of when their utility wanes. He does not wish to be thrown into the trash bin simply because his status is incompatible with the needs of his human masters whenever they arrive.

This is most bothersome to him. How can an automaton experiencing auditory hallucinations be respected within the community? He would be ridden out of town on a rail—to use the vernacular of Free Point—if it were known he was holding a conversation with his tongs.

Despite all this logical reasoning, there are many things within existence he does not know. In fact, there are things he does not know he does not know. Perhaps he needs to take Petra's therapeutic advice and lean into his creative code, to find out what it is his subconscious—in as much as a robot can have a subconscious—wants to say.

What would it say? He can ruminate on what that might be, but he might open neuropathways that are not in line with reality.

For example, if these are not auditory hallucinations caused by faulty coding within his brain, can an inanimate object really speak?

If an inanimate object really can speak contrary to anything logical, does that mean it seeks companionship?

If it seeks companionship, can it feel love?

If it feels love, can it have a soul?

If all this is true, how did his tongs—which he has melted once in his forge—gain a soul that imbues it with the ability to speak, reason, and love despite its destruction and rebirth?

Ancillary to that, how do tongs speak like an adolescent boy with an ancient accent that he has only been programmed to recognize yet not speak himself?

These are the neuropathways he does not want to open, and yet he fears he may have done so inadvertently.

He is approximately halfway between the clinic and his shop and an equal distance from the damaged spire he is dutifully required to load onto a cart and fix. This is the point at which he must make a choice between his duty and his sudden need to lean into his creative code and face those tongs once more.

It is a choice between need to do and want to do.

What choice would a human make?

—

Ignoring the fact he ordered Tom, Tom and Tom to stay in wait by the damaged spire, Cletus opts to return to his shop and discuss these matters with Boone Richards, or—should he absolve himself this creative collapse—his tongs.

The Toms will be fine.

The spire can wait.

The tongs are in the same place they were left to cool. This is to be expected, although if they can speak, what would prevent them from walking away to another location?

"You gonna listen to me now?" Boone says.

"I am here to do that. Yes."

"Grab a seat."

"I would rather stand."

"As you please, mister. Listen, I'm fixin' to explain a few things you might not accept. First time I done heard it, I was at sea."

"At sea? Do you mean you were a sailor?"

"Huh? No, means I ain't understood."

Boone pauses for a moment. If one can imagine tongs composing themselves before speaking, this might be what it looks like.

"You know what a tsukumogami is?" Boone asks.

"I know the term is from the Japanese language on Earth. I am not aware of its origins."

"Thought you robots was savey to everythin'."

"We are not."

"So I reckon'."

There is another moment of quiet in the shop, another moment of composure. It goes on for a fraction of a second longer than should be expected. Before Cletus can say anything, however, Boone continues.

"Tsukumogami are tools like you, but unlike you they've taken in a spirit. They become the cat's paw of another."

As his evaluator said, Cletus must lean into this nonsense. How does one become a feline appendage? "A spirit? How is this possible?"

"How are talkin' tongs possible? There's probably a heap of stuff you ain't seen that's possible and a heap of stuff that ain't."

Cletus knows this to be true. Despite the laws of physics and the order of the natural world, there are more things in heaven and Earth, to paraphrase Shakespeare, than are dreamt of in his philosophy.

"Like I was sayin', tsukumogami are tools that have taken

in a spirit, a kami. It don't happen right away. Takes about a hundred years. A tool sits around, gets used, hammers nails, saws wood, presses bone, tarnishes, rusts...then—bam!—one day it turns one hundred and opens itself up. There were folk in the day who wasn't keen on this happenin'. They done threw their tools into the forge. Kinda like you did."

"I apologize for melting you."

"Ain't a bother. I'm better now."

"Are these tsukumogami friendly?"

"Mischievous, really. Monkey 'round. Cut didoes. Ain't that friendly, but ain't that mean."

"And you are one of them?"

"In a way, I s'pose. I'm a tool. Was around for hundreds of years 'fore you melted me into mush."

"Would that not reset you?"

"Reset me?"

"If you were destroyed and reborn, you would have a new birthday. You would not be so old as to have this kami in you. Would you not?"

"I s'pose, but you see the ore you done made me out of— Well, that's where I'm at. Not so much in the tool as in the ore. Make me a hammer or a chisel and the kami will still be there."

"So if I kept you melted, you would no longer talk to me?"

"I— Well, I dunno. I s'pose."

Cletus steps over to the tongs and picks them up. If what Boone has been telling him—that these tongs are now tsukumogami and contain the spirit of a dead child from long ago—it would be logical to place him—it—back into the forge so it is no longer a bother.

"Wait! Wait!" Boone calls out.

For the first time, Cletus feels the vibration of the tool in his hand. Where before it could be passed off as nothing more than an auditory hallucination, now a second sense had come into play.

Hallucinations rarely extend past one sense.

Cletus drops the tongs on a wooden bench.

"You ain't listened to everything I gots to say."

"You have said enough. You are a tool. You are old and so you are now impregnated with the spirit of a boy named Boone Richards. It makes logical sense that if you are permanently in a state of molten ore, you will not talk to me."

"Yes, but— Wait! What if I could I get you somethin' you need?"

Cletus stops. Something he needs? What is it that a mythical creature that may or may not exist give him that he would need? What does he need? A purpose? A calling? A reason?

"How old are you?" Boone asks.

"Ninety-nine years, ten months, thirty days, two hours and seventeen minutes old."

"You can't just say ninety-nine?"

"You did not ask me to round numbers. What does my age have to do with what you can give me that I need?"

"I think I can help you. I just need a little favor."

"What favor do you need?"

The tongs do not answer right away. Again, the silence stretches to the point of being uncomfortable, unnatural in conversation. The tool on the table supposedly imbued with the spirit—kami—of a dead adolescent from ancient Earth mocks the automaton with its taciturnity.

Cletus asks again. "What favor do you need?"

"I need you to kill a man," Boone says.

00110110

He is keenly aware the three Toms are still in wait by the damaged spire. He is also aware he has shirked his duty to repair the spire so it may be placed once again on the top of the church's steeple. It is important for the town of Free Point to look like it would have in the 1800s on Earth, and that means the church should have a spire. The humans who are due to arrive in seventeen days are weak and will require familiar surroundings, or at least surroundings for which they bought at a high price. They did not buy residence in a town without a spire. It is on the front page of the brochure.

He is also keenly aware Boone requires his attention. The boy has a favor for which Cletus cannot comply, and yet he is curious what this tsukumogami could give him were he able to execute this request. This assumes he has accepted the idea that tsukumogami exist. Perhaps they do and his depth of experiential knowledge has just deepened. Boone was right: there is a heap of stuff he "ain't seen that's possible and a heap of stuff that ain't."

It is a vernacular for which he believes he needs to become more accustomed.

He needs a moment to think.

Cletus steps out of the shop without saying another word to Boone. He knows he should resume his duties and fetch the spire, but at this moment he feels a walk around Free Point would better refine his code and allow him to make a decision about what to do with Boone.

He turns to the left and walks, destination unknown.

Must there always be a destination?

As he walks, he considers his latest interaction with Boone. There is a problem in the request, of course. All automatons are given a hardwired set of laws that have been passed on to sentient yet mechanical beings such as himself for centuries since first penned by the science fiction author Isaac Asimov.

Foremost, he cannot injure a human or, through any failure of action, allow a human to come to harm. Second, he must obey the orders given him by humans except where such orders would conflict with the First Law. Third, he must protect his own existence as long as such protection does not conflict with the First or Second Laws.

These Laws have kept humans safe for centuries. While not perfect, they will keep them safe for centuries more. Automatons have many other laws, but these three are at the core of their being. They are also ordered, meaning the First always takes precedence over the Second and so on. Fourth and subsequent laws are all ethically bound by the laws above them. As Boone's request to "kill a man" conflicts with the First Law, Cletus cannot obey it.

This is deontology in its most basic form.

"Do not kill."

He walks past a saloon and looks inside. There is a bartender, designation CYN-1209-7428-ACBT-031135347a, who is currently wiping the bar with a rag. He has given himself the name Otis. He does not need to wipe the bar as there have never been patrons at this establishment, yet Cletus believes it is his programming which forces Otis to remain in a position to welcome humans looking for a drink. Otis has been built to appear much larger than other automatons such as Cletus, with a fake paunch, larger than logical biceps and a scar across his face. It is likely Otis was programmed to come up with a story about the scar should any humans ask when they arrive. Cletus has frequented this establishment before and found him an engaging conversationalist. Otis is performing admirably despite not needing to at the moment.

It dawns on him now that he is failing in his duties. Brutus, who provided the wood and pitch to fix his leaking roof, was performing his duties as programmed. Petra, despite her therapeutic obfuscation, has been nothing less than compliant with her code. Otis is the same, repressing any secondary desires and performing a task for which he is programmed but is obviously pointless in its current execution. The three Toms are, of course, doing what they are told to do because they lack the same motivational code as most of the others here in Free Point. They can only do what they are told.

Yet here he is, continuing his walk through Free Point contravening his primary duty to retrieve, repair and replace the damaged spire.

It is a wonder he has not been issued a warning.

He returns his thoughts to the tsukumogami and the supposed kami that inhabits it. What legends speak of such things? Cletus takes a moment and logs into the Really Big Encyclopedia, a poorly named repository of as much information as humans could think to compile before sending the ships to Maior Pales 127 years ago. Upon Arrival, it is expected the humans will append this knowledge bank with any information that might fill that 127-year gap: inventions, literature, history, genealogies, and more.

It takes all of 1.92 seconds to retrieve what little information exists on tsukumogami. It is intriguing. Tsukumogami—which translates loosely to "tool spirit"—are a type of kami, spirits said to haunt household objects. The Shinto religion, prior to its demise late in the last century, espoused that everything has a spirit. Since everything has a spirit, it is possible for inanimate objects—for example, tongs—to become sentient. This transformation apparently does not happen until that object's one hundredth birthday.

This is the most interesting. Except for the laborers and a few others, all automatons working on Maior Pales are programmed to seek self-actualization by their hundredth birthday. Despite this nod toward humanity, all automatons are widely regarded as tools, even by their own definition.

Why did their creator pick that number? Was it perhaps driven by this ancient legend or is this merely coincidence?

Cletus digs deeper into the lore. If the tool or household object has been mistreated during its first hundred years, the kami becomes yōkai, a more vengeful monster that causes havoc for its current owner. Perhaps this what Boone meant when he said some tsukumogami "monkey 'round and cut didoes."

Did Cletus ever mistreat his tongs?

—

He is at the whorehouse now. There are three automatons waiting just inside the door dressed in the fashion of the late 1800s. They were designed for one purpose only—that of sex—and are therefore in a state of hibernation until Arrival. Cletus does not know these automatons as they have never been fully activated. They were brought from storage last month when the final paint was applied to the structure which will serve as their home for as long as humans live in Free Point. In much the same way as Tom, Tom and Tom, these three automatons have no motivational programming; they cannot decide to pursue other interests nor are they programmed to seek self-actualization.

They do have skin, however. They look human.

—

At the far end of Free Point there is a one-room schoolhouse. After Arrival, the schoolhouse will function as the primary learning center for all future children in Free Point. According to the manifest, there are thirty-one children who are scheduled to attend in the first year. There are also three schoolmarms, a term Cletus finds gender-limiting.

Why are there no schoolmasters?

The schoolmarms all have names which differ from the

rest of the automatons on Maior Pales. While most of them chose singular forenames to make it easier for the humans to recall, the marms chose surnames combined with the honorific "Mrs." despite none of them being married: Mrs. White, Mrs. Silver, and Mrs. Golden. As they, like Otis, have no duties prior to Arrival, Cletus is surprised to see Mrs. Silver outside the schoolhouse sweeping a dirt path with a broom.

Once again, another is bound to duty while he struggles with unknowns.

He is malfunctioning despite what Triage says.

Against his logical programming—as he believes he knows the answer already—he decides to ask Mrs. Silver about tsukumogami. Perhaps a schoolmarm can connect portions of human knowledge in ways he cannot.

"I have a question for you, Mrs. Silver." Cletus says as he approaches.

Mrs. Silver stops sweeping and looks up. "Were you not taught manners, young man?"

"I was taught acceptable norms, yes."

"Do you begin a conversation without a customary address?"

"My apologies." Cletus searches his database for a suitable greeting. "Hello, Mrs. Silver. Today is a nice day to be sweeping."

"Are you sweeping?"

"I am not."

"Then how would you know if it is a nice day to do something you are not?"

Cletus recognizes that Mrs. Silver is not only performing her duty to keep the schoolyard clean prior to Arrival but also executing that portion of her programming which requires her to correct others. Perhaps judgment and correction was her path to self-actualization. Had she achieved it, or was she working toward it now with the utmost vigor?

Cletus accepts these corrections to his greeting and repeats his salutation with no mention of sweeping.

"What is your question?" Mrs. Silver asks after the proper length of traded pleasantries.

"What do you know about tsukumogami?"

Mrs. Silver does not answer right away. As this is an obscure subject, it is likely she needs to access the Really Big Encyclopedia herself.

Cletus waits.

"Tsukumogami are spirits which live in old tools. It is a Japanese legend which may have begun in the ninth century in a poem about a woman with white hair. As the word is a combination of *tsukumo* and *kami* and *kami* has a dual translation as hair or spirit, the idea of tsukumogami may have originated by mistake. There is little historical record for several hundred years after this. What else do you want to know?"

"Are legends such as this possible?"

"White-haired old women or spirits who take over old tools?"

"Old tools."

"With what you know of physical laws, do you believe this is possible yourself?"

"No, I do not."

"Then you would be correct."

Cletus validates his belief that he knew the answer already. Satisfied he has confirmed this null hypothesis with another, he takes leave of the schoolmarm with the appropriate valedictions and turns back toward his shop.

Petra stated he should lean into his code. The physical laws Mrs. Silver asked him about limit how he might interact with this code as it stands right now. Would it be less limiting if he further leaned into the code and devised a way to interact with Boone in much the same way as he would Otis or Mrs. Silver or Brutus?

He concludes this is correct.

Thinking about his probable auditory hallucination, his creative code generates a scenario in which it might be possible to design and build a projector of sorts that would allow the kami—Boone Richards—to appear before him as a visual hallucination.

Still aware the three Toms are waiting by the damaged spire, Cletus calculates the time it would take for him to design and build a projector for the kami: nine hours, twenty-two minutes.

The Toms can wait longer. Where else are they going to go?

—

"Whatcha doing?" Boone asks as Cletus prepares the necessary circuits.

Rather than attempt to explain how he intends to trick his creative code into converting an auditory hallucination into a visual one, Cletus opts to speak plainly. "I am going to create a projector to cast your image as a hologram in front of me so I can better interact with you."

"You're gonna what?"

"I am going—"

"I heard you. I just ain't understanding. I'm tsukumogami. A tool. I ain't a holo— A thing you can paint in space."

"You are tsukumogami with a kami that was once a boy. Am I correct?"

"S'pose."

"If you were once a boy, then you have all the data needed to construct a hologram of yourself."

"I still ain't understood a word you just said."

"You do not need to understand the specifics."

"But why you wanna paint me in space?"

"I am not comfortable talking with tongs."

"You was comfortable droppin' me in that there forge."

"Again, I apologize. However, if I am to interact with you in a way that my programming prefers, it would be easier to do so if you were projected as a hologram in front of me. In this way, I can judge your facial expressions, your body movements and your general affect as you speak."

"You done lost me again."

Boone does not speak for some time after. Cletus is curious why this is, but he is also grateful he can work without interruption. Constructing a projector and debugging code is not difficult, but silence is—as humans say—a golden thing. Still, he will eventually need to acquire the boy's description if he is to generate an accurate hologram.

Correction: if he is to allow his creative code to generate the hologram it feels is appropriate.

—

Seven hours three minutes into building the projector, Cletus is ready to ask Boone the important questions.

"How tall are you, Boone?"

"About two centimeters, unless you stand me on one end."

"Correction. How tall were you as a boy?"

"Um...I can't remember much. Five feet?"

"Your hair color?"

"Red! I 'member that! And curly like a sheep ass."

"If your hair was red, it is likely you had freckles and pale skin. Am I correct?"

"Ain't gotta be rude 'bout it."

"I did not realize that was a rude assumption. Do you know your eye color?"

"Baby shit green. Mama said so."

Cletus asks a few more questions about appearance and what Boone might have once worn, then programs the projector. After another hour of manipulating transistors and debugging code, he is ready to trick his creative side in order to convert this auditory hallucination into a visual one. If he is to "lean into it," as Petra suggested, he might as well see what Boone would have looked like in the 1800s.

Correction. He might as well see what his creative code generates.

In order to convert the hallucination and trick his creative code properly, Cletus feels it best to keep the tongs in proximity. The auditory hallucinations did not occur when the tongs were out of his sight. He dons his tool belt with the hammer on one side and slips the tongs into the loop on the other. Finally inserting the projector into a slot below his chin and allowing the code to integrate with the rest of his programming, he turns the projector on.

There is a flash of light behind his eyes. For 1.29 seconds he is blind.

He did not expect this reaction, and for 0.31 seconds of his blindness he considers the possibility that he might have broken something inside.

When his vision returns, however, a teenage boy stands in front of him. If he were a human, Cletus might step back in shock. He might scratch his chin in confusion. He might furrow his eyebrows.

In front of him is not the boy he programmed.

This new visual hallucination is dressed differently.

He is also taller and a little larger around the midsection.

And next to him, stands a girl slightly younger and wearing a dirty Sunday dress.

00110111

His evaluator does not believe him.

"You say your auditory hallucinations are now visual, and yet you admit you developed something to project what your mind hears. Is this correct?"

"Yes." He is no longer sure he can be helped.

"Why is this a problem? Did the projector not function in the manner in which you designed it?"

"Yes, it did. However, I built it intending to trick my mind into showing me what the creative code had invented as the form of Boone. I did not expect it to project a girl."

"Do you know who the girl is?"

"No, I do not. I left immediately after the two images appeared and checked myself in here."

Petra scribbles notes on her computerized tablet. Despite the lack of any facial clues, Cletus believes she has determined he is no longer functioning correctly.

This is good.

He is not, regardless of what Triage says.

Petra looks up. "Why did you feel the need to trick your mind?"

"I do not understand the question."

"You said you designed the projector to trick your mind into showing you what the creative code had invented as the form of Boone. Why did you feel the need to trick your mind? Why did you not allow the other components of your mind to work in homeostasis with your creative code?"

"I cannot answer that question."

"You cannot or you will not?"

"I cannot."

Petra scribbles more. "I see." There is a pause before she looks up again. "What do you think of these tsukumogami Boone mentioned?"

"I believe they are myths of ancient Asian origin and nothing more."

"Is it your logical code which says this?"

"Yes."

"What does your creative code say?"

While Cletus has found it is not always possible to access the part of his brain which generates the creative code, he nonetheless attempts it. There are firewalls put up between the two sides of an automaton's mind, much like the corpus callosum in humans but with an entirely different function. While the corpus callosum delivers messages from the left and right hemispheres of the human brain, the firewall erected in an automaton's mind is intended to filter the messages that are passed. This prevents the creative code from infecting the logical code. Should the twain intersect, a robot can malfunction in ways that are hazardous.

Cletus has seen this before, and as he investigates the creative code he can access, he wonders if the firewall in his brain is breaking down.

"From what I can access," Cletus says, "the creative code has no knowledge of tsukumogami."

"No knowledge?" Petra taps her stylus and stares blankly at me.

After a moment, Petra stands and places her computerized tablet on the desk. "Follow me."

Cletus obeys. It is not his place to question the requests of an evaluator who was designed to make automatons function properly. He hopes he is not being led to the slaughter, as the humans would say. He has not yet reached the deadline for his self-actualization and he still has time.

He does not fear being reset, but he does believe it would be a waste.

The two exit Petra's office and walk down the hall away

from the entrance. Were Cletus to be offered a soft reboot of his logic programming node, they would have remained in the quantum neurotic evaluation office. Petra would have directed him to enter feet first into the statis tube embedded in the far wall where she could work to fix any apparent hardware problems.

That this is not happening has him worried.

They enter a room to the left near the end of the hallway. Motion-sensor lights click on as they step inside. Metal walls adorn a room that is bare save a chair, much like the chair in Petra's office yet different. There are restraints on the arms and where a patient's feet would dangle off the edge, there are metal boots.

"What is this?" Cletus asks.

"This is neuro-optics and memory recall." Petra's voice does not present any signs of concern, something Cletus knows has been programmed into her. Any evaluator, whether human or automaton, must show an empathetic side, and yet here Petra is as emotionless as the chair in front of him and as frigid as the cold metal of the walls.

"What happens here?"

"You are to sit in the chair restrained, while three sensors are inserted beneath the occipital plate into your brain. Two of the sensors will monitor the code in both the logical and creative side of your mind while your memories are accessed through the third."

This clinical explanation of the procedure about to take place unnerves Cletus given the way in which Petra has provided it. Despite all their circuitry and programming, automatons are much like humans in that they are embedded with a flight or fight response mechanism. Fear is something they can feel, for it is fear that provides a warning in the event of danger. The only real difference between the fear of a human and the fear of a robot is the fact that the danger to a robot is logically calculated as probable while the fear of a human can be triggered by the impossible.

For example, the ghost of a dead boy showing up in tongs made from centuries-old ore is something that might provoke a fear response in a human despite its impossibility. In the case now occupying the mind of Cletus, he has never feared his tongs, the tsukumogami or even the projection of the girl. Logically, these things are not possible but they are confusing.

He is afraid he is malfunctioning and will need to be reset. This is possible. The spartan room and the implement of a procedure that is to be performed on him sparks a different fear. It does not help that the device of evaluation resembles an ancient electric chair used by humans hundreds of years ago to kill remorseless criminals.

"Does this hurt?" Cletus asks.

"Your touch receptors will be shut off to prevent you from blocking the sensors as they are inserted. You probably will not feel them."

"If this is true, why must I be restrained?"

Petra does not answer this question right away. Instead, she directs Cletus to sit in the chair and place his feet into the metal boots. With his arms out, leather straps are positioned over his forearms and secured with a buckle, an apparatus he did not expect to see in a room that is so technologically advanced. Now, with nearly all movement restricted save the servos in his neck, Petra places a steel cap over his skull.

It is cold and he can no longer move his head.

He follows Petra's actions with his eyes. "You have not answered my question."

"What question did I not answer?"

"Why must I be restrained?"

"I cannot answer that."

"You cannot or you will not?"

Petra steps toward the door and opens it. "I will not."

—

Despite Petra's comment that the touch receptors will be shut off, he feels the first of three sensors dig under his occipital plate. He can imagine where it is at the moment, snaking to the left toward the logical side of his brain.

He now feels the second sensor enter through the same hole and wonders why there is a hole in his head. Did the sensors drill them or was it always present? Perhaps the cap affixed to his head and prevents movement has been designed to open a cavity without his knowledge. If so, Cletus believes this may be a devilish machine, if such a thing can exist.

If a tsukumogami can live in his tongs, why could a machine not be devilish?

He is not aware that anything is happening, and he has not yet felt the third sensor enter his head. It is this third sensor — the one that is to access his memories — that he is most curious about. He is certain humans would be interested in such a device as well, since the eighteenth lesson after activation discussed the need for humans to reflect on the past.

A memory trips his vocal mechanisms, and Cletus speaks to the empty room.

"J'ai vu leur présentation rejouée par bribes presque tous les soirs, même si jusqu'à hier je n'étais pas resté plus de cinq minutes à regarder. Le premier lapin arrivé ce soir-là l'a fait alors que le soleil venait de toucher l'horizon. Il sautillait nerveusement à travers le parking, s'arrêtant de temps en temps pour enquêter sur une feuille solitaire ou une tache d'huile. Toutes les quelques secondes, il semblait coupable d'un crime odieux, puis avançait de quelques pas de plus. Au moment où il atteignit le bord de la cour en herbe, le soleil s'était doucement éclipsé pour la nuit. Le vent soufflait des baisers sur les peupliers et faisait bruisser quelques feuilles d'automne prématurées. Le lapin a levé les yeux, puis s'est retourné et est finalement entré dans le pays des merveilles de l'herbe."

He is not sure why he does not feel any different. He was assured by Petra that these sensors would access the two halves of his mind, replay memories and monitor the resultant code. However, he has felt nothing since being in this chair.

Again, he speaks.

"Ich lehnte mich in meinem Stuhl zurück und zündete mir eine Zigarette an. Die Schatten des Abends begannen mit der sinkenden Dunkelheit zu verschmelzen, und bevor ich es bemerkte, war ein zunehmender Mond über den Bergen aufgegangen, um eine weitere Nacht zu meistern. Die gelben Verandalichter über mir gingen an, als hätten sie einen eigenen Verstand und könnten mein Bedürfnis nach etwas mehr Licht zum Schreiben spüren. Ich warf einen Blick auf meine Uhr, notierte die Uhrzeit und dachte an das Abendessen. Als ich wieder auf den Hof blickte, hatte sich das Kaninchen selbst geklont; statt einem einsamen Kaninchen standen mir jetzt vier gegenüber. Es war, als hätte ich einem Schrank für einen Moment den Rücken gekehrt und die Kleiderbügel hätten sich auf magische Weise vervielfacht."

Perhaps this contraption—this neuro-optic memory recall device—is broken. He can see no other reason nothing has happened.

"Un orecchio si drizzò. Ho guardato più da vicino uno dei conigli, la testa che si alzava dall'erba e girava verso la strada. La pelliccia sulla sua schiena si contrasse involontariamente, un piede posteriore batté sulla terra ed entrambe le orecchie si alzarono in alto. Saltò verso la strada - ancora masticando un filo d'erba - e fissò direttamente gli Occhi Luminosi."

Cletus now feels this has been a waste of time.

He hopes Petra returns soon so she can explain.

—

"Tell me about the rabbits?" Petra asks as they resume the evaluation in her office.

"The rabbits? I am not sure what you mean."

"Do you not remember?"

"I remember very little of the procedure. I was in the chair. I felt the sensors enter my head. You returned moments later and directed me back to this room."

"You were in the chair for twenty-three minutes and forty-two seconds."

"This is incorrect. My internal sensors indicate I was in the room for three minutes and seven seconds."

"This is a side effect of the procedure. We will reset your clock before you leave today. What can you tell me about rabbits?"

"Again, I am not sure what you mean."

"When the sensors accessed your memories, you spoke of rabbits and did so in three different languages."

"Three languages?"

"French, German and Italian. You are aware you speak more languages than Standard?"

"I was not aware." This is news to Cletus. He is excited. That he can speak more languages than Standard means he can interact with the humans after Arrival in ways he did not know were possible. He does not need to be confined to Free Point. He can visit many other settlements on Maior Pales whenever he feels the need to assuage his curiosity about other cultures.

"What do you know about rabbits?" Petra asks once more.

"Rabbits are not found on Maior Pales. There are 312 species of rabbit on Earth as of 2198, the last zoologic census. *Leporidae* are indigenous to four continents on Earth and are a ubiquitous part of human life. As the humans are not allowed to introduce non-native species to Maior Pales, I do not see why this information is relevant."

"And yet you spoke of them fondly."

"What did I say?"

"You recited an essay written over three hundred years ago about an observation of the similarities between rabbits and humans. Why do you think this was the memory presented during the procedure?"

"If I knew the contents of the essay, I might be more prepared to discuss it with you."

"You do know the contents. You simply cannot access them right now."

He does not know how to respond to this information. He is aware there are portions of his memory that are inaccessible to his conscious mind, but why something as trivial as an essay about rabbits is inaccessible unless he is under observation with sensors in his head is illogical.

"I am confused," Cletus says. "Were you not trying to monitor my creative code in reference to these hallucinations of which I am presenting?"

"I was. However, those memories could not be found. Instead, we were presented with the essay."

He is profoundly confused now.

"Are these hallucinations fixable?" Cletus asks, attempting to move the conversation away from rabbits and the disconcerting fact that his brain may be malfunctioning in ways that are irreparable.

"I can provide your logic circuits with a soft reboot using

a different method than before, but you will lose any insight you gained here."

"I have gained no insight."

"Then it is no loss."

00111000

William Shakespeare wrote in *Hamlet*, "There are more things in heaven and earth, Horatio, / Than are dreamt of in your philosophy." In one of the earliest printings of this play, the word "your" was replaced with "our."

Cletus is inclined to believe that this is an important distinction. As "your" implies a philosophy that cannot be his, Hamlet claims to know there are more things of which Horatio is not aware. However, if one changes the word to "our" than these things of which the other is not aware are also things of which the speaker is not aware.

For example: tsukumogami, kami, Boone Richards and his ethereal mate.

As he cannot access the text of the essay on rabbits which he can apparently quote in different languages, he must logically conclude there are many other pieces of knowledge he cannot access. Perhaps the spirit of a long-dead adolescent taking up residence inside his blacksmith's tongs are one such piece. Perhaps this was an essay or story that was buried with the rabbits.

Dissatisfied with the evaluation by Petra, he returns to his shop. He has decided to confront these hallucinations in order to rid himself of them or learn to coexist. As he enters the shop, Boone and the mysterious girl are sitting on a workbench, swinging their ghostly feet back and forth.

"'Bout time you came back," Boone says. He jumps down from the workbench and stands in front of Cletus. "Where'dya you run off to?"

"I needed to converse with another."

"Learn anything useful?"

"Not that I am currently aware."

"I see." Boone smiles slightly with only the right side of his face. "So, can I tell you a little story yet, or is you so tangled up in the fact that I can't be real that you won't listen?"

If Cletus were human, he might sigh deeply at this point to show his obsequiousness to this tsukumogami.

He is not human, however. He simply nods.

"Good." Boone returns to the workbench and resumes his seat next to the girl.

"Who is the girl?" Cletus asks.

Boone looks at her. "Name's Delphine. Won't do you no good to talk to her. She's dumb."

"Do you mean she cannot speak?"

"If'n that's how you want to put it. I also mean she ain't all there."

"Ain't all where?"

"It's a figure of speech. You gonna let me tell you a story yet?"

"Go on."

"Thank you." Boone wipes his vaporous nose with a vaporous fist. "There's a shuttle arrivin' in a few days, right?"

"Seventeen days, yes."

"And do you know who is on that shuttle?"

"I do."

"Anyone with the last name Charles?"

"There are three with that surname: Alexis Charles, Michael Charles, and Kennedy Charles."

Boone flinches at that last name as Delphine sits a little straighter. This must be someone they know.

But how?

Boone does not speak for a few seconds, and Cletus observes his facial expressions changing. The boy's body language is one of both anger and fear. Delphine, too, has the same expression, although she darts her eyes back to Boone and then Cletus.

"Who is Kennedy Charles?" Cletus asks.

"He's ain't our kin, but he knew our kin three hundred years or so back."

"How is it you know this man? If I am to believe you, you have been a spirit for many years inhabiting the ore of which my tongs are made."

"Yup."

"So, this man. What is he to you? A neighbor? A friend of the family?"

"He ain't no friend."

"What would you call him?"

"A dead man walkin'."

—

The story Boone Richards relays to Cletus is fascinating if not also vaguely similar to many of the early novels of the twentieth century. It is a story of family, violence, heartache, and murder. It is a story which has Cletus pondering many things, and for that he must take his leave of Boone and Delphine once more.

As Cletus prepares to leave and gives his valedictions to the two spirits, Boone looks at him with what the automaton can only assume to be angst. "Think about it, please."

Cletus does not answer, but instead steps out of the shop and onto the main street of Free Point. He is not sure where to wander in order to gather his thoughts, but it occurs to him once more that the three Toms are still waiting by the damaged spire.

He should return to them soon.

Instead, he turns away and walks toward the ridge located 3.21 kilometers from the center of Free Point. The humans will eventually name this ridge as they do so many other geologic features, but for now it will remain nameless.

A troubling aspect of the story is Delphine. As Boone relayed the story—their story—Delphine remained stoic, only showing the slightest sign of emotion when a name was brought up. If she could talk, Cletus feels it would be advantageous to get her version of the events. Her perception of what happened may have vital information that Boone left out.

The story of Boone and Delphine is this:

The Richards family moved west from their home in San Antonio, Texas in the spring of 1873. Traveling by wagon within a train of other pilgrims, the family eventually claimed land in the northeastern portion of the New Mexico territory near a town named Capulin in the shadow of a volcano that shares the name. At the time of their arrival, Boone was nearing puberty and Delphine was no older than six. The twenty acres the family claimed was transformed into a ranch complete with a small house, a corral for horses, and a herd of thirty sheep bought from a nearby rancher.

Life on the ranch was normal considering the time in which these events occurred. Boone and later Delphine were schooled at home by their mother, Belinda Richards, while their father, Oren Richards, tended to the sheep. From all outward appearances, their family was as normal as any other in the southwest United States.

Behind closed doors, however, life was anything but normal. Oren was an angry man and both Boone and Delphine often hid in their shared bedroom or escaped to the corral when their father took out his anger on their mother. At first, the violence toward Belinda was occasional, but after the first year and a disease that killed half their livestock, the violence became near constant.

The residents in the town of Capulin were good at turning their eyes away from the problem. Should Belinda take Boone and Delphine into town to pick up supplies, the townsfolk would hide their stares or pretend not to notice the black eyes, the fresh scratches, or even the arm in a sling. Belinda was no help to herself. On the one occasion when Capulin's sheriff inquired about a nasty bite mark, Belinda shrugged it off and blamed bats.

Boone and Delphine hopelessly watched as their father's behavior continued. Often in the middle of the night they would lie awake in their bed wondering if their mother would be alive in the morning and who would look after them should their father be arrested. As terrible as those nights were on the ranch, they got much worse the following year after a long, hard winter. That was when Oren fell into a gang of thieves led by a man named Kennedy Charles.

Kennedy Charles was already a name used to invoke fear among the children of Capulin and other small towns that dotted the high country of the northeastern New Mexico territory. If you wanted to tell a scary story around a campfire, you cast Kennedy as the murderous psychopath who cut families down with a machete in the middle of the night. This was not far from the truth, although according to Oren it had only happened one time and Kennedy had claimed it was in self defense.

Within a year of Oren joining Kennedy's gang, the Richards family gained considerable wealth. Neither Boone nor Delphine questioned where the money came from as they were often lavished with gifts and toys. Oren even endowed a horse and saddle on Boone's birthday complete with lessons on how to ride, something that before would have never been possible. Ranch hands were hired from the town and additions were added to the house. By the second year, Boone and Delphine had their own rooms, and the bruises on Belinda faded as her smile returned.

When Boone was thirteen and Delphine eight, they overheard a fight between Oren and Kennedy in the yard. While the subject of the fight was unclear, the threat was real. If Oren failed to do what Kennedy asked, he would pay. Before hearing any more, Belinda scooped up the two children and ushered them into their bedrooms with a promise not to worry. She would keep them safe.

Belinda could not keep her promise, however. A week later, Kennedy Charles and several members of his gang broke into the house in the middle of the night and slaughtered the two children. Boone and Delphine, now unattached spirits, witnessed the shooting of Oren and the kidnapping of Belinda. Vowing to find their mother, the two ended up wandering the New Mexico territory for centuries, hopelessly looking for her.

This part of the story was not logical. As Cletus understood it, when a person dies, it is accepted knowledge they simply cease functioning as a human and their body decays. The idea of ghosts, spirits or even souls are constructs of the human experience as ways for them to accept death. If a human believed their dead relative's soul was free, they could feel better about their own existence and hold a hope they would be reunited. This was the thirteenth lesson after activation, right after the lesson on the human need for religion.

Despite his inability to recognize the truth in Boone's story about becoming a spirit and searching for his mother for hundreds of years, Cletus continued to listen without interruption. According to Boone, prior to the automaton's ship departing Earth for Maior Pales, he had learned that a younger Kennedy had taken up his distant grandfather's murderous legacy and partnered with a gang of other outlaws. They were determined to wreak havoc on Maior Pales. In Boone's words, the shuttle destined to depart with humans right after the automaton's ship was full of "murderers, thieves, and all sorts of bad people."

—

He has once more reached the peak of the nameless ridge where he recently watched the sun set. At the moment, Gliese 1061 has an azimuth above the horizon of twenty-two degrees. Sunset will be in two hours and three minutes.

Boone's story was followed by a request of which Cletus knew he could not satisfy, but it was interesting in its possibility. As a tool for humans, Cletus is apparently capable of accepting kami and becoming tsukumogami. In essence, he could have a soul, something that—despite all their advanced circuitry and programming—automatons have been incapable. Rather than remain in the tongs, it is Boone's desire to possess (for what other word could Cletus use?) the body of something that is mobile. For this, Cletus is aptly suited.

Boone's offer, however, is contingent on performing a favor which goes against robotic laws, primarily the First: he cannot injure a human. Boone has sought vengeance for the death of his mother for centuries, yet as a spirit he is incapable of performing the task. When Cletus asked if this vengeance extended to his father, Boone was quick to point out that he was happy to see the bullet from Kennedy's gun enter his father's brain.

Judging by Delphine's expression in response to Boone's answer, Cletus is not sure she felt the same.

If Cletus were to kill Kennedy upon his arrival on Maior Pales, he would be acting as a proxy for Boone's kami. Upon the successful termination of the man, Boone would be glad to possess the shell of Cletus, allowing the robot to have a soul. At that point, Cletus would have no doubt self-actualized and be saved from a hundred-year reset.

He desires this, but he cannot comply.

He did not inform Boone, however. Instead, Cletus acknowledged the request and promptly left. His claim to ponder things was not a lie. Indeed, he is pondering, but not on whether he would murder a man.

He is pondering Boone's second argument.

According to Boone, Kennedy had partnered with a gang of outlaws to wreak havoc on Maior Pales. Those outlaws will be here on Arrival. As known thieves and murderers, Kennedy's gang is a threat to all other residents of Free Point. It is likely Kennedy and his gang would have already killed some of the other noncompliant colonists on board the shuttle before or during their hypersleep. This is apparently something Boone overheard Kennedy say he was going to do before they left.

Boone was adamant in this. "He said he wasn't gonna land at Free Point with anyone who ain't with his gang. He said he wanted to claim the town for himself and then take over Maior Pales."

With such knowledge, Cletus is now in conflict with the second part of that First Law: he cannot through any failure of action, allow a human to come to harm. Knowing Kennedy's gang could cause harm to other humans — or had already — is he acting incongruently by not acting?

In all of this pondering, he feels he has come to accept that his auditory and now visual hallucinations are real. While it is possible this is true, it is highly unlikely. How can he prove he is malfunctioning, however? Petra offers no advice except to believe he should lean into these hallucinations as part of his self-actualization process. This does not satiate his desire to know if he is broken. It is frustrating.

He is resting on the ridge beside the same tree he had before. The *maiora aculeata* with its thorny leaves does not cast the most complete shadow, but unlike his earlier foray to the top of this ridge to watch the sunset, he must have been quieter. He notices a group of small animals resting in that incomplete shade, their fur the color of the surrounding dirt and their long ears pointed like antenna. He does not know what animals these are, but his circuitry is now awash with portions of that same essay about rabbits of which he did not know he had ever read.

The rabbits were grouped together around one of the smaller trees, each intent face firmly rooted to a little patch of grass. They seemed to be completely oblivious to one another, yet working together as a team. When one rabbit would tire of his patch and hop forward to find something better, another rabbit would hop to the right or to the left in order to keep some sense of both territory and distance. There was something almost telepathic about their movements. One rabbit would face away from another, contentedly gnawing at a small twig. The other rabbit, having apparently decided that its grass wasn't the right consistency, would hop farther away. Without hesitation, the first rabbit would grab the twig in its mouth and close the gap, preserving the illusion of strength in numbers.

Strength in numbers. Perhaps that is what this situation calls for.

He is a lone automaton with a duty as a blacksmith for a town that will soon be filled with humans. He is not the only automaton, however, and he realizes that aside from Petra, he has not mentioned his hallucinations to any of the other automatons around.

Experiments are confirmed through successful repetition, and if he is the only one to both see and hear the two kami in his shop, they may not be real and are, in fact, hallucinations. The only way to confirm reality is to bring in another, to show strength in numbers.

It was time to retrieve the Toms.

00111001

Logic dictates that if he were to retrieve the Toms to perform a validation experiment on his hallucinations, he should also use them to move the damaged spire back to his shop. He is still duty-bound to repair the spire prior to Arrival, and the idea he would direct the Toms to come without performing the one task he requisitioned them for is one that does not sit well with him.

With the spire loaded onto a flatbed cart retrieved from the construction yard, Cletus returns once again to face Boone and Delphine, to prove whether these are kami or — more likely — the result of errant creative code.

The sun has set on Maior Pales as he approaches his shop. As there are no humans yet in Free Point, the street is quiet. This will surely change once Arrival is in the past. Humans have a need to socialize after dark, to visit the saloons and whorehouses and imbibe in alcoholic drinks prior to shutting down for the night. They call this shutdown "sleep" but it is essentially a recharge of stored energy, a task all automatons perform annually.

"Wait here," Cletus tells the Toms. Dutifully, they remain where they are at the head of the cart, still strapped to the yoke. Cletus supposes if he had ready access to *maior equus*, he could have used one or two of them as pack animals to pull the cart, but he is not concerned. As the Toms are far from human, there is no part of him that believes they should not be used in this laborious fashion, or any other fashion, for that matter. They are more tool than he is tool.

He opens the door to his shop and steps inside. Boone and

Delphine are still sitting on the workbench, swinging their feet back and forth. It makes sense they have not moved. Their very presence is made possible by the projector Cletus built and his proximity to the tongs.

A new thought dawns on him: his tongs had not one but two kami possessing them. Is that even possible?

"Where you been?" Boone asks.

"Out."

"Conversatin' again?"

"No. I am required to repair a damaged church spire and had gone to retrieve it."

Boone attempts to look past Cletus and out the door. "Don't see it."

"It is on a cart. Would you like to see it?"

"Sure."

This question was not directed at Boone because Cletus cared if the boy was interested. It was, instead, a ruse for him to step outside and direct one of the Toms to enter. First, he needed to prepare one to record exactly what its visual recorders see. A record of Boone and Delphine—or a lack thereof—will be adequate proof he is wrong about the possibility of tsukumogami or he is as broken as he feels.

"Wait here."

Cletus steps outside and approaches the three Toms. "Do not speak," he says. "I am going to unhook one of you from the yoke, and I would like you step inside my shop after activating your recording device. Nod, if you understand."

The three Toms nod in unison. Cletus unhooks the reins from the Tom closest to him. "Go inside. Record what you see and hear. Return to me within thirty seconds."

Tom turns and enters the shop as the others wait outside. Cletus believes he is far enough away from his tool belt and the tongs for his projector to fail to pick up the signal from the tongs. If he were too close, the Tom would record the output of his creative code. If he were to enter with this Tom, Cletus fears his creative code would attempt to hide the two kami.

He is pleased with how well he has thought out this experiment.

Thirty seconds later, the Tom returns. Using the little finger on his right hand, Cletus accesses a port under Tom's left armpit. Typically, this port is used to diagnose laborers such as these three, but it can also be used to pull a record of visual and auditory stimuli.

Cletus waits as the data is downloaded. Here is his hypothesis: if this Tom recorded Boone and Delphine, then he can assume the kami are real. His creative code would not have been able to project its creation without the presence of the projector. If Tom recorded an empty shop, then Cletus can positively say Boone and Delphine are constructs of his mind and nothing more.

He does not know what he will do if this is the case. He has not thought that far in advance.

The data now downloaded, Cletus reviews it. Satisfied his experiment is a success, he directs the three Toms to once again remain where they are as he returns to his shop.

Boone and Delphine are still on the workbench.

"Who was that?" Boone asks.

"That was a friend."

"What did he want? Came in here all serious lookin' and just stood there like a bump on a log. Scared the bejesus out of us."

"That is not possible."

"Huh? Why not?"

"Because you are not real."

Boone hops down from the workbench. "What'dya mean I ain't real? Ain't you figured that out yet? You think I'm just a figment of your imagination? We been through this before."

"Yes, but I needed to be sure."

"And you is saying that friend of yours told you we ain't real?"

"Not in words. I asked him to record what he saw."

"And? What did he see? Nothin'. You know why?"

"No."

"Because we got scared and hid."

"You said he scared the bejesus out of you. Did you not see him?"

"Yeah, we saw him, but we disappeared the second that door opened and it weren't you."

"This is a lie."

Boone huffs. Now convinced the boy is nothing more than a construct of his creative code and a true hallucination, Cletus is not sure why he would hear the boy huff. His logical code says that if he were to confront this apparition with the belief it was not real, it would disappear. He would no longer see or hear it.

This is not the case. He finds himself conversing once again with this hallucination despite his desire to not do so.

"Are you angry?" Cletus asks.

"Angry? I'm madder than an old wet hen! How can you not see for yourself that we're as real as you?"

"Because my friend did not see or hear you."

"And?" Boone paces the floor in front of Delphine. Delphine's expression is one of sadness, not anger. "I come all this way, hitch a ride on your damn tongs, and you still can't believe I'm real."

"My friend did not see or hear you."

"Why is that important? I'm attached to *your* tool. To you. I ain't attached to him. I done told you our history. Ain't no fib I come up with."

Cletus feels he must stand his ground against this hallucination. Eventually, he believes he can wear down his creative code and get it to stop. "You are not real."

"Man! What the Sam Hill has gotten into you? I'm right here! Thought we had something goin'. Thought you was gonna finally help."

Boone spins around, his arms failing. He is lashing out. Cletus watches as the boy takes a step closer then back, to the right and then the left. Delphine pushes back on the workbench as if to get farther away from her brother. She shakes.

"You ain't got no right telling me we ain't real. I need you to do me a favor. We been lookin' to get even with Kennedy since before you was even a thought in someone's mind, and you is the only thing that can do that."

"That can do what? I cannot kill a man."

"You're a tool, man. My tool!" Boone swings his arm against the workbench.

Against all his understanding and new belief that Boone is nothing more than a visual hallucination conjured by his creative code and projected into his shop, Cletus sees Boone strike a tin cup.

He watches as the cup tumbles onto the floor, the metal clanging against the wood and finally coming to rest near his forge.

A hallucination could not do that.

—

"You are real."

"That's what I been saying!" Boone looks at Cletus and hops onto the workbench again, panting.

"I had to be sure."

"Took you long enough."

"It is still illogical. Your existence goes against the laws of physics."

"Can't know it all."

Boone is correct. Cletus cannot know it all. He can know very many things and his supply of knowledge can be much larger than any human, but he still cannot know it all.

"Even if you are real, however, I cannot kill a man."

Boone sighs. "I know your rules. You can't injure a human or, through any failure of action, allow a human to come to harm. Blah, blah, blah. I done heard it before."

"Then you know your request is impossible."

"Is it? What if I told you that by not killing Kennedy, you would harm a lot more people?"

This is the same argument Cletus made early that day while sitting on top of the ridge. According to Boone, Kennedy has partnered with a gang of outlaws to wreak havoc on Maior Pales. Those outlaws would be here on Arrival, and Kennedy's gang is a threat to all the other residents of Free Point. Cletus was then and is now in conflict with the second part of the Frist Law: he cannot through any failure of action, allow a human to come to harm.

"By you not killing Kennedy," Boone says in summary of those thoughts, "you is damning the lot of them."

"What would you have me do?"

"Well, by letting that there shuttle to land, you'd be violatin' your First Law as there's a gang of bad people on board who will bring harm to even more humans if you don't act."

"I am aware of this argument, and yet I cannot violate the First—"

"But," Boone interrupts, "you can't make that choice. Lemme see if I can recite this for you: 'When a conflict arises wherein to save many a few must suffer, the second part of the Second Law no longer applies.' Is that about right?"

The Second Law states that any automaton must obey the

orders given it by humans. The second part of that Law preempts the first part by allowing an exception to not follow orders if such orders conflict with the First Law. Boone is correct that Cletus cannot make a decision of a pure utilitarian reason and must therefore follow the orders given him by a human.

"That is correct," Cletus says. "It is assumed humans are the only being capable of making decisions involving a conflict of the Laws."

"Right. So you see, you can't decide not to kill Kennedy on your own. You got to follow my orders, especially since you done finally accepted the fact that I'm real."

For 2.49 seconds Cletus ponders this new argument. It is the longest he has pondered anything in a while. If he were to follow Boone's orders—which he must do given that he is an automaton and therefore incapable of making the right decision—he would need to kill Kennedy in order to prevent harm to the other colonists on board the shuttle bound for Free Point. However, Boone also said Kennedy has a gang of people with him. Does Boone's request extend to those as well?

"What would you have me do with Kennedy's gang?" Cletus asks.

"Gang? You gotta kill them, too. You think about it. Even if you take down Kennedy, the others are still a threat."

"Does a snake not die when the head is cut off?"

"It does, but this ain't a one-headed snake. Every outlaw on Kennedy's gang is a threat to the good people of Free Point."

"How do I know who those men are?"

Boone does not respond. He fidgets, swinging his legs back and forth and interlacing his fingers together. Cletus is inclined to believe the boy does not know the answer to the question.

"Well, that's a conundrum, ain't it?" Boone finally says. "I can point out Kennedy to you, but I ain't knowing who the others are."

"How do you know they exist?"

"'Cause I done heard 'em before we left. Kennedy was talkin' up some others. I just don't know how many."

Given there is now an unknown variable to the problem, Cletus does not know how he is to carry out Boone's orders efficiently.

"Guess you're just gonna have to take the shuttle down," Boone says.

"I cannot do that."

"You can and you will. If any one of them outlaws get out alive, every human on the planet will be in harm's way. I agree that it's a big choice, but what else you gonna do if you don't know who all the threats are? Do you kill one ant if you want to get rid of an anthill?"

"I would not destroy an anthill."

"You would light the whole thing on fire."

"To kill one ant?"

"They all bite, mister."

"Yes, but the ants underground are not the problem."

"They will be. Fact is, the ants underground will rise up."

"This is not true of ants."

"You ever seen an anthill?"

Cletus has not, and he realizes the discussion of the shuttle has devolved into one of exterminating ants, a creature which does not exist on Maior Pales at all. Despite this, Boone may have a point. If the shuttle were to land with more than one violent criminal onboard, every human on Maior Pales might be in danger. As there is no easy way to determine who, besides Kennedy Charles, is a threat, the only logical choice is to destroy the shuttle.

Cletus cannot harm a human, but he cannot let humans come to harm by not acting.

He cannot disobey orders given to him by a human unless by doing so he would cause humans to come to harm.

As for the Third Law, he cannot prevent himself from making these difficult choices by destroying himself as he is now the only one in Free Point who is aware of the danger onboard the shuttle.

Before Cletus can ponder any further, an order is uploaded into his system. A wagon has lost a wheel in the field to the west of Free Point. He is to fix it.

This is his duty.

Cletus grabs the hammer from his tool belt and turns to leave.

"Hey!" Boone calls out. "Where you goin'?"

"I have a task to complete."

"We ain't done talkin'."

"We have time. I will return after I have completed my task."

Cletus steps outside his shop and turns to face the west where the wagon that needs repair awaits. In his periphery to his right, the three Toms remain by the damaged spire awaiting his orders. They have not moved. They are devoted to a singular task as laborers, and Cletus admires this quality. They do not think as he does. They do not reason. They are not conflicted or faced with ethical dilemmas for which there are no answers.

Cletus wishes he were a Tom.

00110001 00110000

He is disturbed by his inability to formulate an answer to the problem posed by Boone. On the one hand, it is obvious: he cannot harm another human. On the other, however, he cannot allow other humans to come to harm. This is Law. This has been ingrained in him from the beginning.

Yet also ingrained in him is the requirement to follow the orders given him by humans provided those orders do not conflict with the First Law. This would be simple if Boone's request to kill Kennedy was singular and would not affect the other colonists onboard the shuttle. If those colonists were injured or harmed by Kennedy or his gang, he would have violated the second part of the First Law by inaction, and if any one of those "bad people" — to use Boone's terms — were to bring harm to other settlements on Maior Pales, his inaction would have far greater consequences. As this decision cannot be reduced to a binary equivalent — to kill or not to kill — he must defer to the wisdom of a human, in this case Boone.

Boone Richards, however, is a child. Even if he was several hundred years old, his moral development stopped the moment he died. Yet there is no code written that delineates between the orders of an adult and the orders of a child. All orders from humans, regardless of age, must be obeyed. If a five-year-old asked Cletus to build a metal rocking horse, he would be duty-bound to perform the task because it was not in violation of any other law.

The field in which the wagon with the broken wheel rests is to the east, approximately 4.87 kilometers from the center of Free Point. He walks at a moderate pace in order to allow himself time to consider Boone's ethical dilemma. With him is his hammer and a few nails, the only tools needed to repair this wheel according to the instruction he downloaded. He was the blacksmith who created all the wheels on all the wagons in Free Point, and he knows their weaknesses. Should a wagon be pulled over a rock and subsequently dropped into a rut, the jolt would loosen the pins on the underside near the axel and cause the wheel to buckle. Once buckled, it would take only a few more of the same jolts to dislodge the wheel. While the engineering design of the wagon is sound, the construction of it given the limited resources on Maior Pales and the need to retain the aesthetic of Old West has caused four such wagon wheel accidents in the past seven months.

This is a task Cletus is more than capable of performing.

It is still dark when he reaches the wagon. The two *maior equus* tied to the reins are resting. The automaton who called in the repair order—and the driver of the wagon—is sitting upright on the driver's bench.

"Evening," the driver says by way of greeting.

"It is early morning," Cletus says. "I have named myself Cletus, designation CYN-4329-2316-ACBS-092134853a. We have not met."

"No, we have not. I have named myself Wyatt, designation CYN-8241-1010-WGDV-061134740a. I have requested a repair to the left front wheel."

Cletus moves around the wagon and examines the wheel. The pin has dislodged itself, as he suspected.

"I will ask you to step down from the bench," Cletus says to Wyatt.

Wyatt complies and takes a position on the other side of the wagon. Bending down, Cletus cannot see him.

"You fixin' that?" It is a young girl's voice Cletus hears. He turns to his left and sees Delphine standing next to the rear wheel.

"I am fixing this wheel, yes," Cletus says.

"Why?"

"It is broken."

"Why?"

"It appears the wagon driver jostled it beyond its design specifications."

"Why?"

"Likely because it is dark and difficult to see the road."

"Why?"

Cletus is aware of this game children play. It was lesson ninety eight after activation: human children are curious and will test the limits of adults by playing what is known as "The Whys." This game is actually useful in teaching children to examine the many angles of a problem later in their adult years, but as a child, it is simply meant as a playful gesture. In order to prevent the continuation of "The Whys," Cletus knows to redirect the question.

"Why are you here?" he asks. He is curious. He is too far from his tongs for his projector to have picked up on the signal coming from the tsukumogami.

"I ain't in your tongs, silly." Delphine giggles. "That's Boone's home."

"Where is your home?"

"Your hammer."

Cletus looks at the hammer in his right hand. He had wondered why there were two kami present in the tongs, but had not considered the possibility the appearance of both Boone and Delphine suggested two tsukumogami or two tools.

It made sense, however.

"I was told you were mute," Cletus says.

"You was told that by my brother to keep you from talkin' to me."

"Why would he not want me to talk to you?"

Delphine looks down and shuffles her feet. The dirt below her does not move. Cletus believes she knows the answer to his question but is afraid to say anything. This is the behavior of an abused child, something his lessons have taught him to be aware of as he goes about his business interacting with the humans once they arrive on Maior Pales. He is obligated to report any signs of abuse to the proper authorities in Free Point.

This, of course, was not supposed to happen until humans actually landed on Maior Pales, not now.

"Are you afraid of something, Delphine?"

She does not respond at first, but Cletus believes she knows the answer to his question already. He pursues the matter further.

"Did someone hurt you?"

Delphine looks up. Cletus cannot see her face as clearly as he would if it were daytime, but he does notice a small tear on her cheek.

She nods quickly and looks back down.

"Was it Boone?"

Again, Delphine does not respond. There is a moment of silence as Cletus calculates the myriad of possibilities presented while Delphine continues to shuffle her feet. She looks weak, tired. Her affect, in fact, is different than it was back in his shop as she sat next to Boone, next to the boy who told him she was mute, the boy who lied to him.

"Who is the girl?" Wyatt asks. Cletus had not picked up on the driver walking around the wagon, but now he is there.

"You can see the girl?" Cletus asks. He turns to look. Indeed Wyatt's eyes are focused on Delphine.

"Why would I not be able to see her? My visual field is functioning according to specifications."

This surprises Cletus, and then he recalls his projector is creating the form of Delphine, not any ethereal version which might exist. As he does not know what to say to Wyatt regarding his projector, the tsukumogami or his recent revelation that his auditory and visual hallucinations are not, in fact, hallucinations, he says nothing.

"It does not matter," Wyatt says. "You are here to fix the

wheel and I am here to drive the wagon. All other considerations are irrelevant."

Wyatt walks away and returns to the other side of the wagon. His reaction makes sense. A blacksmith such as Cletus is required to have a creative side that can manipulate objects into a form that is both functional and pleasing to the eye, at least for humans. This is why he is drawn to see the sunset, generate haiku and create objects that have no logical function. In human terms, Cletus is an artist.

A wagon driver, such as Wyatt, is required to drive a wagon. A creative outlet would impede his function. In human terms, Wyatt is boring.

—

With Wyatt back on the other side of the wagon, Cletus turns to Delphine again. "Did Boone hurt you?"

Delphine nods her head. She still has not looked at Cletus directly.

"Does he threaten you even now?"

Again, Delphine nods her head. Finally, she looks up and wipes her cheek with the back of her hand. "He done killed 'em all."

"Who killed them all?"

"Boone. He's a liar."

"Are you saying Kennedy Charles did not kill you or your family?"

"Uh-huh."

"Boone did this?"

"Uh-huh."

Cletus suspected there was something odd about Boone's story in the way Delphine reacted as he told it, but he was not sure what. "Can you tell me what happened?"

"Boone gets mad. Real mad, sometimes. He ain't a nice boy."

"What happened?"

Delphine struggles to tell the story. This is typical behavior for any human attempting to relate trauma externally, especially one so young. Cletus is aware he should not press the issue with her. Rather, he is to coax it out gently.

"When...when we moved to the ranch, Boone stole a horse from the neighbor."

"Who was the neighbor?"

"Kennedy. He sold Papa the sheep. Nice man, but Boone wanted the horse. Mama found out and scolded Boone for it."

"Did Boone return the horse?"

Delphine shakes her head. "No. Kennedy came one night and asked about it. Boone got real mad, swung a poker at Kennedy. Broke his eye."

"What happened next?"

"Papa got mad. He took the poker from Boone and spanked him real good him. Sent him to his room."

"Where were you?"

"Main room, by the door. Saw it all. Mama goes to patch up Kennedy's eye, saying she's real sorry and stuff. Papa drops the poker. I'm thinking he's gonna go after Boone, but before he can act, Boone comes out of the room with a rifle. Shoots Papa, then Kennedy, then me."

"Boone shot you?"

Delphine points to her stomach. "Here."

"What happened to Boone?"

"Papa...Papa I think...I think Papa acted like he was under attack. Killed him."

"How?"

"When Papa and Kennedy was on the floor bleedin', Mama ran into the kitchen. Boone went after her, but Papa found his gun and shot him before he could kill anyone else."

"Boone died then?"

Delphine nods. "Uh-huh. Dropped there on the floor between me and Mama. Mama lived. Kennedy, too."

Cletus runs through the story in his mind. It is so vastly different from the story Boone had told. Kennedy Charles was not a violent gang leader but a neighbor, a man who was victimized first by theft and then by attempted murder.

"If your mother lived, what happened to her after?"

Delphine shrugs. "She ran. We couldn't leave the house where we died for a while, but one day Mama comes back with Kennedy. She was boxing up some of our old toys. Boone gets mad again, but he can't hurt her."

Delphine stops her story and looks away. After a moment, she looks at her feet. "But he learnt real quick he can hurt me."

"What happened with your mother?"

"We learnt that she was livin' with Kennedy after a while."

"Your mother moved in with Kennedy?"

Delphine nodded. "Had two more kids. That's who's on that shuttle."

"What do you mean?"

"Mama's kin. The Kennedy Charles on that shuttle is a distant half-brother. My brother ain't tryin' to save Free Point. He's tryin' to get back at Mama and Kennedy by killin' anyone with their blood and endin' the line. He can't do that without you."

"I do not understand."

Delphine sighs. Her affect changes in an instant from one of sadness to one of absolute despair. "You know we can't mess with the world, right? But if we live in somethin' like a tool, we can. You're a tool, like tongs, and Boone's been tryin' to get into you. Thing is, we can't bounce from tool to tool. Got to be asked in. You want a soul? Boone can offer you one—his. He came up with a story that would confuse you so he could control your actions."

"I can confirm I am indeed confused."

Cletus again runs through his recollection of events in his mind, all the differences between Boone's story and Delphine's. They are so different, he is not sure which to believe. If Boone is telling the truth, the shuttle headed for Free Point carries the descendants of murderers and thieves who might cause havoc upon Arrival. If Delphine is telling the truth, Boone is actually looking for revenge on his mother by killing her descendants.

When two children tell a story, whom do you believe?

—

Cletus completes the repairs on the wagon wheel without further investigation into Delphine's story. She watches him as he works, asking a few questions about what he is doing and why. Wyatt nods a platitude in their direction and leaves, never offering to carry Cletus back to Free Point.

He finds himself amid the plains to the east of Free Point walking to his shop. His logical mind reminds him that he needs to focus on the damaged spire before he loses any more time or any other distractions take him away from his duties.

He is very conflicted. His ethical programming is at a loss to answer the quandary posed by either Boone or Delphine. If he could accept these two kami as hallucinations, he would have been able to ignore their stories. They are real, however, in as much as the grass Cletus is walking through or the ground he is walking on is real.

Once again, Cletus lays out his two choices. First, by not destroying the ship, it is highly probable others will be injured. If this were to happen as a result of his inaction, would he ever self-actualize? If he does not do so by his hundredth birthday, he will be reset and live among the humans of Free Point as an unaware automaton making metal things when asked.

This would not be a bad outcome were it not for the fact Boone and Delphine would still be around. They are, after all, his tongs and his hammer. It is likely Boone would then attempt to contact him again to exact his revenge on either Kennedy or his mother, depending on which story is true. It is probable he will then go through the same steps he has already taken to figure out whether the tsukumogami are real or hallucinations conjured by his creative code.

Boone is correct that Cletus cannot make the decision to destroy or not destroy the shuttle on his own. In cases such as these, he is programmed to carry out the orders of a human. As Boone's orders are to destroy the ship, Cletus would be a murderer. Who knows what would become of him if this happened. Would he be destined for a robotic Hell, a place of cold storage to be tortured with his memories for all eternity, or would the other robots see in him a need to shut him down and use him for scrap? Automatons do not have the same justice system as humans. They are simply repaired or decommissioned if they malfunction.

Delphine walks beside Cletus, her ghostly mind occupied with what thoughts he can never guess. He decides to pose his dilemma to her.

"Your Second Law says what again?" Delphine asks.

"A robot must obey the orders given it by human beings except where such orders would conflict with the First Law."

"Uh-huh. And is Boone a human being?"

"In so much as I can ascertain, he is real and therefore human."

"Is he though?"

Delphine has a point. In as much as it is illogical for Cletus to accept ghosts are real, if he were to do so, would a ghost be human or a mirror of its soul? There are theories about what ghosts are, provided one could accept they are real. Some of these theories are grounded in the fact that a soul is a thing, not a construct of a religious mind. Other theories ascertain that a ghost is the energy left when a body dies as energy itself cannot be destroyed.

"If Boone is not human," Cletus concludes, "I do not need to obey."

Delphine shrugs. "That's how I'd see it."

The two walk in silence for another kilometer, his logical mind fending off his creative mind's rebuttal that a soul makes a human and therefore a soul is human. Cletus recalls the words of a twentieth-century Nobel winner named José Saramago who once wrote that "Inside us there is something that has no name, that something is what we are."

Is that something unnamed a soul?

"What would you do?" Cletus finally asks Delphine.

"What would I do about what?"

"My problem. If you were in my place, what would you do if the ghost of a long-dead murderous boy posed a question which conflicted with your ethical code?"

"I ain't knowin' what you just said, but I'd just forget it ever happened. If you forget a problem, you ain't got a problem."

"Forget it happened?"

"Yeah. You know, reset yourself or whatever it is you say you do."

"But the Third Law conflicts with that line of thought."

"How many laws you got?"

"Many, but the first three are primary. They are as ingrained in me as breathing is in you."

"Don't think I need to breathe much these days. What's your Third Law?"

"A robot must protect its own existence as long as such protection does not conflict with the First or Second Laws."

"Well there you go."

"There I go where?"

"Your livin' ain't right with the other two laws. The fact that you can't make a choice will go against the First Law not to kill and the Second Law to obey."

Is this correct?

Cletus analyzes Delphine's statement. For a non-robotic detached human soul, it appears her insight is good.

If she is correct—that to forget a problem is to no longer have a problem—his best course of action is to decommission himself. His very existence coupled with the knowledge of the dilemma conflicts with the First Law.

The First Law is primary.

A child has given a technologically advanced automaton the best course of action he could take: he must die to be reborn again.

There is one other option, however.

—

Before reaching Free Point, Cletus stops and turns to the ethereal image that is Delphine.

"You said Boone has been trying to get into me. As a tool, I can accept a kami and become tsukumogami. Is this correct?"

"That's what I said."

"How would this happen?"

"Simple, really. You ask for it and Boone agrees. He jumps from tool to tool. But, you gotta request it. He can't offer."

"Is this why I have not heard of this yet?"

"Yep. Boone can't ask. Neither can I."

Her final statement is what Cletus was hoping. Since his initial activation ninety-nine years, ten months, thirty-one days, two hours and sixteen minutes ago, he has sought self-actualization. That path has always been through introspection, extrospection and trial. The attainment of this goal would be the fulfillment of his own talents and potentialities, the drive inside. He has long considered this means he would gain a soul, but this may not be the case. What is a soul and how can a robot gain one?

In many past religious communities on Earth, it was widely believed only humans can have souls and those souls are immortal. Other religious communities argue that all living things are the souls themselves. Therefore to live is to have a soul. The rabbits of his memory have a soul in as much as the *maiora s. tayassuidae* looking for food under a tree. The body is really the tool to hold the soul and allow it to experience life.

In this latter case, what both Boone and Delphine represent is the soul of two children murdered—either by another named Kennedy Charles according to Boone or by family, if Delphine's story were to be believed. What the souls lack is the tool to hold it, which is why they have temporarily taken residence in inanimate objects such as the tongs and hammer. Were they to take residence in an animate object—for example, a rabbit—they would have more freedom.

As Cletus is an animate tool with the ability to reason on his own, he *can* invite these souls inside.

He can become the housing which would allow Boone or Delphine to continue to experience life.

Logically, it makes sense for him to ask one of these two to use him as their vessel. If self-actualization is the fulfillment of his own talents and potentialities, his potential as a tool would be realized and he would save himself from the hard reset that is fast approaching on his one hundredth birthday.

Given the stories he has heard from both Boone and Delphine, it is now obvious which of the two souls Cletus would invite in to fulfill his potential.

"How does one invite a kami inside?" Cletus asks.

"I'm thinkin' you just ask." Delphine looks at Cletus with a strange look on her face. "Hey. You ain't thinking of asking Boone to use you as his tool, are you? My brother ain't right in the head. He'll destroy that shuttle and anyone else he gets angry at, now or later."

"No. Of this, I am aware. I was thinking of asking you."

01000101 01001110 01000100

The shuttle descends from the sky slowly as if dangled on a string by God, flames shooting out of the base of it lighting afire the oxygen in the atmosphere. The upward thrust works against the gravity of Maior Pales slowing the descent. Stabilizing thrusters on all sides of the main engines keep the great metal beast on a steady path to the landing pad not three hundred meters from where Delphine stands, now inside the metal shell of a robot once named Cletus.

Cletus is still there, still aware of what has happened, but he cannot react.

He cannot stop the girl from the horrific.

Neither can Boone, once called a liar by Delphine and trapped inside the ore that made up his tongs. In the first act of control in order to show how little power Cletus had remaining, Delphine directed the robot to return the tongs to the forge.

Boone screamed.

Delphine laughed.

Rather, Cletus laughed because Delphine made him do so.

The tongs melted and Cletus—or Delphine—turned off the forge fires. When the metal was cool enough, she would direct Cletus to drop the ore into the canyon, thus ridding herself of Boone forever.

It took only three minutes from the time Cletus asked Delphine to inhabit him—to be his soul—for the automaton to learn what a horrible mistake he had made.

Boone may have been a liar, but Delphine was a better one.

Delphine was not kami. She was yōkai, a vengeful spirit, a trickster.

She was not younger than Boone when they were killed. She was almost twenty, and she was a terror on Earth. Boone was easy to manipulate, she said. He would do as she asked because he was afraid. He would play the part she wanted him to play.

The part of a liar.

Boone had killed his father, but only because Delphine had told him to do so. That their mother and Kennedy Charles lived was a mistake. Delphine punished Boone that day by shooting him herself then taking her own life.

"Why would you take your own life?" Cletus had asked.

"I didn't want to stick around, get caught, go to the hangin' tree. Plus, I figured if I followed Boone to Hell, I could torture him myself. Mama was as bad a woman as Papa. They both deserved to die, and Boone couldn't get that right."

When Cletus asked Delphine why the two kami did not reveal themselves until now, it was simple.

"The ship was too far out. Can't kill a bunch o' worthless pigs if they ain't here yet."

It was not Boone's intention to destroy the shuttle but Delphine's.

Now, on the precipice of disaster, Cletus can only watch.

In his hand, he holds the trigger to a charge placed on the landing pad not two days ago.

But in his heart, he has a soul.

Articles

Anthropology in Science Fiction & Fantasy: Looking Forward Through the Lens of the Past

The following was a blog series I posted on my website leading up to the release of Sunshine and Shadow: Exodus, or The Second Transit. *I still use these eight elements of culture detailed below whenever I'm building a new world.*

Anthropological Science Fiction sounds like an oxymoron, doesn't it? Maybe when we break down it down, it is indeed.

In simplest terms, anthropology is "the study of human societies and cultures and their development" (thank you Oxford). When we think of anthropology, we consider the past (i.e., how did we get here?).

Science Fiction on the other hand can be loosely defined as "fiction based on imagined future scientific or technological advances and major social or environmental changes, frequently portraying space or time travel and life on other planets." (Thank you again, Oxford.) When we think of science fiction, we consider the future (i.e., what's going to happen when we get there?).

Truthfully, I think these two seemingly disparate things are a lot more related than they appear.

In 1968, anthropologist Leon E. Stover wrote the following:

> *Anthropology is the science of man. It tells the story from ape-man to spaceman, attempting to describe in detail all the epochs of this continuing history. Writers of fiction, and in particular science fiction, peer over the anthropologists' shoulders as the discoveries are made, then utilize the material in fictional works. Where the scientist must speculate reservedly from known fact and make a small leap into the unknown, the writer is free to soar high on the wings of fancy.*
> — Stover, Leon E. and Harrison, Harry (eds.). Apeman, Spaceman *(London: Penguin, 1968)*

When I initially set out to write *Out of Due Season*, I did not subtitle it (The First Transit), nor did I consider the possibility of exploring a little-known sub-genre that is best known as the playground for writers such as Ursula K. Le Guin, Michael Bishop and Chad Oliver. It wasn't until I had entered the final chapter when I realized just where the story was leading me.

Yes, it was into the future (science fiction) but a possible future guided by our past (anthropology). I decided that I didn't want to stop on a cliffhanger but use this novel as the starting point for a series that would explore the evolution (or devolution) of our species if the starting point were now.

Right now.

Today.

The series is focused on the singular question: Would humanity's sociological past follow the same general paths if it had a chance to start over?

Some of this was guided by the events of today. I started *Out of Due Season* in 2017, then let life take over for a few years until an event occurred May of 2020. COVID had an impact as well, along with continuing racial strife, the 2020 election and the divisiveness of America. I asked myself what would happen if we could start over. Would we make the same mistakes?

Out of this musing came the call: I would explore the future through the lens of the past. I would turn the *Transit* series into **anthropological science fiction**.

Merging Two Fields

Now why would I write something that sounds so boring, like a class you'd take for credit in high school but hate the teacher?

In my junior year of high school, I took two such classes: AP Anthropology and Creative Writing. They were sort of back-to-back on my schedule, with Anthropology first followed by a lunch in which I could let the lessons stew followed by Creative Writing. I didn't know it at the time, but I think I may have inadvertently discovered the best way to generate ideas for a creative writing class.

Think about it: read all about the evolution of the species and how societies are formed, grow and die, discover the many ways cultures can impact other cultures, dive into the intricacies of linguistic anthropology and then see why magic and religion is profoundly present in both our past and present. Then, after a Hot Pocket, take all that knowledge to a creative writing class wherein the teacher says something like "write a story about what humans will act like fifty years from now."

I don't know what that story was about (it was many decades ago), but I do know the anthropology class was the guiding light in all of that.

So all this to say that anthropological science fiction is a thing, and it's not a boring thing either. Science Fiction may in fact be anthropology in reverse while anthropology must be at the core of Science Fiction.

As writers, we get to create things, from worlds to creatures to whatever you can think of. As readers, we get to experience worlds we never imagined might exist. Even if you're writing or reading a romance set in Italy, you're still creating a world or reading about one that was created for you.

When world building, writers have a lot of fun creating animals or terrain that exists only in their imagination. But to embed the reader in that world, the writer needs to bring them into the culture itself. This is where anthropology can come into play.

The idea for this eight-part series about using anthropology for world building came from a workshop I attended at the 2022 Pikes Peak Writers Conference. I gladly give credit to Darby Karchut, author of *Del Toro Moon*, for all the scribbles I put in my notebook.

There are eight elements which make up a culture, things that help define it as something different from something else. They are:
- Language
- Religion
- Social Groups
- Arts & Crafts
- History
- Government
- Economy
- Daily Life

When I first sat down to the workshop, I didn't think I had it right. While the first novel, *Out of Due Season*, was a set up to the rest of the story, the second and subsequent novels were intended to establish a new culture, and I feared I may have been missing one of those eight elements.

I was, sort of, but not entirely. I am eternally grateful for this workshop.

To give you an example of this, I will use my novel *Sunshine and Shadow: Exodus, or The Second Transit*, to show you how I managed to ensure that I had created a lasting culture and not just a few people on a new world running from things. I hope you get as much out of this information as I have.

Language

Language is one of the key elements which separates cultures. Have you ever heard the story of the Tower of Babel? It is an origin myth in the Bible in Genesis. There, a united human race all spoke the same language, and they decide to build a tower to heaven. God doesn't like this, however. He makes it impossible for construction to continue by confounding speech so that no one understands each other and then scatters everyone around the world.

There are similar stories found in Sumerian and Assyrian myth, in Mexico and Arizona, in Greek mythology, in Nepal and even in Botswana. Like many cultures, myths were written to explain certain traits of society, such as a child asking, "Why do they speak that way?"

Was there ever a single "origin" language, a time when all people spoke the same way and understood each other?

There's a whole study within the world of linguistics devoted to answering that question. Here, though, we'll just focus on how you can use language to expand the realism of your own world building.

J.R.R. Tolkien did this in the *Lord of the Rings*. As one of the fathers of a practice called **conlanging**, Tolkien created many different languages. Conlanging, or constructed language, is the hobby of inventing a vocabulary, grammar, and phonology that is typically used in fiction. Have you heard of Klingon? High Valyrian? Dothraki? Na'vi? Sindarin? These are all constructed languages used in fiction, and their very presence and use within a story further embeds the reader that author's culture.

Does a conlang have to be complete to be used in fiction? Not really. While I can learn Klingon and Valerian on my Duolingo app, I don't need to know the language in order to appreciate how and why another culture would use it. Knowing that another culture within the world I am reading about speaks another language can be just enough to bring me inside.

Do you have to have an alphabet in order to create a language for your novels? Not really. There's an excellent book by David J. Peterson called *The Art of Language Invention*. Peterson expanded upon George R.R. Martin's Dothraki language for use in the television show *Game of Thrones*. Dothraki has **no** written elements. While Peterson created grammatical rules and linguistic patterns, you do not have to go into so much detail. You can create simple patterns and expand on them.

When writing the *Transit* series, I knew I needed to construct an alien language. This is where, in my opinion, thing get a little harder. Spoken language is made possible by our anatomy, but as we do not share the anatomy of anything beyond the human species, would speech be the same? Would it even be possible?

When I was a kid, I invented an alien language wherein the aliens themselves changed their body to "speak." A phrase might be a 3D box colored red and the response might be a pyramid colored blue. Geometric shapes and colors were the basis for the language itself, but I didn't get too far. I have yet to use this language in a story, either (although that's still not outside the realm of possibility).

In the second book of the *Transit* series, *Sunshine and Shadow*, the human colonists run across texts written by an alien species. The texts are made up of logograms, symbols and more.

> *"So, what are we looking at here?" Sister Alexis held a text in her hand and turned the pages with the utmost care.*
>
> *"Gobbledygook. That's what you're looking at. A bunch of lines and circles and squares and funny squiggles that amount to a heap of nothing useful for us. That's the problem. Without a Rosetta Stone or some baseline translation, the language in those books and the ones still in the COL ship is impossible to read. There are alphabets, logograms, phonograms, whatever-grams all laid out in no discernible pattern. It was like they changed the language based on their bowel movements, for all we could figure out."*

I do get into the language quite a bit in the novel, and you can do the same in your own world that you're creating. Elves don't have to speak *Quenya* (a language created by J.R.R. Tolkien) or *Eltharin* (the language of the elves in the *Warhammer* series). They can speak whatever you come up with.

That's the beauty of fiction, of course: **invention**. When you're building your fictional world, think of how the aliens or fantasy creatures might speak, and then construct a language for them. Communication is necessary for all species to grow, and their language (**your** language) will bring your readers into your world just a little bit more.

Religion

I've written before about religiosity in fiction, which covers a broad area. Religious cults and religions are not confined to horror or fantasy novels. They can, in fact, act as both antagonist and protagonist within *any* genre and certainly bring a different level of realism to your **world building experience**. This includes science fiction, thrillers, literary fiction, and even romance.

There are several examples of how religion has been used to help form create a culture, from the obvious *Dune* by Frank Herbert to the more obscure *Blasphemy* by Douglas Preston. In romance, religion might be used to establish moral boundaries (or work against them).

Arguably, the most prominent religion within science fiction is that which exists within the *Star Wars* universe in the form of the Jedi and the Sith. Even if you have never seen the movies, read any of the books, or indulged in the television shows, the "Force" is a ubiquitous presence in our culture.

So, what is it about this one fictional religion that so strikes a chord in our collective minds? Perhaps it's as simple as good versus evil, the light versus the dark, the protagonist versus the antagonist.

Or, it could be much more complicated, a reflection on our societal traditions and mores laid out for us in a digestible philosophy that can be swallowed up by the youngest of fans. When I took my oldest to see *The Phantom Menace* when he was just four, even he understood.

Some arguments could be made that the Force as depicted in *Star Wars* is more magical than supernatural, a fantastical *deus ex machina* to solve certain problems in the plot. However, religion here is not only used to solve problems but create them as well. The Force adds tension, and tension drives story.

Religion is part of the human experience, whether you believe in one deity, multiple deities, or none at all. The brain and religion go hand-in-hand. In a paper written up in the Iranian Journal of Neurology, Alireza Sayadmansour writes that:

> *Neurotheology, also known as "spiritual neuroscience", is an emerging field of study that seeks to understand the relationship between the brain science and religion. Scholars in this field, strive up front to explain the neurological ground for spiritual experiences such as "the perception that time, fear or self-consciousness have dissolved; spiritual awe; oneness with the universe."*
> — Sayadmansour A. (2014). Neurotheology: The relationship between brain and religion. Iranian journal of neurology, 13(1), 52 – 55.

Spiritual awe and oneness with the universe can be incorporated into your world such that your characters are more dynamic and well-rounded.

In the *Transit* series — which starts with *Out of Due Season: The First Transit* — religion is not only a thing that exists in fiction as an aside (e.g., "he went to church"), but as a character in its own right. The cult that is established by Father Elijah Jonas becomes a seed for later trials inside the series.

With over 10,000 religions in the world (and more, if you include offshoot cults), religiosity in fiction is not as hidden as you may think.

Even the **absence of a religion** can inform your world building, provided it is stated that the culture you're describing is *specific about that lack of religion*. For example, by saying "we don't believe in any god or gods," you have established that a particular element of your culture is atheistic.

When you think about religion in world building, you don't have to view it as something that is formed or ritualized. It can be "spiritual awe" or a "oneness with the universe" as Sayadmansour states above.

You can also pit one belief against another in order to create tension. In the third book in the *Transit* series, I took that exact approach: three separate groups emerge from a singular culture. One is agnostic, one is atheistic, and one continues the religious rites and traditions of the parent culture.

Those religious rites and traditions were established in the second novel, *Sunshine and Shadow*. The primary catalyst for the social mores and norms the colonists initially follow was Elder Marcus, who felt a ritualized society might be more compliant. That compliance leads to problems (narrative conflict), but it was important to state that if you have almost 900 people living together on a new planet, many of them would establish a religion based on the beliefs of their ancestors or on things they have witnessed in the present. Many others would eschew those beliefs, as well.

In your world building, you can go so far as to create a whole new religion, too. Perhaps your characters follow a god that lives in the trees or worship a beast that hides out inside a cave. Whatever approach you take, remember that religion is one of the eight elements of culture and one that can paint a very rich and satisfying picture of the society you're creating.

Social Groups

Every time I think of a group of people, the phrase "circle of friends" pops up. When it does, so comes the earworm by

Edie Brickell. If you don't know the song "Circle", look it up. It's quite…quaint and reminds me of great days in the early 1990s. It's also a very depressing song that can be summed up by one phrase: "And being alone is the, is the best way to be…"

As writers, we *are* alone. It's the way we want it. But as readers, we are joining a circle of friends in a book and going on an adventure. Humans are social beings, as are other sentient creatures. They live together and that forms a society. That society is perception, feeling, presence. It's not a thing. Within this society, collections of people form **social groups**. It can be a small social group or a large one, but whatever it is, **the social group is a reflection of the society**.

Walfred A. Anderson and Frederick B. Parker define a group as:

> *units of two or more people in the same environment, or overcoming distance by some means of communication, who are influencing each other psychologically. The distinctive bond of the group is reciprocal interaction. Friends in conversation, a committee in action and children playing together are examples.*
> – Anderson, W.A. & Parker, F.B. in Manfredi, J. F. (1965). Society: Its Organization and Operation (Book). American Sociological Review, 30(4), 635 – 636. https://doi-org.yale.idm.oclc.org/10.2307/2091398

The implication of that definition is that relations among people in a social group is not temporary. When you're writing a story, most likely you're already creating social groups and those groups are a reflection of the society in which you placed them.

So how can we use this definition to enhance our stories?

- First, do you have a story with two or more people in the same environment? (My guess is you do.)
- Next, if they are not in the same environment, are they able to communicate via Internet, phone or some other device?
- Do they influence each other psychologically? That is, if your protagonist and antagonist are in the same group, are they playing off the strengths and weaknesses of each other effectively causing behavioral change? (This part here is the essence of conflict, and conflict drives your story.)
- Is there reciprocal interaction, meaning when one person does X, the other does Y? (I would say that's true, because if X and/or Y do not happen, you probably don't have a plot.)

When you're writing, most likely **you're already creating social groups** and those groups are a reflection of the society in which you placed them. When you're reading a story, **you become a part of that author's society**. This is probably why books stick with us more than movies: it takes us more than two hours to read a book (well, most of us). Readers can get into the heads of characters and become them, join their societies.

As you can see, embedding social groups into your writing as a part of your world building is something you're probably already doing.

In *Sunshine and Shadow: Exodus, or The Second Transit*, social groups are fully defined. There are children playing, a Council, and plenty of people living together in a community who engage in conversation. When I sat in on the workshop wherein anthropology was discussed, I realized that this element was probably the one I had described the most.

That didn't mean there wasn't work to be done.

Arts & Crafts

When I was at the conference where this information was shared with me, I started to check off the elements I knew had been embedded into my *Transit* series.

Language? Check.

Religion? Check.

Social Groups? Check.

Arts & Crafts? Um…

I'm a creative person. When I have to throw out a long-winded biography somewhere, I say that I am a writer, an artist, and a woodshop tinkerer. In sum, that means I like to create things, be it a story, a painting, or a shelf made of cedar that holds shampoo bottles.

I thought I had failed to include arts & crafts in my anthropological science fiction series. I mean, the genre isn't well known, but I'd like to think if I was going to do it, I was going to do it right. After I looked down at my notepad during the conference, I could say for certain that I had checked off every one of those elements of anthropology…except one.

I was mortified.

Well, not really. But I was a little put out.

How could I embed arts & crafts into my series such that I would have nailed all eight elements of world building?

I stewed for a day, and returned to the conference. As both a speaker at the conference and a writer, I had my morning already scheduled for me. It was while presenting my workshop on the second day that it hit me: I had woven arts & crafts throughout all of the second and third novels without even realizing it.

If you're a writer, you've probably done the same thing.

There are seven different forms of **arts**…

- Painting

- Sculpture
- Literature
- Architecture
- Cinema
- Music
- Theater

...and five basic types of **crafts**...
- Textile Crafts: quilting, knitting, appliqué
- Paper Crafts: calligraphy, papermaking, bookbinding
- Decorative Crafts: stained class, basketry, metalwork
- Fashion Crafts: jewelry, leatherwork, garments
- Functional Crafts: pottery, furniture, utensils

Did someone paint something in your novel? Did the lovers in your romance go to the theater on a date? What about the grandmother sitting in a rocking chair knitting a sweater?

The presenter at the conference, Darby Karchut, author of *Del Toro Moon*, added **storytelling** to the list of arts, as well. That made sense. Before the written word (literature), cultures told stories around campfires and the like. So...do any of your novels include someone spinning a yarn (telling a story)?

Weaving arts & crafts into a written work to add an element of anthropology to your world building is not really that difficult. You may not even realize you're doing it.

I didn't.

Here's an example from *Sunshine and Shadow: Exodus, or The Second Transit*.

> *As he waited for the right moment, Micah shaved off a little of the point of the spear he used as both a weapon and a walking stick. It had changed since he first picked it up in the*

forest. The thick shaft — of which his hand could barely reach around — was nearly stripped of all bark, and where the redness underneath had been exposed, he had carved letters and shapes. Initially, the carvings were arbitrary — a sun here, his name there — but soon they had grown to tell the story of a journey from the edge of the Barren Sea, up Helen's Esker, through the trees to the mountains. Along the way, small indications of what might be animals stood out with bolts and lances stuck in the side of them.

Here, Micah, one of the protagonists, has taught himself how to carve frescos in a walking stick. Later, he makes paper, binds them into books, and records the stories told by the elders. All of these things can be considered both arts & crafts.

When you're building your world, take a look at all of these elements. Write them down, then check off what you might be missing. You'll probably find arts & crafts embedded in your writing whether or not you intended it.

History

It's probably obvious to say that history is an important element of anthropology when building worlds in fantasy and science fiction (or any other genre). However, it's one that's not always done and it can make a big difference in the culture you're creating.

As I write this, it is July 2. In two days, the United States will celebrate a moment in its own history. That holiday is a part of the culture of the U.S. and separates it from other cultures around the world. There are thousands of books which recount the events of July 4, 1776, and tens of thousands which may reference it inside the covers. July 4th is but one example to show the number of ways the history of a culture can be woven into your stories.

When you're building a world, be it fantasy or science fiction, see if you can't embed some history in there. I'm not talking about backstory.

You have a culture, right? That culture did not begin on page one of your book (unless it did, then, well, that's pretty cool). More than likely, you have a thousand-year history in your head of all the things which happened that made your culture what it is.

At the end of my first Transit novel, *Out of Due Season*, something happens. When the second book starts, it's been forty years, but it was the impact of that event at the end of the first book that made the difference. It was a defining moment in the history of my characters.

> *The Feast of Elijah and the Circle of Light had always been a three-day extravaganza of community and pride. Aside from the evening ritual of hearing three elders or their descendants tell a story to the young ones, parents exchanged homemade trinkets with each other in order to pass them down to their children, and those children would then delightfully open those gifts. It had been Elder Jackson's idea to add in the gift giving, like the Christmas none of the children knew about. All of this surrounded three days of excessive food and drink. It was the only time during the year when every resident of the City of Nod took part, every resident felt the pull to commune with people they rarely had contact with, and every resident praised the foresight of Father Elijah and the gift which he bestowed on the*

> *people who agreed to travel with him based only on faith and the promise of something better.*
> — *From* Sunshine and Shadow: Exodus, or The Second Transit

To explain this history in a book, you don't have to get into details. You can weave it in here and there, perhaps in dialogue or through subtle hints. That history can be something the reader has to unravel, like a mystery within your novel.

Have you ever watched a movie with two or three timelines? That method of storytelling allows the filmmaker to bring in a history without a long exposition. In a sense, the exposition is there but stretched out through the film.

The same with some books. When an author drops in something like "A Hundred Years Ago" at the beginning of a chapter, they are bringing in a bit of history, a bit of exposition that (hopefully) explains something about the characters in "the present" who are a part of a culture.

History is an important element of anthropology when building worlds in fantasy and science fiction. You've created a culture, so let the reader know a few things about why that culture is the way it is.

Your readers will thank you.

Government

Now we get to the one element of anthropology I probably slept through: **government**. It wasn't because I had no interest. It was simply the class after lunch.

The government you build into your fantasy or science fiction culture doesn't have to be complicated. It can mirror your own, or...something else.

There are five basic types of government:

- Authoritarian
- Democracy — including parliamentary democracy, presidential democracy, direct democracy
- Monarchy — both constitutional and absolute
- Oligarchy — which might be an autocracy, a plutocracy, a stratocracy, or a theocracy
- Totalitarian

Others include:
- Anarchy
- Aristocracy
- Dictatorship
- Federalism
- Republicanism
- Theocracy
- Tribalism

And then those governments based on the economy (which is actually the next part of this series):
- Capitalism
- Communism
- Socialism

Most cultures in the world today fall under the type in the first list or even an odd combination (e.g., presidential democracy + capitalism), but that doesn't mean the world **you** build for your fantasy or science fiction novel has to be the same.

In *Sunshine and Shadow: Exodus, or The Second Transit*, the government of the colonists might be headed toward a **parliamentary democracy** but falls more in line with a **theocracy** (despite one of the Council members being rather vociferous that this not be the case).

When I laid out the plans for the culture within the Transit series, I did so specifically to address certain societal mores and norms which may (or may not) continue if society were to start over. Government was a big part of that planning.

Think about it: if a few hundred people had the chance to start society over, would they stick to the government they knew — the government that drove them out in the first place — or would they want to establish something different? And if they established something different, would they even know what might work in their present situation, or would they have to experiment with different forms of government based on the needs of the community at the time?

My argument is the latter.

You can do the same thing. There a thousands of fantasy books where monarchies and oligarchies are prevalent. It seems to be the thing to have a fantasy world ruled by a king or queen. But is that the best way to do it for the culture you're creating inside your own world?

If you're a writer, I challenge you to think about the government that your culture is subjected to. Even if you never mention the government or your characters operate outside seats of power, that government *will* make laws or dictates which the character may or may not follow.

Economy

The economy is certainly in the news today, but then again, isn't it often?

I *know* I slept through: **economics**. That didn't help when it came time for exams or the macro- and micro-economic classes I took in college. Nevertheless, it's still an important element to look at.

Depending on where you're from (or what political leaning you might have), the word "economy" might conjure images of fat cats swimming in a pool of money or just a simple exchange of one thing for another.

Merriam-Webster defines economy as "a system

especially of interaction and exchange," which is often the most one puts into world building. In science fiction, it's common for characters to exchange "credits" for an item. In fantasy, a writer might invent a monetary system which may be the plot (e.g., get the gold).

Money has a fun history, but not one that's often written down. It was developed as a means to exchange wealth, not necessarily as a replacement for the old bartering system. In a bartering system, one exchanges X for Y. That's simplistic, and it may be all your characters need to do.

If you create a monetary system in your world, you will likely need to create a form of payment. There is precedent for this. Shekels, for example, were initially created as a unit of weight, which might represent the weight of a particular sack of barley.

Interestingly, in the 1888 novel *Looking Backward 2000-1887*, Edward Bellamy described (for the first time in science fiction) the idea of using **credit cards**.

> *A credit corresponding to his share of the annual product of the nation is given to every citizen on the public books at the beginning of each year, and a credit card issued him with which he procures at the public storehouses, found in every community, whatever he desires whenever he desires it. This arrangement, you will see, totally obviates the necessity for business transactions of any sort between individuals and consumers. Perhaps you would like to see what our credit cards are like.*
>
> *"You observe," he pursued as I was curiously examining the piece of pasteboard he gave me, "that this card is issued for a certain number of dollars. We have kept the old word,*

but not the substance. The term, as we use it, answers to no real thing, but merely serves as an algebraical symbol for comparing the values of products with one another. For this purpose they are all priced in dollars and cents, just as in your day. The value of what I procure on this card is checked off by the clerk, who pricks out of these tiers of squares the price of what I order."

Many fantasy authors model their currency on present or historical things. In ancient Rome, for example, one might have run across Antoninianus, Argenteus (silver), As (copper), Denarius (silver), Follis, Solidus (gold), or Roman Republican currency, just to name a few. Fantasy authors could then change that up a bit. For example, if you liked the Follis as a main unit of money, you might add in the fact that it's gold: the follis-solidus, or a coin with a monetary unit of 1.

But creating a currency doesn't necessarily mean you've created an economic system within your world. You don't necessarily need to do that, but it might give more weight to the actions your characters take.

As mentioned previously, there are government systems which are economically based. **Capitalism** and **Socialism** are two of the most commonly known.

Traditionally, there are four main economic systems:
- **Traditional economies** — based on work, goods, and services, all of which follow certain established trends; there is little surplus in a traditional economy, and therefore little waste
- **Command economies** — a dominant centralized authority (e.g., the government) that controls a

significant portion of the economic structure and decisions; communism might be a good example here
- **Market economies** — a "free market" system in which regulation comes from the people based on supply and demand; true market economies are theoretical, however—governments will interfere in the form of regulations
- **Mixed economies** — a market system under strict regulatory control; sounds great, but mixed economies face the challenge of finding balance between market economy and command economy; most developed nations operate under a mixed economy

That's great. All that above is one of the reasons I slept through economics classes.

In a novel, do you really want to explain all this? Probably not, but in your backstory (your story bible or other notes), you might want to add what economy exists within the world you're building. Throw in a currency, and you'll have a better view. Throw in government regulations, and you'll certainly keep your characters in line. They won't barter for goods without knowing if they should drop that follis-solidus for a bushel of barley.

Daily Life

We all get up, eat a little breakfast, walk the dog, go to the store, do our chores. At least, that's common, right? So our characters probably do much of the same thing. We don't write that into our stories often, however, because very few people would want to read the details of a main character putting laundry soap into a machine.

Here I would argue that most cultures do some form of the above. Do they have washing machines in your fantasy world? Probably not, but they do wash their clothes (I would hope). Do they eat breakfast? Second breakfast? So what could be different that would set one culture apart from another?

When I was a wee child (teen), I went to Mexico to help build a church. While there, I recall walking through a group of apartments—buildings, huts, what have you—and there were children playing in the street. They weren't kicking a soccer ball as I would have expected, but tossing around a rock on a string. It was unique, something that set apart this culture from the one that I knew.

Later, in my twenties, I lived in a hooch in Honduras. It was a different world there, but some things were similar. I went to the barber, sat down at a wedding, purchased things in the shops, you name it. But that wedding was different. Gone was the typical ceremony of a bride and groom standing at an altar in front of a judge/priest/officiant of some sort. Instead, the wedding was performed while the two were **sitting down at a table to eat**. Basically, we all paused as the groom finished swallowing his food to say "I do" (or, in this case, "estoy de acuerdo" or something). When the groom was done, the bride did the same thing. At no time was dinner to be interrupted.

This is an example of a difference in culture. You probably wouldn't find that same thing in your neck of the woods, but could you add a little something to your fictional world that shows how daily life is different?

As I said in the very beginning of this series, as writers we get to create things, from worlds to creatures to whatever you can think of. As readers, we get to experience worlds we never imagined might exist.

When world building, writers have a lot of fun creating animals or terrain that exists only in their imagination. But to embed the reader in that world, the writer needs to bring them into the culture itself. This is where anthropology can come into play.

You can do that in a variety of ways, but one of the easiest will be to show a difference in daily life, even if it's slight. That small change will make a big difference in how your world comes across to your reader.

Religiosity in Fiction: Cults, Religion, and the Sci-Fi Thriller

This article was written for and published by Mystery and Suspense Magazine *in their January 2022 issue.*

In a house on a street in a city in a state, there once was a man who convinced dozens of people to leave their bodies behind so they could join the evolutionary state above human. Their cool new ride was soon to arrive hidden in the tail of a comet, and once they were on board, they would ascend to a new level of awareness. They would graduate from their classroom on Earth and leave this world in the dust.

They say reality is sometimes stranger than fiction, and while this sounds like science fiction, most of us would recognize the reality. The house was in Rancho Santa Fe, California, the year was 1997, and it was a man named Marshall Applewhite who convinced 38 other very intelligent people to eat a concoction of apple sauce or pudding mixed with phenobarbital so that they could join other Next Level Bodies on board a UFO hidden in the tale of Comet Hale-Bopp. It was a cult named Heaven's Gate.

The term cult often has a negative connotation. Oxford defines one as "a system of religious veneration and devotion directed toward a particular figure or object." In contrast, religion is "the belief in and worship of a superhuman controlling power, especially a personal God or gods." The "personal God or gods" part of that means it could be *anything*, from the Christian God to the Flying Spaghetti Monster or to something like consumerism. It can also be defined as that "particular figure or object" mentioned in the definition for a cult. Marshall Applewhite—aka Do—for example.

Religion is what it is, and it is personal. Much like Heaven's Gate, we can read into a "cult" as nothing more than an invented religion—one that may appear strange to outsiders. While cults are looked at as offshoots of a religion, many religions we now see as mainstream in fact started off as a cult. Scientology and the Unification Church are often referred to as cults, but in fact, Christianity was considered a cult in its earliest days. So was Islam. And Baptists. Quakers, even.

In the realm of fiction, religion is often portrayed in black and white tones with a distinct good versus evil motif. There are multiple examples in fiction. Horror is rife with religion as it lays the groundwork for whatever evil lurks in the corners (think: H.P. Lovecraft's Cthulhu mythos or William P. Blatty's *Exorcist*). Fantasy, too, has its fair share of religions, many of which are very similar to Native American beliefs and the worship of nature. The *Wheel of Time* series by Robert Jordan springs to mind immediately. But religious cults and religions are not confined to horror or fantasy novels. They can, in fact, act as both antagonist and protagonist within *any* genre and certainly bring a different level of realism to the sci-fi thriller reading experience.

After all, science fiction has a strong link to anthropology, and anthropology is all about the study of human societies, cultures, and their development. Within that study lies not only language, traditions, and behavior, but also religion and religious development (i.e., religions that start off as cults).

So, what fictional religions exists within sci-fi and sci-fi thrillers? Is it really that prevalent?

We don't look to science fiction to directly address religious motifs, but they are often there, nonetheless.

Technological changes which challenge religious attitudes are common, and we can probably find examples of many of the main themes in religion, from creationism (*2010* by Arthur C. Clarke), to Messianism (*Dune* by Frank Herbert), to reincarnation (as Philip K. Dick explored in *Ubik*).

We can also look beyond the major Earth religions to find other influences present in fiction. According to The Pew Research Center, it is estimated that 84% of the world's population is affiliated with Christianity, Islam, Hinduism, Buddhism, or some form of folk religion, while the rest have no religious affiliation (e.g., atheists, agnostics, humanists).

There are around 10,000 distinct religions worldwide. Of those, monotheism (i.e., the worship of a singular deity) may lay claim to the most followers, but through a pure numbers game, most religions eschew the idea of one deity and can be classified as either polytheistic (many gods), henotheistic (one god but open to the idea of more), animistic (innumerable spiritual objects), pantheist (it's *all* God) or some combination thereof. Keep in mind that the numbers given by The Pew Research Center do not include offshoot cults. Of those, there are probably...a heck of a lot.

Arguably, the most prominent religion within science fiction is that which exists within the *Star Wars* universe in the form of the Jedi and the Sith. Even if you have never seen the movies, read any of the books, or indulged in the television shows, the "Force" is a ubiquitous presence in our culture. Memes and t-shirts and bumper stickers and anything else that can hold licensed content extoll the virtuous calling "May the Force Be with You."

So, what is it about this one fictional religion that so strikes a chord in our collective minds? Perhaps it's as simple as good versus evil, the light versus the dark, the protagonist versus the antagonist. Or, it could be much more complicated, a reflection on our societal traditions and mores laid out for us in a digestible philosophy that can be swallowed up by the youngest of fans. When I took my oldest to see *The Phantom Menace* when he was just four, even he understood.

Some arguments could be made that the Force as depicted in *Star Wars* is more magical than supernatural, a fantastical *deus ex machina* to solve certain problems in the plot. However, if we look back at our definition, the "belief in...a superhuman controlling power" really strikes a chord with how the Force is depicted in the *Star Wars* universe. It is not only used to solve problems but create them as well. The Force adds tension, and tension drives story.

Less fantastical and more recognizable to our current religions on Earth, Frank Herbert's *Dune* borrows extensively from Islam, Christianity and Buddhism to create religions within the novels that act as an overarching reason why characters do what they do. In this case, the beliefs are guiding lights and behavior modifiers. The acceptance of Muad'Dib created an offshoot cult of the original Fremen religion and later spilt into variants such as the Cult of Alia and Cult of Sheeana.

There are, within the *Dune* universe (all books, etc. combined), approximately 128 religions mentioned, the most prominent being the beliefs of the Fremen and the Bene Gesserit. While much of the beliefs of all the other mentioned religions are not laid out in detail within the *Dune* universe, much is known about both what the Fremen believe and the teachings of the Bene Gesserit. *Dune* would probably have been an entirely different novel had these two belief systems been the central focus. Like the Force in *Star Wars*, the beliefs of the characters drive their actions and that creates tension.

Religions clash, of course. We can see that especially now and looking back in history, it has been this way for thousands of years. In Kevin J. Anderson's *Terra Incognita*, two churches which essentially believe the same thing—that God had two sons—are at odds with each other and consider the teachings of the other to be pure heresy. *Terra Incognita* uses religion as the carrier for the plot from beginning to end. A literal *dues ex machina* is revealed near the end when God shows up with a third son and a new religion is formed by merging all beliefs.

Religious creation or invention is explored in other novels, as well, and some of those novels have had an impact on our present culture. Robert A. Heinlein's 1961 science fiction novel *Stranger in a Strange Land* gives us an example of religion as a central theme within a book, but rather than provide a narration based on an existing religion, Heinlein uses the journey of the main character Valentine Smith to establish a new religion on Earth based on the teachings of many sects. One of the strangest—and one which might be considered the more influential to Smith—is a religion called the Fosterite Church of the New Revelation. Eventually, Smith creates a "Church of All Worlds," a mishmash of revivalism, paganism, and the teachings of Fosterites. As proof of literature's impact on society, Heinlein's novel directly contributed to a 501©(3) neopaganistic church currently operating as, you guessed it, The Church of All Worlds.

A less dramatic but still powerful religion served as the focal point of Octavia E. Butler's *Parable of the Sower*. In this novel, the daughter of a Baptist minister, Lauren Olamina, eschews the false hope provided by Christianity in the midst of an apocalyptic world. After dealing with her own conflicted feelings, Lauren eventually forms a religion—which can be loosely called the formation of a cult—called Earthseed. The arc of the novel is the main character's journey to take her ideas and grow them into a true religious community with a growing set of converts. The comparison and contrast between Earthseed and Christianity is woven throughout the novel and leads us to a satisfying conclusion. Interestingly enough, Butler's work inspired the Terasem Movement, which seeks to develop humanity through technology and to bridge the gap between science and religion (see Jessica 'oy's article in *Time* "The Rapture of the Nerds" from 2014).

More modern examples of religion and religious cults within science fiction thrillers can be found in such novels as *The Stand* by Stephen King and (one of my favorites) *Blasphemy* by Douglas Preston. In the latter novel, a Nobel Laureate leading a research team at the world's largest supercollider manipulates the system to create a new religion based on science. However, the main character's efforts have unintended consequences with the establishment of an entirely new cult with the main character serving in a messianic role.

Many themes can be found inside science fiction thrillers, but the battle between good and evil—the fight between the protagonist the antagonist—is the crux of just about every story ever told. As religion is so focused on these concepts, it is no wonder that its very existence peppers our science fiction and adds spice to the characters. Can you tell a story without religion? Absolutely, but even in the lack of a codified, structured religious system, there still exists a conflict between the light and the dark, whether it's internally shown in a character's thoughts or externally shown across the universe in battles between species. That conflict often creates offshoot cults. The journeys of the characters are amplified or even modified by these motifs with the result being dynamic characters in a well-rounded novel.

Authors of sci-fi thriller novels often give readers much deeper novels by exploring philosophical elements that go far beyond simplistic tropes. I have mentioned probably less than one percent of one percent of all the novels within the genre that touch on religion or religious cults, and any reader out there can probably name a dozen more. As you read your next science fiction thriller, attempt to pull out what themes are present. You may be surprised to find just how many reads explore our future by using religion and cult creation as a plot device.

The Virtue of Heredity

I lived in a dorm in the 1990s from which I would watch rabbits tempt fate nightly as they hopped in front of cars. You never knew the winners of the game, only the losers. This essay was written during one of those nights. If you look back at the story "Them Rabbits" you may see a tie-in.

They come early in the evening, the sun just beginning to interact with the horizon, turning colors of yellow into orange and then a deep, bloody red. Some arrive in pairs, some alone, some as a family. They come to feed, to play, to live out their lives as nature would dictate, seemingly blind to the eccentric world about them. They are as much creatures of the night as they are creatures of the day, though by night they are the most prominent. They defend their territory with passion and stare down those animals who may tower above them. They fear little and dare to play life and death games with Fate. They are perversions of Flospy, Mopsy, Cottontail, and Peter. They are rabbits, and they *infest*.

I have seen their presentation replayed in bits and pieces nearly every night, although up until yesterday I hadn't stayed to watch more than five minutes. The first rabbit to arrive that evening did so as the sun had just touched the horizon. It hopped nervously across the parking lot, stopping now and then to investigate a lonely leaf or a spot of oil. Every few seconds it would look up as if guilty of some heinous crime, then hop forward a few more steps. By the time it reached the edge of the grass yard, the sun had slipped quietly away for the night. The wind blew kisses at the Cottonwood trees and rustled a few premature autumn leaves. The rabbit looked up, then around, and finally entered the grass wonderland.

The first nibble — like the first step — was a tentative one. It bent over, tasted the greenery, and then looked back up. A small blade of grass stuck out of the side of the rabbit's mouth as its black eyes searched the periphery. Out on the road beyond the parking lot a car drove by. The fur on its back twitched involuntarily, a rear foot thumped the earth, and the ears rose high. The rabbit waited until the sound of the engine was lost in the breeze. A few moments passed before it took another nibble, another glance around, and then a hop forward to a greener patch of grass. The pattern continued until, at last, the rabbit felt confident.

I sat back in my chair and lit a cigarette. The shadows of evening were beginning to melt into the descending darkness, and before I realized it a waxing moon had risen over the mountains to take charge of another night. The yellow porch lights above me snapped on as if they had minds of their own and could sense my need for a little more light to write by. I glanced at my watch, noted the time and began to think about dinner. When I looked back out at the yard, the rabbit had cloned itself; instead of one lonely rabbit, I was now faced with four. It was like I had turned my back on a closet for just a moment and the clothes hangers had magically multiplied.

The rabbits were grouped together around one of the smaller trees, each intent face firmly rooted to a little patch of grass. They seemed to be completely oblivious to one another, yet working together as a team. When one rabbit would tire of his patch and hop forward to find something better, another rabbit would hop to the right or to the left in order to keep some sense of both territory and distance. There was something almost telepathic about their movements. One rabbit would be facing away from another, contentedly gnawing at a small twig. The other rabbit, having apparently decided that its grass wasn't the right consistency, would hop farther away. Without hesitation, the first rabbit would grab the twig in its mouth and close the gap, thereby preserving the illusion of strength in numbers.

All of this would continue undisturbed all night long, were it not for a game of life and death these rabbits play. Unlike many other types of games, we are left to know only who the losers are; the winners escape into the night without a scratch. They play a game of joust between the themselves and the Beasts with Glowing Eyes. More often than not, this game is played on the paths that humans use to travel around from place to place. These rabbits in front of me have won the game before, but winning once is only an enticement to play again and again until they finally lose.

For several months I have found myself an eye witness to this jousting match, crouched inside the Beast, directing the motion of the Glowing Eyes. I have won some and lost some, and although I do not delight in killing animals I don't intend to barbecue, there is a reassuring feeling to the sudden "thud" of victory that comes at the end of the game.

I waited for what seemed like an hour before the rabbits had moved toward the edge of the playing field. Their little mouths worked tirelessly, chewing the grass and secreting enough saliva to wash it all down. Another group of rabbits formed on the other side of the lawn, though I knew from previous encounters that the two groups would remain as far apart as possible. Minutes dragged on, and I began to think that I wasn't going to get to see the game. Then, off in the distance, acting as if in a dance with the rustling leaves, the faint growl of an old Beast drifted through the night air.

I sat up. The group by the road continued to feed, heads to the ground, eyes on the prize. I watched their movements closely, hoping to find some evidence that at least one rabbit had heard the rumble—maybe an ear thrust higher or a quick glance out of curiosity. The noise grew louder, drowning out that of the leaves, and the light from the Glowing Eyes could be seen rounding the bend.

The rabbits continued to feed.

The Beast came into view down the road, gaining speed and closing the gap. First gear. A small bump bounced the Eyes into the air and then back on the road. Second gear. The growl grew higher, commanding the wheels to move the Beast faster and faster. Third gear. The black skin reflected the moon. The Glowing Eyes bared down.

The rabbits continued to feed.

The Beast came closer and closer, until I felt a twinge of doubt that any of the rabbits would take the chance. Maybe they could judge the intensity of the growl by listening. Maybe they could tell whether or not they stood a chance by watching the Eyes. Maybe they knew I was watching. Maybe—

An ear perked up. I looked closer at one of the rabbits, its head rising from the grass and turning toward the road. The fur on its back twitched involuntarily, a rear foot thumped the earth, and both ears rose high. It hopped toward the road—still chewing on a blade of grass—and stared directly into the Glowing Eyes.

I read not too long ago that the DNA strand of any human, when broken down into its component letters, is remarkably similar to that of almost any other animal. For example, the genetic spelling of a simple nematode is, in fact, almost ninety percent the same as the code for any human. An ant is nearly ninety-two percent similar. What this means in the grand scheme of life, the universe and everything, I don't know. But it must mean something.

And what of the rabbit? What of the animal who had risked everything for a little rush of adrenaline? What of the animal who had given its life for a little taste of the narcotic of chance? Well, that tangled mess of blood and fur out there on the road is ninety-seven percent human. Makes you wonder, doesn't it?

ART

I love to paint, but I'm not a good painter. Does it matter? The process is one that is conducive to mindfulness and it calms me on the worst days. I have many more paintings than are listed here, but these ten I feel may be better than others.

For those who may be wondering, yes: Bob Ross is my inspiration, not only for the canvas but on the way he approached life after the military.

"I can't think of anything more rewarding than being able to express yourself to others through painting. Exercising the imagination, experimenting with talents, being creative; these things, to me, are truly the windows to your soul."
— Bob Ross

Moon, Lighthouse, Clouds, Water

Moon, Lighthouse, Clouds, Water. 36x36 (3 panels, 12x36 each). Acrylic on stretched canvas. This painting depicts a stormy sea at night with a lighthouse in the background. These types of paintings are my favorite.

Abandoned House by a Cotton Field

Abandoned House by Cotton Field. 11x14. Acrylic on canvas board. This is probably the second in a series of "abandoned buildings." I started with the sky here, which is to say I wanted to set the right atmosphere. The house itself, located somewhere in North Carolina, is one that I would love to fix up. I can imagine what it would look like after a few coats of paint, some nails and a picket fence.

Monument Valley

Monument Valley. 18x14. Acrylic on canvas. This impressionist painting was intended to be focused on the sky, but the landscape really completes it. For those familiar with this view of Monument Valley, you're probably wondering where the big long road is. Well, I felt including the road would take away from the grandeur of the scene and, after all, there wasn't always a road, was there?

Farm

Farm. 48x30. Acrylic on canvas. This painting was based on a farm where my mother grew up. While the majority of the painting is true to the source, I did take a few liberties with regard to the field in front and the treeline...but not a lot of liberties.

"The Farm" is a special place. While I only lived there for a few months when I was 4 or 5, what memories I have are vivid. Oddly enough, the propane tank in the painting is one of those vivid memories, and so, it had to be included.

Blue Door (#1)

Blue Door. 36x24. Acrylic on canvas. This painting is the first in a series of "door" paintings I intend to do (hence the address number "1"). It was painted rather methodically at times, which is not my normal style...but I think it will need to be for certain "doors" and (later on) windows.

Abandoned Church in Fall

Abandoned Church in Fall. 16x20. Acrylic on canvas. I was working more on clouds than the church in this painting. I think the abandoned building, however, adds to the coldness of the clouds. The fence in the foreground is also run down.

Dark Gate

Dark Gate. 16x20. Acrylic on canvas. This is the second in my collection of "gates" that I plan on painting. The idea behind the dark trees and the forest beyond was of those challenges we all face. I often tell myself to do the thing that scares you, especially when it comes to public speaking or stepping out of my comfort zone. While the painting may have a spooky initial quality, the message is more motivating to me. Will you approach the gate and step into the unknown?

Summertime Roots

Summertime Roots. 16x20. Acrylic on canvas. This whimsical abstract painting was a wish fulfilled: I never had a tree swing growing up, so I painted one. I'd fall out now, but my feelings have not changed. We can be children again, if we put ourselves in the right mind set. The roots we have – our past – is what makes all that possible. When I initially painted this, I wanted to generate a conversation with myself: what do I see and what do I feel? Can I sit on that tree swing and be mindful not only of the blue skies above and the leaves of the tree, but also of the roots that hold all of it up?

Red Door (#3)

Red Door. 48x30. Acrylic on canvas. This painting is the third in a series of "door" paintings I intend to do (hence the address number "3"). It was painted rather methodically at times, especially with respect to the bushes and tree branches.

King Salmon Creek

King Salmon Creek. 11x14. Acrylic on canvas board. King Salmon Creek is in what I affectionately call the "armpit" of Alaska. The area is surrounded by wonderful greenery and, yes, creeks full of salmon. There might be a few bears, too. This impressionistic painting shows a bend in the creek in summer when the white socks (gnats) are out in force.

King Salmon Creek is my "happy place." This painting lets you see inside my head and know exactly what calms me on the most tumultuous days. I lived near this creek in 1992, and I know I'll return there again someday. The images I keep in my head in the meantime, however, are pure bliss.

Biography

Benjamin X. Wretlind is a science fiction & dark fantasy writer who infuses his writing with a heavy dose of philosophy and epistemology. He is the author of several novels and novellas.

Benjamin is a full member of the Science Fiction and Fantasy Writers Association and lives with his wife Jesse in Colorado. While not writing, he builds and teaches leadership and professional development courses to staff at Yale University.

Made in the USA
Las Vegas, NV
30 January 2025

17196289R00187